- Scripts -

Brandon Knightley

I0751017

LAVENDER SKY PRESS

Paperback: ISBN 979-8-9943423-0-5
eBook: ISBN 979-8-9943423-1-2

Publisher: Lavender Sky Press

Best to be like water,
Which benefits the ten thousand things
And does not contend.
It pools where humans disdain to dwell,
Close to the Tao.

Lao-tzu, *Tao Te Ching*
Translated by Stephen Addiss and Stanley Lombardo

Be intent on action,
not on the fruits of action;
avoid attraction to the fruits
and attachment to inaction!

The Bhagavad-Gita
Translated by Barbara Stoler Miller

Do good and disappear.

Nun's Saying

Reading One

"Victory" by Marla Kraft

[A couple standing face to face in their bed-room, leaning forward slightly.]

Alan: Come on, let's go! We'll be late.

Ellen: No.

Alan: What do you mean, no? They'll be waiting.

Ellen: Let them wait.

Alan: What?

Ellen: I said, let them wait! What part of that didn't you understand? Let them wait until they don't want to wait anymore. Or go by yourself.

Alan: Look, Johnny and Julie are expecting us. If we weren't going to show up, we should have called...

Ellen: <u>You</u> should have called. You made the date; you made the arrangements.

Alan: We always go out with them--every second Friday night! Why shouldn't you want to go tonight?

Ellen: Wrong question, you damned fool: Why should I ever have wanted to go? They're <u>your</u> friends, and they're fools, too.

Alan: I don't care what the hell you think! We are going! <u>You</u> are going! We are not about to stand up two of our best friends, two people who--

Ellen: Two people who enrich our lives by sitting around with us for hours at some awful stinking bar, until he gets drunk enough not to care whether she catches him looking at the breasts, legs, and asses of every woman in the place--including mine!--and until she's had enough beer and cigarettes that every five-word sentence is punctuated by at least as many of those damned little gulping burps of hers. Oh, yeah, I treasure their company. And the best part is listening to you relive high school with Johnny. God, I just <u>love</u> that! Especially how you pulled the underwear off that kid in the gym class who didn't want to wear a jock. Christ Almighty, why would I want to miss hearing <u>that</u> again?

Alan: Go to hell, lady! Just go to hell!

Ellen: Where do you think I am, you stupid bastard!

Alan: You're my goddam wife, and you're where I put you! You're nowhere else...and <u>nothing</u> else but what I say you are!

Ellen: Am I? And what are you? What have you been doing all these years? What you wanted? No, you've done nothing but work at a job you hate--and you've done it for me. Because of me! That's why you hate me as much as that job of yours, and that's why I've won!

Alan: Won? Won what? According to you, we both lost. We both lost the day we met.

Ellen: No, I got what I wanted. I've ruined you for what you did to me.

Alan: What <u>I</u> did? That I loved you? Because I loved you?

Ellen: Oh, that's a crock! You use the word as if it meant something noble. Let me tell you what your love amounted to, buddy boy: The end of any kind of romance. The end of any kind of being myself. The end of any chance of becoming something.

Alan: If that's how you feel, then how did <u>you</u> win?

Ellen: Because I knew it before it started. I knew what I was getting into. I expected that and nothing more. I was ready for it! But you weren't. You thought our life, our love--Oh, God, that sounds so stupid and horrible!--our love would mean something. You gave away a lot for that, and <u>that's</u> why I've won.

Alan: You can't mean that. You're not smart enough, and even you aren't bitch enough to mean that. Nobody is.

[Ellen smiles.]

Helen looked at David, who was still breathing hard. Her dress was disarrayed around her shoulders, but her hair had its usual metallic precision. "That was good," she said. "Our best ever, I think." They were still standing in their places in the central area of their living room, a space defined by a sofa and two chairs set at right angles to it.

"Yes," he replied. "God, I really thought you were going to kill me.... I really thought you hated me. I really thought I hated you." His voice trailed off. They looked at each other, a trace of something unexpected in both pairs of eyes.

"You want to read another one?" she asked, her eyes bright. He nodded soberly, as if they had reached some profound agreement. "But let's have a drink first."

"Okay." He settled on the sofa. She walked over to the bar, filled two glasses with an inch and a half of bourbon, returned and handed one down to him. She sat down, too, in one of the fat chairs and they stared across each other's line of vision.

"Anything much happen at work today?" she asked, still not looking in his direction.

"No. Started the new contract. Anything new here with you?"

"You mean that big job?" Without waiting for a response, she went on to answer his question. "Oh, I don't know. Mona came over for lunch with some new crisis in her life, but I didn't much listen."

"Your sister?"

"What other Mona do we know?"

The silence held until most of the bourbon was gone—not in the least a strained silence, but one that carried, for both of them, an odd sense of nascent guilt. Then she leaned forward eagerly.

"Ready?"

Chapter One

Charlie walked out from the bedroom and left the apartment without a glance or a word. Arlene stood looking blankly across the living room. She was used to it, but still didn't understand it. She grabbed her glasses from her face in a characteristic gesture: if they weren't smudged before, they certainly were afterwards. She wiped them repeatedly using a pleat in the skirt of her tan dress and replaced them, never taking her eyes from the blank, silent door. At least ten hours stretched before her until Charlie would return from work.

Their flat was on the second floor, a southwest corner apartment overlooking the intersection of two streets that were not really busy and yet less than quiet. She looked out the western window knowing that her husband would be out of sight, heading up the other street where his car was usually parked. It was late enough in spring that sunlight shone through the early leaves of the trees that had been deeded small rectangular cut-outs in the double-width city sidewalks.

Arlene had been up and dressed for almost two hours. She walked into the kitchen, which so far had been left undisturbed by the new day. Charlie wouldn't give her the satisfaction of making him breakfast, which he hated anyway. Absently she heated some water, stirred in some low-quality instant coffee, and prepared a piece of toast from a three-day old loaf of white bread. She buttered the toast, smeared a bit of marmalade on with the convex face of a worn teaspoon. She seated herself at the kitchen table, an unprepossessing construction of scratched chrome and a Formica top: a scatter of tiny open shapes reminiscent of boomerangs superimposed on a faded, cream-colored background. The table was built to accommodate four and therefore could serve twice as many as had ever used it since its move to this particular apartment.

One slice of toast was quite enough for her. In the extraordinarily unlikely event that Arlene ever found herself in a police lineup, she might well have been identified as "that stringy blond." While somewhat above average in height, she was decidedly below average in weight. Her neck, arms and hands were long; the two open buttons at the neck of her dress showed pronounced collar bones that terminated in two prominent knobs. Her breasts were obviously slight, and her hips, had they not almost always been lost in the lines of her clothing, would have shown an almost preadolescent angularity. Her hair could offer little help: it had the exact color of hay, and, worse yet, was of similar texture. The large round glasses with their translucent pinkish frames only improved things to the extent that they detracted from her sallow, coarse complexion.

Yet if Arlene's lines, colors, and textures were some eccentric's rendering of female unloveliness, the artist contradicted himself in three important particulars: Her hopelessly nearsighted eyes, while merely blue—and by no means startlingly blue—almost always suggested a sense of cheerful serenity in their clarity and symmetry. Her mouth, just slightly on the wide side, with pale lips that were neither full nor thin, could be, at times, no less than fascinating: it took on an odd life of its own whenever she was sufficiently engaged with something. She simply forgot to control her lips, so that their movement and shape reflected her every emotion and projected her inner life instant by instant with an irresistibly attractive innocence. Finally, her legs, had she dressed less conservatively, would hardly have been described as stringy or ill-formed, but rather as long, graceful, and altogether sexy. Arlene knew she had nice legs, but it would have surprised her to think that this might matter in a woman's life. Yet whatever the root of this failure of pride where pride was entirely justified, it served her well in taking correspondingly less account of her obvious physical shortcomings.

She finished her toast and took her coffee over to the other window, the one that faced south and was always safe from her husband. Another day to be faced. She gazed steadily out through the glass, her eyes somehow focused without seeing anything in particular. Her accustomed mix of activities—straightening the apartment, washing, ironing, shopping—were reckoned in terms of fractions of hours, not days. Indeed, these were things she did to keep *herself* centered, for Charlie seemed not to care, and Arlene understood well the more precise truth: he could not notice or speak of such things, even to criticize them, without implicating her as something that mattered. Hence, he said nothing. And so once again Arlene found herself, a full-grown woman of more than average intelligence and competency, in the middle of a life that could properly have been characterized by an outside observer as lethargic. But from the inside, the description simply would not fit: her continuing minute observation not only of what little passed in those hours but also of her own state of mind–-of how *she* endured their passing—was itself an intense form of activity, although Arlene could not have identified its intention.

She finished her coffee, placed the cup in the sink without rinsing it and went to the bedroom. From the closet she took a worn white woolen sweater with pearl buttons. She put in on, pleased to feel its familiar embrace and comfortable warmth, and crossed back through the living room. She picked up her small purse from the corner of the kitchen counter and her keys from a hook on the cabinet above, and then left the apartment.

Arlene was four when her parents brought her for a weekend to her aunt's house. It was July of 1936, and the world had just begun once again to solidify around her, and this sudden change of locale might have been a setback but wasn't. A year earlier her life had changed, completely and incomprehensibly. Her parents one day had carried her away—forever—from the rooms that had defined her first consciousness of space. After a period of confinement and confusion that had all but completely disappeared from memory, a time of clinging to her mother with her whole body, with eyes closed tight against all the surrounding disorder and unfamiliarity, there was again a sense of settled coherence. But she knew her world had changed. And, more than that, the words she heard and was expected to speak, the very sound of speech itself, had altered ineffably. Even her name was different; it had become shorter…but heavier.

She had wandered out the back door of her aunt's house unopposed. The three adults were speaking excitedly, seriously, but the words, while still familiar, were formed from the sounds of that abandoned place and were no longer comprehensible to her. She thought of asking her mother what had happened, but suddenly changed her mind and slipped away.

Her aunt's house was old, its structural members no longer quite making right angles where they should have, and the leaf-green paint was peeling in narrow ribbons along the grain of wooden siding. Arlene liked it—she intuitively preferred the organic texture of the old wood to the harsh grittiness of the brick buildings with which she was more accustomed—and was fascinated by its locale. Set back from an old and entirely neglected road that threaded its way through miles of similar rural decay, the house stood in an isolation that she had never experienced before. The backyard was unfenced and untended, and only defined by the relative absence of dense brush and trees. She followed a slight trail from the yard to a smaller structure that was once intended for a garage but now served as a storage shed for things that were no longer of any use. Arlene peered into the vertical crack between the shed's padlocked doors, compressing the right lens of her glasses against her eyebrows and cheekbones, and then stood back. She turned to her left to make her way around: perhaps there was a window.

About midway along the left side Arlene found her window, but the back of some tall, badly used piece of furniture completely obscured her view. She exhaled at this small frustration and continued a few steps further, at which point she found her intended path completely blocked by a shooting fountain of grass, dense and substantial, but softly waving in its full, seed-laden maturity. She glanced up at the sun, as if to gather energy, and then pushed her way through, experiencing a warm and delightful thrill at the sudden and unexpected sense of total envelopment by another life form. The smell and texture of the grass saturated her senses; its immediacy compressed her range of vision to mere inches. Then it was gone: she had broken through, standing alone in a new space, blinking through her large glasses, a slight figure whose pale skin made little contrast with the faded yellow of her second-hand sun dress.

A minute or two later, Arlene sat down, back-to-back with the shed, and drew up her knees to her chin, looking forward, coming to terms with how she felt. Her view was cut off both right and left by the luxurious high grass. To the front she could see a little way through some bushes, but not enough to compromise the delicious sense of isolation. What was different and new was a sense of security that did not require the presence of her mother. She was alone, but not lonely.

Arlene continued sitting in this place for a long time. She would never return here, and never speak of it. Yet the memory remained intact and vivid whenever she chose or chanced to recall it, seeming always to belong not to her childhood self, but to the person she would become.

Madison Elementary School lay twelve blocks north of her apartment. It was an unimaginative, rectangular two-story structure made of large tan stone blocks roughly the same shape as the building taken as a whole. Across the street to the west was a modest park, not large enough to provide any real separation from the city, even at its most interior point. The only children present were too young for school and under supervision. A few pedestrians crossed diagonally through the park merely as a shortcut to their destinations.

Arlene sat on a bench that looked into the park, away from the school. She neither needed her sweater nor was made uncomfortable by it. The sun warmed her hair agreeably, lofting its natural scent into the slight breeze. She felt the lightest trace of drowsiness.

"…It would serve him right if she went out one day and never came back, is what I say."

Arlene looked over at the woman who had sat down next to her about twenty minutes earlier, realizing that her mind had been drifting.

"Excuse me, Mrs. Forney, but I was distracted. Why should your niece leave her husband?"

Mrs. Emma Forney wore a billowing green topcoat over a drab paisley dress that was dominated by the color of rust. The topcoat had nothing whatsoever to do with the weather. Her husband had died in the first months of America's engagement in the war, and with him had passed away any thoughts of family, direction, or meaning in her life. No one, not even Mrs. Forney, knew what she weighed now. The topcoat at some incomprehensible level hid, at least from herself, a massiveness born in reciprocity for all of those losses. About the only thing left to her was a niece by a much older sister, also dead, now five years.

"I was telling you," continued Mrs. Forney, "that the bastard slapped her—he called her a whore and then he *slapped* her!—because she was rushing to fix herself up and didn't get his eggs right. He's always doing something like that. My Harry treated me like a damned princess in comparison, and Lord knows he was no prince!"

Arlene sat quietly for a few moments. She had heard such stories before from Mrs. Forney, who seemed immoderately bent on prying her niece loose from her marriage. Distracted now in an entirely different way, the younger woman's mouth twitched as she reflected for a moment if she would prefer verbal abuse and light violence to contemptuous invisibility. But then she realized there was nothing to be gained in making such a comparison.

"Do you think your niece would really want to leave him? Would she not be afraid?"

Mrs. Forney delayed any answer for a few moments of her own. She caught herself once again—these two had been meeting incidentally in the park since spring had first taken hold this year—enjoying Arlene's voice, her manner of speaking. She could not have said exactly what quality it was, certainly not an accent of any kind, but there was something precise and almost musical in the way Arlene formed sentences. And in the thoughts themselves. She could have wished for a closer connection, but then Arlene was really nothing to her, while her niece was her only remaining family.

"Oh, she'll never leave him, you can bet on that, missy. All he's got to do is smile at her and you can see her start to melt. I guess how he treats her just don't mean as much to her as it should."

"Ah, is he so romantic and handsome then?"

Mrs. Forney compressed the corners of her lips. "I suppose he's not bad looking."

Arlene smiled, and then they were both suddenly looking in the same direction, their attention caught by something midway across the park. Two highly vocal little girls, who seemed, respectively, about three and four years old, were wheeling a baby carriage around the peanut-shaped asphalt path that enclosed a modest play area: swings, sandbox, some enormous wooden bugs and birds mounted on thick coils. Arlene saw that the girls' mothers were in urgent conversation about twenty yards away, standing almost toe to toe, the taller one holding a cigarette which was never allowed to move more than a few inches from her mouth, a protruding oval distinctly outlined in deep red lipstick. Both had penetrating eyes, made all the more so by the intensity of their exchange. Clearly the children could expect little attention, barring some sort of an emergency.

"I said no, and that means no!" intoned the older girl. She wore matching shorts and top, a pattern of daisies on a light green background. The irrepressible cheerfulness of the outfit contradicted the serious—indeed, almost threatening—set of her jaw.

"Oh, we'll see about that!" answered the younger, with admittedly less volume but even greater presence. Her tiny orchid dress, shiny black shoes and white cotton socks better suited the dignity of her rejoinder. As she spoke, she took her hands off the baby carriage and placed them demonstratively on her hips.

What amused both Arlene and Mrs. Forney was not the words, but the total delivery. Even the airy, irresistible sweetness of their little-girl voices could not mask that they were earnestly imitating an adult exchange, some variation of which they must have heard again and again. The cadence of their speech, their postures, their gestures: all worked together effectively, if not altogether consciously, in selling these roles to their accidental and unnoticed audience.

Arlene's pretty mouth was still wriggling in mirth when Mrs. Forney suddenly turned back to her.

"So, how's it with you and your fellow then?"

Her lips went still, as did her eyes, as Arlene looked steadily and politely into the distance, no longer seeing the two children. In the space of a few seconds, she somehow managed to dispose of the question with neither answer nor acknowledgement. Mrs. Forney was disappointed, but not surprised. She knew that Arlene had been married less than a year, knew that her husband worked locally at an unimportant job in a small luggage factory, but she had never been able to learn anything about the nature of their relationship that might not have appeared on the kind of application she and Harry had once filled out to buy some furniture on credit. To her vast dissatisfaction she was thus denied the kind of vicarious marital drama she could share so easily with her niece.

They sat in silence for the next five minutes. The two little girls had answered a summons from their mothers and departed.

"I think it must be nearly half past ten, Mrs. Forney, and I think I must be going. It's always nice to visit with you here."

The older woman just nodded. Arlene arose and slanted off across the grass behind the bench. When she reached the sidewalk, she headed south to the intersection and then turned east. Mrs. Forney watched her, subconsciously admiring the subtle athleticism of her gait, as if the spring in her young legs had to be controlled, lest she begin running.

A minute later Arlene disappears into the morning traffic. A woman sits alone in her green coat, thinking about her niece.

Reading Two

"Graduation Night" by Marla Kraft

[A school athletic field, almost midnight. A nicely dressed young couple walking at some distance from a dozen or so celebrating classmates.]

Laura: It's been a really nice night, hasn't it?

Paul: Oh, yes. The unstructured conclusion of four very structured years. I guess that's got to be nice.

Laura: What's wrong, sweetie? You haven't been yourself this whole evening. Is it some sort of melancholy? You know, the end of high school and everything that goes with it... People going their separate ways? Can't you just enjoy the night, and that we're all still together?

Paul: I'm sorry, Laura. I didn't mean to ruin anything for you.

Laura: [Takes and squeezes his hand.] Oh, you didn't. I just want you to be happy along with the rest of us.

[They go on for a minute in silence.]

Paul: Laura, when the others are ready to go, would you stay here with me, just for a little while...and then we'll walk home?

Laura: Oh...Okay.

Paul: I know it's a long way--

Laura: It's really okay, sweetie. I only hesitated because--well, never mind. Of course, we can stay.

Paul: Okay.

[A girlfriend pulls Laura into a free-for-all game of catch played with a tattered graduation cap. Laura takes off her shiny, stiff shoes, runs across the grass. She returns a few minutes later.]

Laura: Oh, God, that was wet! [Stops and bends down.]

Paul: My God, Laura, do you always do that? Just reach right under your dress and take off your stockings like they were nothing more than a pair of gloves or something?

Laura: Well, only on graduation night. It was fun, though. Didn't you want to play?

Paul: I guess not.

[The game ends, and the others depart, leaving Paul and Laura alone on the field.]

Laura: Lord knows what they were all thinking when you told them we wanted to stay. But it's fine--I don't care.

Paul: Me either. Let's go over there near the end of the stands and sit down.

Laura: [Nods slightly.] I hope this means you're going to tell me what's on your mind now.

[They climb to the top benches and sit under an encroaching tree limb. Paul looks off across the deserted field. Laura looks at Paul.]

Paul: Look, you're right, Laura, I have something to say, something important, but I can't quite come straight at it.

Laura: Oh, don't worry. You can tell me anything you want, any way you want. I'll be alright.

Paul: Laura, it's not...Okay, let me find a place to start...I guess that would be long before we started going together these last couple months. You know, you've lived around the corner from me since third grade. I don't know why we never knew each other much as little kids.

Laura: I don't either. I suppose we just weren't ready to. But that can't be what you're so upset about, that it took so long for us to get to know each other.

Paul: No--well, maybe in a way. It's just that it took so many years before I even began to notice this very pretty girl walking by my house all the time. Especially in summer, in those short, airy dresses. And then, this year, just when it was beginning to turn warm enough to bring out those dresses again, I did start to notice. And pretty soon we were taking walks together and you were bringing me cookies from the bakery in little white bags and calling me sweetie as if we had been together for twenty years.

Laura: Ah, now I see the problem, Paul: you thought I was pretty, liked my clothes, liked the cookies, liked that I called you sweetie, and then we started going out together. Who wouldn't be upset? [Smiles broadly.]

Paul: Laura, don't make fun. Oh, I know you didn't mean it that way. It's just that when all of this started, it was great, but I never thought that anyone could get hurt.

Laura: Paul, I know what this is about! About you going away to college, and that will be the end of us, and you just don't want to say it! That's why you've been acting so--

Paul: No! No, you don't! You don't know at all what this is about!

Laura: I'm sorry...

Paul: Everything has changed so fast! What I thought I wanted, where I was going, even where I was in the whole business of growing up. All of it has changed.

Laura: Please tell me what happened--what's happening!

Paul: I will. Remember that very pretty girl that used to walk by my house? She's gone, Laura, and in her place there's now this heartbreakingly beautiful one who's become, without any warning whatsoever, the indispensable center of my life.

Laura: But Paul, if that's how you feel, why...

Paul: Laura, almost nothing that mattered to me before matters now, and nothing matters now except that I want us to stay together--and to be married. We're not too young. I'll get a job first and work and save as much as you think we'll need. That's what I want to work toward now. That's all I want to work toward. Everything else can wait.

[She places her head on his neck and says nothing. He remains rock still. Finally, she draws back a little.]

Laura: Sweetie... Sweetie, listen to me. I would marry you right here, right now, if it were possible. I never hoped that you'd feel that way about me so soon, but I did hope you would eventually, even though tonight I thought what you wanted to tell me was just the opposite.

Paul: Oh, Laura, I'm so sorry for acting so badly. But I'm just not used to being me anymore, and I was so afraid of losing you. And everything depends on you now. Can't you see that?

Laura: Of course, I can, Paul.

Paul: Then we can do this?

Laura: Of course, sweetie.

"Is that you, Aaron?" Holly looked up from the oven toward the front of the house.

"Yeah, who else?" She heard him put his keys and attaché case down. "Where're the kids?"

"With my sister and John. She let them each bring a friend for a cook-out: hamburgers, hot dogs, marshmallows. Johnny had the day off. They've been there for most of the afternoon already." She peered into the oven again, where a shallow pan held a small roast and some potatoes. "This is about ready to come out."

"Okay, just give me a minute."

Holly had just finished setting out the last of the food and utensils when Aaron returned. She smiled as she sat down across the table from him, but he was looking over the meal and missed it.

"Mr. Howard was really happy with those new pressure tables," he said, as he transferred several slices of meat and about a half dozen small potatoes to his plate.

"Said they should save the power guys days of work on their next design."

It's funny, thought Holly, helping herself in turn. *He does this over and over, knowing that I don't know or care anything about the airplane business.* "That sounds pretty good," she said aloud.

"It's even better," he continued. "I think I can adjust for temperature next with only a slight expansion of the table of parameters, and that should really save them some time. In fact, it seems to me that…"

Holly was afraid to pretend to stop listening, not because he might become angry, but because, she felt certain, he wouldn't notice. They had met in his last year of college, and everything that followed seemed completely natural. No, she thought, not natural, but what? Mechanical? Routine? None of those words quite fit. She was the first girl he had ever dated. That alone should have made things more romantic, more special, but nothing could be further from the truth. Aaron was smarter than most—certainly better with mathematics—but he wasn't any kind of distracted, towering intellect. He mowed his lawn, washed his car, even played with his children sometimes, like any good man would. True, their marriage had cut short her own college education, but she had accepted that fact from the first as part of the system and really didn't mind either the abortion of her own education or its consequences.

She waited until he seemed done with his technical monolog, at least for the moment.

"Aaron, we have the next couple of hours to ourselves."

She glanced up briefly to see the uncomfortable expression on his face.

"No, not that," she added quickly. "But I was down at the library today and Janie let me make a copy of the new script she got hold of last week. She said it's really good, about a young couple just at the point of engagement—"

"Jeez, Holly, you know I hate those things. Can't we just watch some television?"

She felt something change in herself. She could no longer quite maintain her deep and habitual pretense of respectfully tiptoeing around his sensibilities—and emotional torpor. She took a deep breath.

"And just what would be special about that?" she asked. "Watching other people's emotions? Oh, I suppose with the kids gone, you think we could really let ourselves go."

"Well, those dialogs of yours or scripts or whatever you call them aren't exactly our own emotions either, are they?" He, too, had felt a change. Although still certain of his control, he was no longer quite the accomplished, assured, dispassionate professional at home and at leisure. He was annoyed—and even more so at being annoyed. All of this was most unfair: he was a good man, who worked to take care of his family, hardly ever spoke sharply to anyone, and his attentions to his wife and children were regular and predictable. "I mean, aren't we just reading what someone else wrote for us?"

Holly had to think for a minute. "Aaron, that's stupid. That's like saying that acting in a play is no different from watching it. That can't be right."

"Well, we're not acting, we're just reading out loud to each other."

"No, we're not! You know it doesn't work that way. We bring our own experiences and, yes, our own emotions to it and…" She was crying now. "And that's more real than any of the stupid things we usually talk about, no matter what you think!" She looked at him across the table, watching his too placid face. "Don't you dare pretend that you don't understand!"

"Yeah, I understand, but I still think you're wrong. The kids, my work, this house, they're all real, even if you don't think they're worthy of your fabulous emotional capacity. I'm sorry life is like that—No, I'm sorry that *you're* sorry life is like that. I don't think you understand the alternative." He spoke with the condescension and contempt that adults often reserve for dull children.

"And I don't think you understand what this is like for me! All this safety and comfort…You think the only alternative is danger? You've got it wrong, Aaron, and I got it wrong when I married you. Safety and danger aren't the only way to look at things. There's also what's real—not just what's reality—but what's real and honest and truly ours in ourselves!"

"So, none of this counts?" Aaron's face was now red and swollen. "Nothing we made? Not the house, not the kids, not the marriage?"

"You know I'm not saying that, you damned fool!" She took another deep breath and spoke through its exhalation. "Why can't you read with me? Where's the danger? *Why can't we just remember for a few minutes what it was like to love each other?"*

The last shreds of control that held her voice to something less than a scream gave her words a sincerity, a finality, an authenticity that overwhelmed him. He rose halfway out of his chair, and for a moment she thought he would come around the table, hold her, comfort her, give her something of what she needed. But instead, he sank back down, put both hands on the table, and looked off to the side, shaking his head minutely. A minute later he resumed eating his supper.

Holly looked down at the table again, knowing that if she continued just to sit there, she would always sit there, and that his way of seeing things would be proven right. She thought of Paul and Laura:

"Then we can do this?"

"Of course, sweetie."

She sat there as a single tear rolled from her eye, fell to the napkin in her lap and was absorbed and lost forever.

Chapter Two

Dolores elbowed the woman working next to her. "See, what'd I tell you? He does that all the time." The new girl looked up from her work to see a slight fellow of medium height surveying the workroom. The hum of twenty machines and as many women was hardly noticeable to anyone who had worked here for more than a month, and certainly not to the sandy-haired man who had worked here for six years, almost from the day he had finished high school. The small factory produced limited runs of specialty luggage items, such as cosmetic cases and small satchels. Most were made of high-quality leather and designed by the owner, who spent very little time in the establishment.

"What's he looking for?"

"It's just a damned show," answered Dolores. "Whenever he's about to leave the room, he looks us over like that. Like he's making sure we know better than to slack off when he's gone."

"But he's not in charge of anything but the machines, is he?"

"That's right, honey."

"Then it's all sort of silly, isn't it?"

"That's right, honey. Cheese Boy Bruce is just preening for the boss and us ladies," replied Dolores with such exaggerated intonation that she was virtually singing.

"Why do you call him that?"

"If he ever comes over to speak to you after lunch, I guarantee you won't wonder anymore."

The girl nodded dubiously and looked down again at her work. "Cheese Boy or Superman, I hope he stays away from me," she mumbled.

Charlie heard Bruce come in, but he didn't turn around. "Almost lunch time?" he asked.

"Yep," said Bruce. The drab, windowless room was a mess. Long ago it had been painted a lusterless olive green, and unfortunately some descendant of the original color still remained. Crooked bolts of heavy fabrics, much of it cheap, brittle leather with its tangy reek, leaned into corners and against the wall shelves. The shelves themselves held a magnificent disarray of tools, spare and broken parts, machine assemblies and subassemblies side by side with stacks of material catalogs and brown cardboard boxes of orders and invoices. Two desks were set up roughly in the middle of the cramped space. The small one was used mostly by Charlie and was so overloaded with papers and catalogs that not a square inch of its heavily nicked blondish wood surface was any longer to be seen. The larger, a battered piece of gun-metal gray office furniture that had seen its respectable days vanish with the onset of the Great Depression, was Bruce's worktable. Here the disarray could not be held to two dimensions and broke into a third, so that whatever he was fixing was generally surrounded on all sides by unstable mounds of electro-mechanical paraphernalia.

Bruce moved a low bench away from a wall and the two reoriented their chairs so that the bench served as a lunch table. Charlie brought out something he picked up on his way to work that morning—on this particular day, nothing more than a bag of pretzels and a small carton of orange drink—while Bruce reached into a wrinkled brown sack to retrieve his invariable sliced cheddar cheese on dry toast, wrapped in wax paper.

The two had been reluctant friends for almost a decade, with the kind of reluctance seen in the less prepossessing couples at a high school prom. Neither had been much favored either athletically or intellectually, or in looks or personality. They drifted toward each other in lunch, gym class, study hall, and somehow a friendship that seemed to have been at best born moribund managed to persist beyond school. After graduation, Charlie went to fulltime status at the independent grocery store where he had worked for the last few years, while Bruce, who had long ago learned some basic mechanics from his father, and had some real intuition about it, went to work tending the heavy-duty sewing machines in a nearby niche luggage factory. When the owner of the factory mentioned that he could use someone to take over the manufacturing paperwork, Bruce recommended his friend Charlie, who shortly thereafter came over for the same pay he had been earning in the grocery store. Both considered themselves well above the common lot of the machine operators and were openly smug about the privilege of working—and taking lunch—in their own private space, such as it was, at an obvious remove from the operations floor and the ladies' common room.

They each took a few bites before Charlie asked, "So how's it goin' today?"

"Not bad," said Bruce, gazing levelly into Charlie's face to give his words credibility as well as emphasis. "I think that new girl—the one Dolores is training—has her eye on me."

"Uh, huh," was the only response Charlie could summon. Bruce talked a great game, but he had never known anyone so shy of women.

"I never could figure why you got married, Charlie. I mean, why you didn't want to look around a little more."

"I told you: it seemed like a good idea at the time. I thought it would work out." Charlie saw Bruce shake his head minutely as he took another bite of cheese and bread into his mouth. He knew what Bruce thought of Arlene, that she was weird "and a real dog besides." Charlie could even laugh along with him when he said such things or prove the quality of his wit with his own cuts at her. But he could never—would never—attempt to explain, even to Bruce, the closest thing in the world he had to a friend, how that marriage had ever come about.

"What did you ever see in her?"

"I don't know," said Charlie, sipping from the limp carton that was no longer perceptibly cooler than room temperature. But I *do* know, he thought, looking away as if he were watching something out on the production floor. Charlie had never been as afraid of girls as Bruce had, and some element of aggressiveness in his personality had even been attractive to a few that he had met in school and later at work. But these girls reflected back something in himself that he loathed, something that, in some vague sense, he understood as both unclean and impotent, and the few intimacies that resulted from these acquaintances had only made things worse. As adolescence rigidified into adulthood, Charlie settled physically somewhere between ordinary and good-looking. He was of better than average height—but by no means tall—and fit, with soft black hair. His mouth might have seemed a bit tightly set, but that was contradicted by his eyes, the color of which was a low-intensity mix of green and brown. Charlie's eyes were remarkably bimodal: they could seem soft and sympathetic, although that was almost always illusory, and then shift into the look of disgusted scorn that generally much better reflected his true interior state. He knew Arlene was funny looking, funny sounding, and the first few minutes in company with her ancient wreck of a mother had been more than enough to discredit her lineage. And yet, she was so unlike these other girls. Charlie was delighted when she seemed to return his interest, could not believe his luck when she accepted his proposal, but shortly thereafter, his feelings began to change. His invariable operational mode became that of a man who had been tricked into marriage by a woman pretending to be something other than she was, while *he* was nothing less than honor personified. But inside, he knew otherwise, although beyond that vague truth he permitted himself no coherent self-examination. The self-loathing smoldered, made somehow more intense by the very presence of his wife.

"Well, I don't say Arlene's the worst girl in the world," said Bruce, crumpling the paper in which his sandwich had been wrapped and throwing it toward a dark brown, open trash can that stood grimly in one corner of the room, "but she sure ain't near the best." The crumpled ball banked off the wall and fell into the can.

It was about eight-fifteen that night, after her morning conversation in the park with Mrs. Forney, when Arlene heard the apartment door open and close. After their unremarkable lunch, Charlie and Bruce had gone out after work to a local bar for some unremarkable beers.

Their apartment, otherwise quite standard, with one bedroom, bathroom, and kitchen, all of which opened off the central space of a living room, had one odd architectural feature whose explanation had disappeared with the building contractors. At what should have been the corner of the living room formed by the exterior wall and the bedroom there was a doorway, but no door, into a space stolen and disconnected from the bedroom. Had it opened to the bedroom rather than the living room, it might have been appropriate for a walk-in closet, except for the presence of an ordinary-looking window—but exactly the kind that one generally does *not* find in a closet. Artificial illumination, when needed, was provided by the harsh light of a ceiling fixture: a naked bulb operated by a short, tarnished, dangling chain. The space was large enough for a modest loveseat facing the window; this was of the thin, continental type, without removable cushions, upholstered in lustrous moss-green velvet, and very much second hand. In front of the left side of the love seat, stood a small, oval-shaped, walnut table, supported by a multi-segmented spindle that branched into three gently contoured feet. Finally, there sat a squat wooden cabinet in the corner opposite the table and at right angles to the window. This low cabinet had a single door that opened outward on a set of hinges to the left, and was made of quality wood, although its surface was now thoroughly marred. To these three modest pieces of furniture, Arlene had added a sepia block print bearing the portrait of a young girl whose face held a compelling beauty and yet was empty of any emotion, a window box now bursting with gold and orange marigolds, and a gathered curtain to substitute for the omitted door. The curtain was her own work, and the only thing she had ever done to which she might herself have ascribed artistic merit. The fabric was a very fine silk that showed an iridescence of pale lemon, white gold, apple green and coral rose in various relative intensities depending on the angle and quality of illumination. On this she had embroidered in vivid blues and indigos, sharp magentas, and gentle lavenders a vast number of highly symmetric, abstract floral patterns of minute and exacting detail. These patterns appeared to have been flung, almost randomly, but with an exquisite sense of balance, across the expanse of silk, which was then folded on itself so that the reverse side remained forever unseen. The result had the luminous depth and opacity of an opal. Once an Avon lady, a bird-like woman of early maturity, with a valise of cosmetic samples—but she knew at a glance that she was not going to make a sale at this particular door—had exclaimed in sustained wonder at this superb creation.

"I only started it," responded Arlene quietly. "Afterwards, it just took on a life of its own." In contrast, the window dressing consisted of nothing more than two cuts from a simple print and had been only an hour's work.

In this space, with the embroidered curtain drawn and only the soft fading pink of the sky for light, Arlene had been sitting ever since she had finished her dinner and put the kitchen back in order. She had left a warm plate for Charlie in the oven, with no expectation that he would even look for it. She listened for the direction of his steps after he had closed the door without yet turning on a light. She knew that this was the hardest part of their marriage for him. In the morning, he could outwait her in bed and leave in perfect isolation, as he had this morning. But coming home at night, unless he stayed out extraordinarily late, it was harder to ignore the fact of another living presence in so small a space. Her retreat into the misbegotten closet made things only slightly easier: they were nonetheless bound to cross paths before he went to sleep.

She heard him stop in the middle of the living room. He knew where she was. He decided to get it over with, walked to her corner, pulled aside the curtain. He just stood there for a few seconds, looking in at her as the light continued to fade.

"How were things at work today, Charlie?" The light was insufficient to see much more than his posture; as she looked up from the loveseat, his dark face showed only its outline. She had said, "Charlie," but that strange enunciation of hers with nearly equal stress on both syllables made it more formal, closer to Charles.

"How long you been in here?" His voice was dry and low. Even though this miniscule space allowed him disproportionately more isolation from her than had they been without it, she knew he didn't like to see her in here. She understood: in the rest of the apartment he treated her implicitly as an intruder, and that alone could justify his hostility; here perhaps she presumed some right to privacy. Besides, he didn't like that sketch, and the elaborate embroidery of the curtain touched yet another raw nerve.

"Since dinner," she answered simply. "I left something in the oven for you. I'll be happy to set the table if you'd like. Or maybe fix you a tray in front of the television." There was that funny accent again: two much stress on the second syllable of "television." Her smile, even in the near darkness, was sweet and sincere. He knew she would do whatever he wished.

"No, you just sit here."

"Are you sure then?"

This passive cheerfulness was more than he could take, and suddenly the muscles in his neck went taught. One hand still held the silk curtain aside, the other pointed stiffly, vaguely toward her. His voice expanded in depth, rose in volume, and took on the clipped precision with which he was wont to express anger under demonstrably careful control.

"I said no, and that means no!"

Arlene smiled—a smile of delight, with no trace of irony, mockery, or malice. She thought back to the little girls in the park. Her eyes sparkled, and in a voice that reflected the mirth of her face she answered.

"Oh, we'll see about that!"

Charlie stood there frozen: the discord between her facial expression, tone, posture and the meaning of her words left him without physical or verbal response for a good ten seconds. Arlene thought for a moment that she had better explain her odd behavior before one of his ugly explosions, and yet she was fascinated by the effect of her own words—a mere six syllables that she had lifted from the lexicon of a three-year old who had in turn, no doubt, borrowed the phrase from one of her parents. The corners of her mouth began to twitch; she quickly regained control of herself, lest she make things worse. Lowering her eyes to her hands, which lay crossed in her lap, she sat in quiescent composure.

Charlie let the curtain fall back into place, crossed the living room again, and disappeared into the bedroom. Arlene was paying no attention, however. She continued sitting quietly in her accidental retreat as the last of the light drained out of the sky. Her hands remained crossed, but her eyes had lifted to the lower pane of the window, where the silhouettes of her marigolds were bobbing ever so slightly in a gentle evening breeze. But she had no attention for their dark, dancing heads either. Her great idea had come.

Mary stood on a kitchen chair, arms high in the air, and, while her brother watched, first her auburn hair and then her round sweet face emerged from a cloud of stiff white mesh and limp satin that slid over her tiny waist, hips, and bare legs as her mother pulled the dress down around her. She smiled at him, amused at the awkwardness of it all, and he quickly looked away. At one of the back legs of the chair, a mostly charcoal-colored, faintly tiger-striped cat stropped. Mary made an effort to look back over her right shoulder, softly calling out, "Hey, Booper Girl."

"Stop squirming!" warned her mother, as she completed the placement and smoothing of the garment. She stepped back a few feet, squinted critically. "What do you think, Charlie?"

"How the hell should *I* know?" He stalked sullenly out the screen door from the kitchen into their small yard, an unkempt rectangle rudely enclosed by a series of rotted vertical planks held together with a few equally decrepit cross pieces. He heard a dull clap as the rusty, sluggish spring pulled the door shut behind him. He was prepared, should his mother have chosen to give chase, to shift into a sprint and, long before she could lay a hand on him, to have disappeared through any one of the many low triangular gaps in the fencing. But he knew that these days she was less and less likely to follow him, no matter what he said.

Charlie's mother had watched for years as this sullenness had become a dominant attribute of her son's behavior. She knew only too well what was happening and could almost fix the minute at which point her cheerful, if somewhat uncertain little boy had begun this painful descent. Mary was three and a half, Charlie just over six, and Mrs. Sloan was walking the two of them home one Saturday afternoon from a birthday party at one of the neighbor's houses, a party for a little girl named Julia who just about split the difference in her own children's ages. Charlie had only been to one such party previously, and it was Mary's first. The event was only a few blocks away, but since there was one major street to be crossed, it seemed prudent to escort them. They walked on a broad sidewalk into a brisk yet still warm October wind; each child kept a hand in one of their mother's coat pockets. They were passing various storefronts—a pet shop, a meat market, a beauty parlor––all closed at this hour, when Mary spoke out in her clear, almost musical, but very serious voice. Looking up at her mother she said, "It would have been better if Julia's mother hadn't talked so much about that dollhouse. She didn't have to do that. I don't think Julia liked it."

Mrs. Sloan had, of course, not attended the party, but she knew Julia's mother well enough to comprehend her daughter's words immediately. Julia's father, a slight man with impeccably groomed hair and mustache, was a small-time lawyer with a small-time inheritance, but both sources together put his family well beyond the means of his neighbors. In consequence, Julia had clothing, toys, and experiences undreamed of by her friends and classmates, and these in turn were used routinely by her mother as tokens of a decisive superiority. Mrs. Sloan could well imagine how the other children, particularly the older ones, had been made to feel in having their attention forced on something so far out of their own reach, and the discomfort that Julia herself might have intuited at seeing her friends put so ill at ease. Yes, she could imagine that all too well, but she could not have imagined that Mary would grasp it. And so it was at that moment that this and other, prior instances of her daughter's unusual emotional perceptiveness crystallized, and Mrs. Sloan smiled down at her with unreserved tenderness and appreciation. When an instant later Charlie withdrew his hand from her pocket, hunched his shoulders, and walked on ahead in a posture of stiff hurt at his mother's all too obviously uneven affection for her two children, she understood. Such spontaneous, radiant affection had never been hers to give him—could never be hers to give him—and he would return its lack with calculated bitterness. From that day on, this particular aspect of the family dynamic seemed fixed, and no amount of overt sympathy or searching empathy of this conscientious woman for her inadvertently affronted son could ever change it.

Now, standing in the middle of her kitchen, Mrs. Sloan watched Charlie's exit with more resignation than exasperation. She turned back to her daughter, who stood quietly on the chair in the white dress. She wondered if Mary's intuition extended to her brother's dark moodiness. But Mary only looked back at her with a faint echo of her own resignation.

"You be sure to thank your aunt and cousin next time you see them," said Mrs. Sloan. "It may not be this dress's First Holy Communion, but it will never be seen on a prettier little girl."

Mary's spontaneous smile, as usual, lighted every corner of the room. She prepared to jump off the chair, but her mother stopped her with a gesture of the hand, walked back over to her, lifted the child, and then gently set her down on the floor.

"You go take that off—carefully!—and hang it up in your closet for Sunday."

Mary smiled again, walking out of the kitchen with notably uncharacteristic reserve.

The following Sunday morning, Mrs. Sloan was surprised to find Charlie making no fuss about getting out of bed and dressing for church. After a stern admonition from his mother to keep clean, he went out to the back yard, where she later saw him playing with an old, rusted baking pan of the low rectangular type appropriate for corn bread or coffee cake. Mr. Sloan was at the table in the dining room—not really a separate room but a portion of the living room given over to a dining room table—quietly reading the paper in a state of comfortable undress, a state in which he would remain until well after noon, when the local bar opened. His wife had made a weak, perfunctory effort to engage him in his daughter's religious passage, but he had waved her off simply by lowering his eyes before she had finished her one and only mention of the affair to him. Now she made one last check of her hat and gloves and her modestly applied lipstick.

"Come on out, Mary! Time to go!" As she spoke, she saw Charlie come in from the backyard, as if he had been waiting agreeably nearby to spare her a further summons. He was carrying the cat in his left arm and set it down carefully on the sturdy jute rug in the middle of the kitchen. It stayed put as he stroked it affectionately. Mrs. Sloan could not see that he was holding a ragged black scrap of cloth balled in his right hand.

Mary's appearance at the door of the bedroom that she shared with her brother—at this age they took turns getting dressed and undressed—may, that fine Sunday morning, by itself have been enough to have convinced her practical, skeptical mother of God's existence. How could this sparkling little round-faced soul in a cloud of white have come from anything else but divine provenance? Yet the events that followed perhaps convinced her of something else entirely.

Charlie looked directly at Mary, as if to be sure he had her attention, and then with his right hand reached for the end of the cat's well plumed tail, forking it with his index and middle fingers. He gave a sharp tug and immediately opened his hand to reveal the dark wad of concealed fabric. The illusion was perfect. Mary screamed in terror: "*Boopers!*" Charlie dashed across the kitchen and out the door, carrying away what seemed certain to be the final segment of the animal's anatomy. Even Mrs. Sloan was fooled for an instant, long enough for her daughter to dash unimpeded after her brother, in a thoughtless panic. She stretched out her arms and lifted the palms of her hands to deflect the screen door, which had not yet closed, and flung her legs horizontally as she crossed the threshold. The closing door blocked her vision so that she could not see and therefore had no chance—none whatsoever—of missing the pan of viscous mud that Charlie had left placed just so on the back porch. One of her tiny white shoes hit the edge of the pan, which then acted as a lever to catapult its contents squarely into the bodice of her dress, with spatters covering her face, underskirts, and legs.

Charlie had stopped, and he turned to watch his sister over the few seconds it took for her to understand what had happened; he saw her face crumple as she began to cry. Then his eyes lifted a little, and for a long moment he and his mother held each other's gaze through the veil of a tattered screen.

Arlene opened her eyes the next morning feeling neither the passage of time nor any interruption of consciousness. She lay on her back, looking straight up, her thoughts flowing in the same delightful stream as six hours before when she had sat with the bobbing marigolds. In the limited, diffuse light of the dawn seeping around the bedroom curtains, the ceiling looked like grey velvet. She listened to Charlie's breathing. Their narrow twin beds were separated by a low maple table that bore a pink ceramic lamp on a poorly executed off-white doily. She did not need to move her head in the slightest to determine that he was still fast asleep. Sliding her hips to the left, she slipped out of bed and into the bathroom, where she stepped out of her cotton nightgown and made a quick and silent toilet, using only a damp washcloth and a brush. She put the nightgown back on, tip-toed out of the bathroom and across the still darkened room. With barely a sound, she accessed the drawers and closet and then left the room, carrying an aqua dress, shoes and underwear, closing the door as if it were moving through a thick liquid. She quickly finished dressing in the kitchen.

The sun was now almost up, and long, well-defined shadows could be seen in the streets below. Arlene was tempted to leave the apartment right then, even though it would mean hours out on the streets waiting at least until nine o'clock, perhaps later. It wouldn't be so bad––the park or courtyard at the library would be lovely at this hour and in this weather—but she did not want anything this day to appear odd to Charlie. So, she waited, and made coffee as usual, but no toast for herself. She took a cup into the alcove and sat quietly behind the embroidered curtain.

Fifteen minutes after she first heard him stirring in the bathroom, Charlie emerged into the living room, and her plans for a nothing-odd sort of morning collapsed.

"Arlene, you back there? How about some coffee?"

His voice was characteristically gruff but that could hardly counterbalance the uncharacteristic act of his speaking to her at all.

"Of course, Charlie."

She came out from behind the curtain. There was nothing unusual for him to notice about her state of dress. She always dressed as if she had somewhere to go or someone to see, even when she had neither one nor the other. If she seemed a little more excited than someone ready for another day on which nothing at all was expected of her, he didn't notice that either. But when she went into the kitchen, and reaching up into a cupboard, her dress rose an inch or two to accent the pretty line of her legs, that he noticed. He looked quickly away, as if guilty of some perversion.

"Would you like something with your coffee?" she asked, as she stood at the counter pouring and stirring in a little milk.

"No, just the coffee." He sat down at the table.

Arlene hesitated a long moment, somewhat unsure of herself. She was distinctly aware of two mutually exclusive impulses. She wanted to rush back behind her curtain, to be left alone with everything she had been thinking, and yet her husband seemed to be offering her a modicum of normality here in this small kitchen. Wouldn't it be foolish and wrong to shun him? Ignoring the mug that she had left on the table in her private retreat, she poured herself another cup and sat down across from him. There was no newspaper on the table, no radio playing in the background, nothing whatsoever to hide behind.

"Maybe, Charlie, you would like to invite your friend Bruce to come for dinner sometime. I can make something special."

"Why would I want *him* here? It's bad enough I have to work with that louse."

Arlene disregarded the smallness of his words; she knew that Bruce and Charlie had been friends since high school. She was not annoyed that he would say such a thing, but still at sea with his behavior this morning.

"Well, maybe Mary. The company would be a nice change, and I think you have not seen your sister in many months."

Arlene immediately regretted her mention of Mary. It seemed so natural: Mary was, after all, Charlie's only sibling, and even as an only child, Arlene knew that brothers and sisters routinely visited each other. But she knew, too, and had known since she first met Charlie, that there was something horribly strange and unhealthy in their relationship, something she had never been able to understand. If only she could get to know Mary better—no, she thought, that wasn't it. She and Mary had an obvious intuitive affinity for each other, and the weirdness of the relationship with her brother was not symmetric: it was in him. She had never seen Mary on her own, without Charlie, and the tension that flowed from his impenetrable discomfort with her made any but the most trivial conversation with Mary impossible. Whatever the cause, Charlie did not want her in his life.

Abruptly, Arlene's problem was solved: Charlie had picked up the cup of coffee but midway to his lips he set it down on the saucer with a loud, resolute crack. He rose from the table and, without another word, left the apartment, apparently to escape the angry discomfort that Arlene's awkward attempt at socialization had caused. She looked blankly at the door, at first regretfully, but soon that cleared when she thought of what lay ahead of her today.

Reading Three

"Day Blindness" by Marla Kraft

[A hotel garden at dusk. A man and woman, both middle aged, leaning against a railing that overlooks a decorative koi pond surrounded by exotic blooms. A small fountain bubbles at the pond's center.]

John: I won't pretend that I didn't want these few minutes alone with you. But now that I have them, I don't know where to start.

Angela: Come on, John. No need to sound so serious. We're much too old and our past much too distant for anything like that.

John: Angela, you know I loved you, and I know that you loved me. It's not that I want to start anything now... That can't be--there are too many other people involved--but that's not really the point.

Angela: Look here, dear. I'm happy and even a little thrilled to see you again--and, yes, especially alone--but in a few minutes, we are going back into that wedding reception, and the lives we've known for two decades are going to go on as if these few minutes had never happened. So, what exactly <u>can</u> be the point? [She looks at him with concern.] Oh, John, I'm sorry. I don't mean to sound so harsh. I really am glad to see you. [She touches his arm gently.]

John: We both married good people, I think, and we've been much blessed. But we didn't marry each other. I love April, as I know you must love Michael. And yet always when I've thought of you, and now when I'm looking right at you, I am filled with this vast feeling of regret, and failure, and apathy.

Angela: I understand only the first one, John.

John: Do you remember what it was like? The intensity? And--I'm sorry I can't think of a better word--the bipolarity? For all those years we were either wrapped so tightly to each other that there was no space to breathe--

Angela: We didn't need it: we breathed for each other. I've never kissed anyone the way I kissed you.

John: But then always the times apart. I think maybe I understand these cycles finally, but that doesn't matter now, tonight. What matters is that I always wanted to come back and be with you and you always took me back, except once.

Angela: Until the very end, I had no choice. I never thought about it. I wanted it as much as you did.

John: Angela, I had so many chances. You let me back into your life so many times. There was one day...

Angela: John, it's all right. Say it. Whatever it is, we'll both be better off for your having said it.

John: That day was so unrepeatably beautiful. I could feel the sunshine inside me, and there were no words in my head because none were needed. I woke up. I wanted to be with you. I went to find you. That sounds simple enough, but there was no plan, no plausible way to find you. I took a bus to your college and just started walking through the parking lots. And there you were.

Angela: I remember...

John: We sat on that little hummock on a little island of grass in that sea of asphalt. Your head was down and the breeze pushed little wisps of your hair against my face. That smell came from paradise. And that was all it took: we were together again for another time.

Angela: But that was a wonderful day, John! There can be no tragedy there--and certainly no occasion for feeling failure and apathy.

John: Angie, that day--don't ask me if I'm being literal or metaphorical because it doesn't make a damned bit of difference--that day was a miracle and a gift from God. I could have asked you right then to at least think about us getting married. We were old enough and in love enough. But I didn't. I smelled your hair, I watched your eyes, I was happy again, but I stayed a boy and let things go their own tired way. And finally, we lost each other forever. [He breathes deeply.] Everything about that day--it was as if God was giving me this precious gift, telling me what to do, in huge letters written across the sky. But I couldn't or wouldn't read the message. That may not be unforgivable, but it is irredeemable.

Angela: I understand all of this, sweetheart, and I am touched and share your regrets more than I can tell you, now or ever. But your life hasn't been ruined. No matter how much that "failure" somehow still hurts you, you've gone on. You've understood. And now you've shared this with me. That's something, isn't it?

John: Thank you, Angie, but just think: Imagine you've come for a job interview. You're young, you're well qualified, you're brash, you're brimming with confidence--maybe just a little uneasy in the stomach. But in the first minute of the interview you sneeze, and there's sneeze stuff all over your resume and tie. The interviewer rolls his chair back a foot or so and asks you, with a nervous squint, why you think you'd be good at the job. You're so embarrassed that all you can say is, "Well, sir, I'm really not as stupid as I seem right now." And then, as if to leave nothing to chance, seeing all your hopes for the job vanish, you vomit all over his desk and excuse yourself massively, only to experience a second wave of sickness. Imagine that, Angie, and imagine it well. Afterwards, would you care if you noticed on the way out that you had done a really good job shining your shoes that day and there wasn't a spot of sneeze or vomit on them? After all that, would it make <u>any</u> difference how good your shoes looked?

Angela: [Almost whispering.] I don't know... I suppose it couldn't.

John: No, Angie, it couldn't. Not any. Not ever.

"Ellie, I will never know why I did it. Every cell in my body was screaming against it, but I let him go—sent him away. I think I was twenty-one; he was twenty-two. Maybe just once I wanted to be the one who acted, who forced things, who was in charge. He had always come back before. But not this time. I never saw him again."

Ellie looked up from her coffee. Ellie and I were having breakfast in a plain little diner across from the local supermarket. It wasn't unusual. We got together once or twice a week. The morning was dark, dreary with low clouds. The few dim lights within the diner and its wall of glass seemed to invite the gloom of the outdoors inside. But it was warm and, sitting in a warm booth across from Ellie, intimately cozy.

"My God, Raela, I've known you for five years, and I had no idea this thing was inside you." She spoke with a quiet intensity and understanding. "Why is it coming out now? All of it would have happened," she said, tightening her lips and pausing for a moment to calculate, "over twenty-five years ago."

"I don't know. Maybe because I'm old enough to have to face now what my life hasn't been and hasn't had. I look back at that day and see—no matter how foolish this sounds—the turning point. I didn't have the courage to see that love through, and I've never had another love worth speaking of, at least not in comparison to what Richard and I had." I could see before I finished the sentence that Ellie understood the implications.

"But, honey, that must mean the bad times with Richard were *really* bad—or you would never have let go."

Among her many charms, Ellie had one quality that was precious: she could be, at the same time, gentle and sympathetic, sensible, and direct. Still, at that moment I dreaded her directness insofar as it challenged my own. A pair of suede gloves lay on the table. I rubbed my fingertips across the back, to feel a texture that reminded me of the tough softness of the petals of a tiger lily. There was no hope of coherence in what I wanted to say. I didn't think it through. I just let the words come out in an unemphatic tumble.

"Oh, the bad times were more than bad. They were torture. But you never saw two people with such a stranglehold on each other's hearts. And yet that bursting intensity always led to the same place: he would pull away, push me away. Yes, that hurt and maybe I should regret nothing. But I can't help feeling that there was something there, in him, that I never understood, and that *he* never understood. That his love for me was not flawed, but something else in him was, and that sooner or later he would have grown out of that flaw if I had only given him the chance. We didn't have to lose each other."

"Good God, Raela, do you know how many women say that? How many women stay in relationships feeling that that single mysterious, magical change that will make it all perfect is both inevitable and right around the corner?"

"I know you're right, Ellie, and that you're speaking good, sturdy common sense. But every moment and every encounter of our lives is special and unique in at least one way, and sometimes so special that the general principles of good, sturdy common sense just don't apply. Richard wasn't some dashing piece of immaturity who charmed me out of my soul and my underwear. He was already steady and disciplined and bright and direct in his passions. Something he could never express got in the way again and again, but not so much in the way that he didn't always find his way back to me. I was his love, and he was mine. I know that—I knew it then. But there would be other loves, just as intense, without the flaws, or so I thought. There weren't, and so I lost the one love of my life."

"Raela, nobody ever quite recovers from that first love. Isn't what you're feeling just that and maybe nothing more?"

"I wish it were. I wish I weren't so certain about what I lost. But, Ellie, you had a first love." Her head bent forward, and then she smiled shyly and looked up at me from under her eyelashes. "Think about him, sweetie. Picture him. Is he there every day of your life? When you look at your husband, do you measure the distance between your feelings for him and for your lost love? Do you have secret songs that you play only to think about him? Do you sit in the park alone and imagine how your life together would have been?"

"Of course not!" she answered at once. "Are you that obsessed?" She bit her lip on that last word, afraid it was too insensitive—and too clinical.

"Oh, yes…"

We both paused. The cups of coffee sat there undisturbed; their steaming had diminished to the most ephemeral and nearly imperceptible of wisps. Ellie drew in a deep breath.

"Raela, something is missing from what you've just told me. Whatever you once had with this man, nothing can be gained from obsessing on the memories. So why have you held them so long? Why are you doing this to yourself now?"

"You mean, what am I getting out of it?"

She nodded, just the tiniest hint of a smile showing some self-satisfaction that her capacity for tactful directness had not been exceeded.

"I could say that what I get out of it is hope, but that would be lying to myself. I have no idea where Richard is, if he's married, and I've never thought seriously about trying to find him. And I *am* married. If Jim weren't a good man, maybe I could imagine being swept away by a romantic tidal wave—should we ever meet!—but Jim *is* a good man. He's done nothing to deserve the kind of pain that would cause him. No, this isn't about some remote and almost infinitesimal hope.

"I could say that this pain gives me a sense of being somehow special, that no matter what I seem to be from the outside, there, on the inside, I have this great glowing passion alive in me. But that would be doubly stupid: stupid by being mere vanity and stupid because even if there's some pleasure to be found in vanity under *any* circumstances, how can it apply to a mere invisibility? That's just raw self-deception.

"I can only explain it one way. Ellie, have you ever read the same book over again?" She nodded. "Even one that had a tragic ending, but you just loved the story so much?"

"Not a book, but a movie..." I could see her reliving something in the moment as her words trailed off, but she never offered to tell me exactly of which movie she was thinking.

"Why would you do that? You know from the moment you start watching or reading that the ending is fixed and inevitable. There's no hope there, and nothing special about you because anyone can watch a movie or read a book. But there's something else you know when you begin the story yet again: you know it has a sort of living quality, and you accept, on some level, the illusion that it's really happening. And what's alive about it is a sense of choice. Part of you projects into that sense. Do you see? That's what I get from holding onto our story—the story of Richard and Raela—the illusion of a beautiful indeterminate future."

"Raela, do you ever wonder how it is for him?"

I realized that my head had dropped to the point of staring at the napkin in my lap. When I looked up, it seemed that the gloom had saturated the air so that the ambient light itself was sluggish. I reached slowly into my purse and pulled out some worn sheets of paper, a few printed pages folded and stapled together like a short piece of music for the piano. I extended my hand across the table. Ellie took the pages and lowered her eyes to them:

"Day Blindness" by Marla Kraft.

Chapter Three

She might have taken the bus, but Arlene wanted the time to think—but not exactly. In all of their essentials, the key decisions had been made within seconds of her exchange with Charlie the previous evening, while she sat so unthreateningly upon her loveseat as he stood at the curtain. There was therefore nothing of a devising or calculating aspect on her mind. No, not time to think, but time to experience. Somehow her state of mind, as she walked in the pleasant light of mid-morning along the neat but by no means affluent streets of her neighborhood, reminded her of that space behind her Aunt's garage: isolation and novelty, without fear. The shade of her dress, a bright blue suffused with a hint of green, seemed to reflect the mix of the sky and the only just maturing foliage of the few trees that she passed. She did not hurry, but the length and strength of her legs carried her soon enough to her goal.

The edge of the window of the narrow shop front was obscured by the tight pattern of collapsed gray lozenges formed by the metal security screen, now drawn in repose. Arlene stopped and stood there for just a moment before crossing the last few feet of glass and turning into the doorway. She opened the door to the sound of a chime, crossing from sunlight into a space that was dark, ancient, and distinctly sorrowful. Her large eyes needed time to adjust to the light; they passed over low, cloudy glass cases that defined the small central space on three sides. Hints of colors and shapes that did not quite aggregate into separate objects could be seen through the glass, giving a sense of chaotic clutter. Behind the cases were shelves of larger, still dimmer shapes. As Arlene continued to peer into these recesses and finally began to make sense of at least some part of her visual field, one of the shapes from behind the glass case opposite the entrance rose vertically and peered back.

Ordinarily Mr. Sommerstein would have said, "May I help you?" in a voice too mechanical to be heard as politeness, but something in Arlene's appearance or posture carried enough of the brightness of the day outside into the shop that he found himself reacting to the incongruity: "So, what have we here?" His voice was at once low and breathy, as if a large dog had been given the power of speech, and in this particular instance it held an unaccustomed note of human curiosity.

"Hello," answered Arlene after a perceptible hesitation. She had had to identify the moving object as a person and the strange sounds as a voice asking a question. "Are you the owner?"

"Yeah, Sammy Sommerstein. What can I do for you?" He had answered immediately but was slightly distracted by the second syllable of her *hello*. It was somehow too round and too long. The rest of his automatic assessment proceeded without hesitation: a nice kid, but not much to look at, about twenty, married not too long, still no children. What she might want in a pawn shop he couldn't begin to guess.

"I would like a typewriter, Mr. Sommerstein," she said simply. "I don't have much money."

That second sentence did not sound like a prelude to a price negotiation as much as a direct confession intended to spare him any later disillusionment. Sammy Sommerstein could almost appreciate that.

"A typewriter? I got two of them in the back. Before I bring 'em out, I might as well tell you: one is a little portable, a flat, green thing that a college student might use, but I don't know. It'll work, I guess, If you don't plan to work on it for too long at a stretch. The other—it costs more of course—was probably from an office once. Much bigger with nice round keys with some kind of metal rims. It's probably better if you expect to do some serious typing."

Arlene thought for a few seconds. She had owned almost nothing nice in her life and had visions of that second typewriter. Of course, it would be more difficult to hide. She didn't like to waste Mr. Sommerstein's time, but she asked, "Could I see them both?"

The tone of diffidence in her voice was something he hadn't heard in years, and it was accented by the slight distortion of her blue irises as she looked up through her thick glasses. It was really no trouble to bring them both out.

"Sure, honey. You have a seat at that little table over there, and I'll set 'em up for you."

His face softened, but he was too good a businessman to smile—or perhaps the requisite muscles had atrophied. Nonetheless, he realized that he was quite enjoying this tiny shred of human contact.

Arlene went to sit where he had indicated. Mr. Sommerstein disappeared into the back of the shop. There were some random and sporadic noises, and within a minute or two he reappeared with the two machines on the top tray of a dull tan utility cart. He brought the cart over to her and shifted the typewriters onto the table at which she sat in what Mr. Sommerstein took to be an incomprehensible state of anticipation. He handed her a sheet of yellowish blank typing paper.

"Have at it."

Arlene had been assigned a typing class in her first semester of high school. She took no note at the time, but it was the same for almost every girl in the class, since the expectation was that if a young woman was going to work at all before marriage, it would likely be in an office; the class was certainly not meant to anticipate college. She loaded the paper into the smaller machine, being careful at first not even to look at the larger one. She began typing:

`Do good and disappear.`

`Do good and disappear.`

She had, like every other typing student, learned about the quick brown fox and the lazy dog in her class, but still preferred to warm up on these four words. Her mother had told her that they were from a convent somewhere in Europe. Arlene knew that they suited her, and it amused her that in a funny way, they described themselves in their quick disappearance—much quicker than any fox could ever manage.

After a few repetitions she had taken the measure of the dull mint-green portable. It would work, but…

Arlene removed the paper from the portable, shifted her chair a bit and turned to the much taller, much rounder, royal blue office machine. The chrome carriage return lever showed a kind of confident pride in its upward salute. She was much more careful about squaring the paper as she inserted it against the roller. Her fingers rested lightly on keys that allowed for much more emphatic vertical motion:

`Do good and disappear.`

`Do good and disappear.`

She had to grin, enjoying both the feel of the machine and how incongruous her little sentence had become when typed on such a fine device.

Mr. Sommerstein, who shared none of her interior depth—in both senses—saw her smile and scented the sale.

"How much is this one?" she asked.

"Twenty-five," he said at once, and recalled automatically that the typewriter had cost him twelve dollars. Arlene's glasses magnified the disappointment in her eyes, and he wished he had been less blunt but was not in the least sure of why he felt any regrets at all.

"Oh… I have only ten dollars," she said in a small, apologetic voice. "I could get maybe five dollars more. I know that's not enough."

"How would you get that thing home?" he asked. He was temporizing, allowing himself time to calculate, but not in any numerical sense.

"A shopping basket, the one I use for groceries. It has big wheels and folds up."

"Yeah, I get it." Mr. Sommerstein observed that she hadn't noticed that his question was irrelevant to the ten dollars that separated her from the blue machine.

"I'll take the portable then." The tone of her voice didn't quite match the disappointment that had not yet faded from her eyes. Mr. Sommerstein recognized—even if he did not understand—that something in that discord between her tone and her look spoke vaguely to a kind of bravery rather than resignation. He took a quick breath.

"Look, kid, you come back tomorrow with fifteen bucks and your shopping basket, and you take the big machine. We'll say it costs twenty, and you pay me the extra five when you have it. Okay?"

Arlene's eyes responded with a confused, unfocussed intensity. "Oh, yes, thank you." She looked down and then back up at him nodding. "I will see you tomorrow morning, if you're planning to be open then."

"Yeah, I'll be here."

Just before eleven o'clock on the following day, Arlene was back on the sidewalks that connected her apartment to Mr. Sommerstein's shop, now on her way home. The light and air were just as pleasant, and somehow made her feel warm just a fraction of an inch beneath her skin. In front of her she guided her shopping basket with both hands. She had stopped an hour or so earlier at a market to buy a few inessentials, but these were just cover for the blue typewriter that sat at the bottom of the cart, enclosed in its own brown paper bag. Her stomach reacted uncomfortably to the implicit deception. She had no reason to think that Charlie would be anywhere near their apartment when she returned, but just in case she did not want it to be obvious that she had brought home anything unusual or of special value. She understood her stomach's reaction to dishonesty, but she did not understand her attachment to her new acquisition. She had somehow tabled any consideration of her self-assessment of this extravagance until this moment, when it was too late to decide against it.

Mr. Sommerstein had looked at her in open perplexity when she returned to his store less than an hour earlier. Arlene imagined he could not understand what she would want with such an item, but that was in fact the smaller part of his perplexity. He looked at her and there was no mistaking the subtle, almost imperceptible quirkiness that had attracted his attention and sympathy yesterday, but why he had made such a—for him—naïve deal with her puzzled him as much as Arlene would be puzzled a few minutes later by why she had to have the more elaborate typewriter. Still, Mr. Sommerstein felt no real regrets as he took her money and helped her slide the machine into her grocery bag. They parted with a mere blink that ended both the transaction and their association. He would never learn the truth about this particular sale, and his only subsequent thought on it would be a neutral grunt when some months later an envelope arrived at his store containing only a five-dollar bill and a note that said, "Thank you very much for the typewriter."

The little green one would have worked, and it would have cost less—no matter that I paid for it out of the small amount of money that Mutti had given me, not out of Charlie's allowance. Mutti taught me not to want fancy things, not to waste my energy on them. She said that these things "madden the heart." I knew that she was quoting something, but she never told me what. And I believe she was telling me the truth. So why did I want this? To have something bigger to hide from Charlie? It would not make any difference to him; he would hate either one just the same—I mean my having either one. *It's not that.*

Arlene continued her long walk home, automatically steering the wheels of her shopping cart away from the irregularities in the sidewalk. Her vague gaze was neither down nor horizontal, but somewhere in between. She enjoyed entering the lives of others, like those little girls in the park, and she understood that her sensitivity—empathy?—was unusual, if not particularly enviable or useful. But she was much less introspective about herself, and so this present self-examination was not especially pleasant. Her lips alternately bunched and stretched as her inner voice continued.

That typewriter is only a small part of what I want to do, but it's a necessary part. I may not have wanted fancy things before, but I have wanted things—although not objects really. Events? Experiences? And yet I have treated them like fancy things for which it is better to keep your heart at a distance. But now, finally, there is something I want to come true, something I want to do.

She stopped, lifted her eyes, and her lips parted and froze, but not rigidly. She understood...

This machine has made everything harder, but it's also made it impossible to go back.

She bit her lower lip slightly. No, these were not the exact words she had been looking for, but they were close enough to move forward. She was committed. The big, fancy typewriter had cut off any retreat. Its polished blueness was a decision made; the little green one was no more than an incipient wish.

Reading Four

"Fusion -- Part One" by Marla Kraft

[A Caribbean beach in late morning. A woman in her twenties wearing a red, skirted swimsuit sits on a towel with her knees drawn up. A young man, perhaps a year or two older, who had been walking toward the water, stops suddenly about eight feet from her.]

Scott: Oh, excuse me.

Alina: My goodness, for what?

Scott: I didn't mean to be staring like that; it was rude.

[Alina smiles broadly.]

Alina: I didn't mind. In fact, it's nice to be noticed.

[Scott is puzzled and hesitant, and a little fascinated by her slightly southern accent. Finally, he continues.]

Scott: Are you here by yourself?

Alina: Yes. I thought at first my sister might come along, but she decided not to. She's older and more responsible, I guess. I haven't been anywhere, so I came anyway since I had a week off from school. How about you?

Scott: Alone, too. Are you a teacher then?

Alina: Oh, please sit down. The towel is plenty big enough for both of us.

[Scott sits, half on the sand, legs folded sideways toward the water; looks at her.]

Alina: Yep, that's why I went to college. I teach high school English, mostly to ninth and tenth graders.

Scott: I teach chemistry, mostly to freshmen and sophomores.

Alina: At a college?

Scott: Yes, a small one. Chemistry isn't exactly a ticket to popularity. Mostly people just put you down to being some sort of boring drone, so I guess that's why I'm here alone.

Alina: But why are you here at all? I mean, this island, this beach.

Scott: I like to hide, in a way, and this is a good place for it... And something else. The water is so warm and placid here. I am not a good swimmer, but you can just paddle slowly away from the shore and keep going and going. The pink hotel just gets smaller and smaller and the beach disappears completely. When I get far enough, there is just me in this enormous ocean. I lie on my back and close my eyes and feel the sun passing right through me into the water. The boundary between me and the rest of the world seems to dissolve, both in space and time. I can feel things that lived deep in this water millions of years ago. I feel so filled with life and meaning, although I can't explain any of that. Somehow, at the same time, it's as alone and as connected to the world as I have ever been.

Alina: Wow. That's not an answer I would ever have expected. Wow.

[At Scott's evident embarrassment at having said too much, Alina resumes her light, cheerful tone.]

Alina: You know, literature isn't so bad--I mean it doesn't have that 'square' factor.

Scott: I guess not. You've got Jane Austen and J. D. Salinger. We've got Dmitri Mendeleev. It's not much of a contest.

Alina: Yeah, I suppose it's a lot easier for me to talk about what I do than for you, but still, I don't talk to many young men. Just a bit too chubby when chubby is going out of style, I guess. No matter how light and puffy and figure-concealing my dresses are, no one takes a second look. Aside from my responsible sister bowing out, that's probably why I'm here alone.

[Scott's face virtually freezes; about ten seconds pass. Alina watches, bewildered.]

Scott: Alina, I have to say something to you that is completely inappropriate for someone I've only known for about five minutes. You stop me whenever you want, and I promise I will get up, turn around, keep walking, and you'll never have to speak to me again.

Alina: My goodness, this sounds awful!

Scott: When I was walking toward the water, I first noticed your face and thought, there is somebody who makes the world more pleasant. It was just an intuition about what someone must be like who has your peaceful, happy, pretty face. I would not have stopped to stare, let alone speak to you, but...

Alina: But what, Scott?

Scott: It's hard to explain. It's like the visual frame that held your face spontaneously expanded to hold your whole body, or rather your whole person. It was like the fusion of who you were on the inside with your physical presence. That is when I stopped and stared. I couldn't look away. And this is to say that nobody who could inspire such a feeling should ever casually dismiss herself as unattractive--to just accept that as the way of things, as if you don't deserve to be admired.

[Alina in turn is silent, but not calculating.]

Alina: Ahm, that swimming-out-to-the-middle-of-nowhere thing that you do, would it spoil it to bring a guest along?

"Next time, you be Scott and I'll be Alina," said Katie. Her eyes sparkled as she flattened out the manuscript pages with the palm of her hand against the low table in front of their tan and gold brocade sofa.

The morning sun flooded the living room; they had rushed breakfast a little to have the time to read together, and their unseen performance had taken them out of any timeline and into another, pleasantly disconnected psychical space.

"Sure," agreed Jill. "You be Alina. This sofa makes a fine beach, don't you think?"

Katie nodded and asked, "Do you think this would be more fun if we had a man to play the part of Scott."

"Not for us," replied Jill, shaking her head without emphasis. "Anyway, the difference in the parts is not really a matter of male and female, except, of course, that men are usually the chemists and women the English teachers." She waited a few seconds and then asked quietly, "Why do you like this one so much, Kate? I like it, too, but for you it seems like a total immersion from which you don't quite want to return."

Katie looked off, gathering her thoughts.

The apartment was modest in size, with neatly painted, clean pastel walls, rather than wallpaper. There were not many furnishings, but every piece had a sort of above-average elegance, although nothing was expensive. The sofa, despite its fine upholstery, was neither large nor deep, but a simple form given a rich texture. The dining table and coffee table were both made of a slightly greenish poplar, with a smooth but unpolished finish. Both dining chairs were of similar construction, with seat cushions covered in subtle floral designs. The overall impression was an optimistic sense of more space than the apartment actually held, punctuated by objects that attracted both the senses of sight and touch. Katie had brought all this about herself, adding and replacing objects organically until she achieved this peaceful order. Jill had simply watched this evolution without comment, knowing that it would converge to something that she would be happy with.

"You know, Jill, I've never thought about that, and it's hard to say. I *do* have that feeling of total immersion when we are reading it, even though I am nothing like either Alina or Scott. Of course, Part Two is obviously more intense, and we do know it's coming, but everything about this—the sky, the beach, the ocean, their meeting—just feels so gorgeously *elemental* to me. Does that make sense? Alina and Scott are really very simple souls underneath their very civilized educations and professions, and I just like them. I like being them. And

I love that they can recognize something special in each other."

"It does make sense, Katie. And, I suppose, they are both in a way invisible to the world."

Katie understood at once what Jill was saying and why she was saying it. Her pale blue eyes met Jill's soft brown ones, and they shared that understanding for a few moments.

Jill stood up abruptly and Katie followed; the special psychical space of the reading that had surrounded them mostly—but not entirely—evaporated.

"Look at the time!" said Jill. "I'll be late for work."

"Okay."

They kissed simply. Jill took her things and left. Katie stood by the sofa for a while and blinked in concentration, fixing the meeting of their eyes in her memory. She thought how blessed she was that she and Jill could so easily fall in love, again and again.

Chapter Four

As Arlene was carefully and happily bumping her shopping cart up the half dozen steps in front of their apartment building, Charlie and Bruce were just finishing lunch at the central table in the small room that served as makeshift office, spare parts repository, and machinery repair area for their modest luggage factory. Bruce silently returned to a bewildering spread of cogs, belts, pins, and springs at his workstation, negligently disposing of the wrinkled sheet of wax paper that had held his pickle and cheese sandwich. Charlie left the room to check over the floor and to attend to a delicate bit of work for one of the owner's new designs that was not yet ready for production.

Dolores looked up just as Charlie came through the door, and she smiled almost imperceptibly. His sharp eyes were instantly intent on her face and did not waver as he crossed directly over to her. His fists were clenched.

"What was that about?"

"What was what about?" responded Delores, her heart sinking.

"You laughed just now when I came in. What the hell is so funny?" He noticed a girl at the next station was watching them both.

"Oh…" She hesitated, and then added gesturing to her right, "It was just something Yoli said, and I only smiled—a little."

Delores was lying, and she knew that Charlie knew it, but it was hardly the kind of lie that could be challenged. It was not even an ill-intentioned lie: she had smiled, but only in relief that it was Charlie, not Bruce, who would be stinking of whatever pungent cheese he had brought for lunch.

Yoli's eyes were as unfocussed as if in death. "That's right," she said almost mechanically.

Both women needed these jobs to help with nothing more luxurious than the rent and the monthly cost of a telephone in their flats. They thought very little of Charlie and Bruce or their small-minded arrogance, but they would never have confronted either of them, no matter how sharp their banter when the men were at a safe distance.

Charlie's eyes now took in both of them. He took a measured, deliberate breath.

"Listen, Bone Rack and Brown Cow, you keep your mouths shut and just work."

Yolanda had been hearing from her mother about her lack of a figure just as long as Dolores had been hearing from hers about her weight. Yet both were stung by Charlies words, as he had intended, and the degree to which they disliked him grew by the same amount that their feelings must be further repressed.

He glared a few seconds longer for emphasis, and then went on to where his own work was laid out. He picked up a tool, looked down at the piece of leather he was intent on shaping, and suddenly blinked at a fast-growing pain in his chest. He knew what was coming, and waited for the pain to subside only to be followed by another more intense wave. It took all of his will to control his posture and not to show his acute distress to the girls on the floor. He put as much weight as he could on his arms, appearing to be leaning over his worktable as if engaged as usual in the task at hand.

Stupid bitches, he thought. He should never have allowed himself to become so angry so soon after lunch. *This could go on for an hour, dammit!* He knew what he needed, and when the pain became bearable, he walked back to the office-storage-machinery-repair lunchroom, stuck his head in, and said to Bruce, "I just remembered, I need to go out for about half an hour. Be right back."

Bruce nodded without interest and continued his work.

Arlene had been home for about fifteen minutes. During that time, she had stowed the shopping cart and the groceries she had bought as cover for the typewriter, carefully placed the typewriter at just left of the center of the oval wooden table in her tiny, curtained alcove, and sat a neatly squared pile of perhaps twenty blank sheets of paper to the right of it. She had to sit forward on the love seat to be able to type, and in fact the seat was a few inches too low for this purpose. Arlene thought about getting a pillow, but the thought was lost in staring at the keys and giving silent thanks to the architectural mishap that had created this space. She had not yet rolled a sheet of paper into the mechanism and felt no immediate need to do so. She knew she was some way from striking that first key and making the first character on an otherwise blank page. But this condition did not flow from fear or tension. She was simply and passively exploring the inner space that had brought her to this moment, sitting in the broad light from the window just beyond the table and the orthogonal, much softer, and much more textured light that passed through the translucency of the intricate curtain, now drawn, a light that seemed to have created itself. Her posture and face both bespoke a happiness, placid and full, that she had never known in this unprepossessing apartment.

All of this changed in the instant that she heard the apartment door rattle and scrape.

What is Charlie doing home? What could I possibly say if he pulls the curtain and sees me here? I can't move, I can't hide the typewriter—there's bound to be some noise! I could go out and close the curtain behind me. Say hello. Ask him if something is wrong. Try to be natural. No, not with my heart pounding like this, and God only knows what color my face and neck are now. But what have I done? I bought a used typewriter—that's all. But it's mine and I want it to stay mine—and clean, not made dirty by what he would say....

And thus she remained in this uncalculated total paralysis as Charlie closed the door and walked toward their small kitchen.

It usually took Charlie no more than fifteen minutes to walk from the factory to his apartment. They had an old blue-gray Pontiac, but it was not worth starting for such a short trip, and so most days it remained parked on a side street, just around the corner from the entrance to their apartment. Today's unscheduled midday walk home went more slowly as he gauged the waves of pain in his chest. Had he been somewhat older or less familiar with this acute heartburn, he might have been worried about some serious underlying medical problem. As it was, he was concerned only about controlling the pain or, more to the point, not allowing others to see it. He moved with the concentration of someone hiking on a dangerous trail, but not in a way that might attract any attention from any passerby, although he was now sweating heavily.

He reached the apartment door and took his keys out of his pocket. As he inserted the door key into the lock and turned, he felt an unbearable stab of pain just under his sternum. Thus, when he turned the key in the lock, he did not notice that it met no resistance; it had not been locked. He quickly opened and closed the door and stood still, again concentrating on controlling his pain. The acuteness passed, and without any real attention he had made the assessment that the apartment was empty. Arlene must be out doing whatever she did to fill her days. He took a deep breath and walked toward the kitchen; it was off the living room opposite the bedroom. There was no door, just an opening about six feet wide. The wooden floor changed from slightly polished and clearly worn hardwood to dingy linoleum, a pattern of white and yellow, with some low-contrast speckling. The kitchen floor, as always, was spotlessly clean, but that only highlighted its essential dreariness.

Charlie carefully reached up into one of the cupboards for a blue glass jar. The jar was filled with oddly textured, jagged white filaments. He filled a glass with tap water at the sink and spilled some of the contents of the blue jar into the water. They immediately burst into effervescence, a reaction that reminded Charlie vaguely of angry bees. He let the fizzing die down a little and then drained the glass in two gulps separated by one sharp breath. He knew that the pain would subside now in minutes. He stood at the sink for two minutes, body bent at the waist, about a quarter of his weight resting on his arms.

When Charlie felt some confidence that the last of the pain had passed, he stood up straight and walked back into the living room. He crossed over to the window not four feet from Arlene's embroidered silk curtain. He looked out at the street: a few cars passed in either direction, a few pedestrians made their way across the intersection or along the sidewalk, and the sun shared its luminosity with the leaves of the trees that grew next to the curb in regularly spaced rectangular gaps in the sidewalk. His mind was blank; it was just a matter of choosing the moment to let himself out of the apartment to walk back to his job.

Arlene, even in her inexplicable terror, deduced Charlie's reason for being home and his movements from the sounds he made in the kitchen and from his steps. While he stood at the window in isolation, she cowered on the other side of the curtain, covered by thick perspiration, feeling anything but alone. She closed her eyes and tightened her lips until they were drained of all color. She breathed so little that she might have become faint except for the extremity of her fear. Only when, at last—after no more than ninety seconds—she heard him walk toward the door and lock it behind him, did she breathe. But it was more than a breath: she was crying, not loudly, but with shudders. She would not type a single character today on her beloved new machine. When she could control her movements and dry her face and hands, she put it away…

She had purchased the more expensive typewriter so that there would be no way back. She realized in this moment that there was also no way back from what had just happened. This was about more than an unrealized person in a common unhappy marriage. Sooner or later, she would have to think this through, to understand the magnitude of her own reaction. Something had burst in that horrific, paralyzing ordeal. She could feel it, but she could not see it.

Arlene shifted off the loveseat to kneel in front of the little cabinet to its right. There was no need to hurry now, but her movements were those of someone who had near-missed a terrible accident, or perhaps received some desperately tragic news about a friend or family member. With a detached methodical cadence, she removed the short lengths of fabric and sewing implements from the cabinet and laid them neatly out on the floor. She put one folded length of fabric to cover the base of the closet and then stood up long enough to lift her typewriter with both hands and place it at the bottom left corner of the now-emptied storage space. She then returned the other fabric cuts and notions to the remaining available space, and her new acquisition was thereby concealed. She closed the cabinet door, left the typing paper on the table, and pushed through the silk curtain.

She stood for a few seconds where Charlie had stood about twenty minutes ago and then gathered her keys and clasp wallet. Taking nothing else, she in turn left the apartment.

Ten minutes later Arlene sat on an uncomfortable bench outside a small church six blocks from her home. The church faced a narrow street that only permitted automobile traffic in one direction. The city trees were much denser on this street than on the larger avenues, and the church itself was mostly covered on two sides by thick ivy. The leaves were still new enough to not have turned their characteristic deep green, and they carried a sense of coolness and life. The bench was against a side wall of the church with the ivy behind it and thus was between fifteen and twenty feet from the street. It faced the deep red bricks of a rectangular building, mostly occupied by a moribund five-and-ten-cent store. There were few pedestrians, and Arlene came to this place from time to time for its sense of green remoteness from both the city and her apartment. The park across from the school where she had sat with Mrs. Forney was a place to see others, to project herself into their interiority. This was a place to be alone.

Her wits were returning to her after the scare with Charlie, and she felt a sense of relief, security, and some pleasure in her surroundings. Her mind, while calm, remained at considerable distance from the wonderful adventure of this morning and the sheer fright of the early afternoon. She realized that she had had no lunch, but it did not surprise her that she was not hungry. Still, perhaps that explained the growing drowsiness that seemed to creep into her from both sides. She blinked a few times from behind her glasses. The last blink did not rebound. *I'm safe here. I like it here. I'm tired.* A few minutes later, anyone watching would have seen a young woman sitting properly alone on the church bench with near-perfect posture. But that was all pretense; Arlene was fast asleep.

Chapter Five

Somewhere between the ages of four and six Arlene's memories began to solidify and gain continuity. Before this time there were only incoherent flashes of confused images and voices. After this time, she could remember vividly the tiny house in which she lived with her parents.

The neighborhood was unabashedly and unattractively urban, a pastiche of densely packed cities that had grown into each other, so that nothing marked any clear boundary between municipalities. This meant nothing, of course, to the stringy little girl in loose-fitting, pale cotton dresses, with worn shoes and tired white socks. What did mean something to her was the near total obliteration of any green spaces. What vegetation there was could only be found in weeds growing in cracks of the asphalt and some sporadic trees that somehow had not been eliminated.

Arlene did remember that for a short time, a little girl lived on the same street a few houses away. Her name was Miranda, and she was a bit older. On a cloudy afternoon in early September, Arlene saw Miranda sitting on the steps of her front porch. She had a small cutting board and a lump of whitish clay with an oddly sweetish smell. Arlene had stopped about four feet away, still on the sidewalk, and watched as Miranda pounded the lump with an object that looked like a squarish hammer with a stellated face. (Neither of them knew that this was too valuable to serve as a toy or that Miranda's mother would have become decidedly unpleasant had she seen her daughter abusing her much-used meat tenderizer.) The clay spread and flattened, retaining the pattern of the hammer's face, until Miranda gathered it up into a ball and repeated the whole process; she was vaguely annoyed to have Arlene watching through her oversized glasses but was too intent on her work to shoo her away. Then Arlene spoke.

"Why do you have that on your arm?" She indicated a modest adhesive bandage applied horizontally.

"Because I'm in school and you're not!" The tone was defiant and startling. Arlene blinked and her lips trembled; Miranda saw that and thought she might be able to make her cry.

"Because I'm in school, and they have to give you needles!" She had a sudden thought, smiled inwardly, and added almost at once, "And to make sure the needle goes in right, they hit your arm first with this!" She smiled maliciously and brandished the meat tenderizer high over her head.

Miranda couldn't tell if Arlene was crying, but she did take satisfaction in how she spun on her toes and sprinted home, her little dress flying out in every direction. Thus, Miranda's next whack at the clay carried an especially vigorous and delicious impact.

Arlene did start school the following fall and immediately ran into trouble. Her mother took her into an unprepossessing brick building with enormous segmented glass doors at the front, now held open by two oversized doorstops. This entrance was not the one ordinarily used by students, but an exception was made on the first day for new pupils. As usual, her mother kept her eyes down and said as little as possible during her daughter's registration. Arlene was curious and a little tense, but not unpleasantly so. This was an entirely new adventure.

When the paperwork was complete, except for one form given over to each parent, an office assistant directed the pair down the hall, then down two flights of dingy stairs, only to find themselves in a slow-moving queue that led into a doorway. Neither mother nor daughter knew what this was about, and they moved along placidly, hand in hand. At the halfway point to the mysterious door, Arlene's mother, from her greater height and experience, deduced the nature of the process. Completely unaware of the startling impact her words would have, she bent down and whispered something to her child. Arlene tugged so sharply at her mother's hand that she was instantly free of her and ran back to the stairwell, dashing out of sight, leaving her mother as the only adult in line without a child in tow, and wishing she were invisible.

About ten minutes later, Arlene's mother and the same woman who had helped with the registration found Arlene cowering in the gap between the open entrance doors and the adjacent wall. Arlene had squeezed into the narrow space sensing only the physical comfort of being in so unlikely a place. The glass, of course, made any concealment hopeless, and her mother could easily see her there. There was no anger in her look, just a hint of surprise at this micro rebellion and a more pronounced expression of sympathy, although she still did not know why her daughter should be so frightened. Arlene wriggled free of the space and took her hand again. This intensely silent woman would ask no questions in a public area, so they quietly traversed their former path to rejoin the line with the registration assistant trailing a few steps behind. A look of terror coalesced on Arlene's small face.

Two women, both employed by the school, had been talking near the door toward which the line was directed. One of them, dressed in her nurse's uniform, stopped abruptly and walked over to Arlene and her mother. She pointed at Arlene but spoke to the adult.

"Is this the little girl who ran away?"

This was met with only the barest of nods.

"Then follow me. It might be easier on her."

The nurse led them to a second door about twenty feet beyond the one on which the line converged and into a smallish room of no obvious purpose. Arlene looked around to see a number of metal cabinets, one straight-backed chair, and a steel table. It did not help that the table reminded her of those she had seen at the butcher's shop. The nurse gestured toward the chair, and Arlene's mother obediently seated herself. Arlene was then lifted onto the cold table by two strong hands. After settling the child down by gently stroking the hair along her neck and left shoulder, this trimly uniformed woman turned to the chair and took the form that

Arlene's mother had been carrying since they left the registration desk and glanced at it.

"I'm Nurse Dyer, and I think it will go easier if we handle things in here. Will that be alright, Mrs. Zirner?"

Again, a nod.

"Just give me a few seconds, Arlene. This will all be over in a minute or two." Her voice was steady and comforting without the false, cloying overtones that adults often take with children.

Nurse Dyer disappeared through a back way that led to the larger, more obviously clinical-looking room in which the children were getting their first vaccinations—or at least the first that any of them would ever remember. She returned to see an intensity in Arlene's eyes that dissolved almost at once into a passive relaxation. *There's no pointy hammer like Miranda told me!*

The nurse began to frown in bewilderment with a question just at the point of reaching her lips but then returned to her usual expression of unstressed competence.

"Ready?"

"Okay," murmured Arlene.

A feeling of coolness from an alcohol swap, a small sharp pinch, and then the band aid. That was all.

Nurse Dyer scribbled her name on the form, handed it back to Mrs. Zirner and said, "Take her to Room 204, where Mrs. Rosen will be assembling her new class. You can pick up your daughter outside at about a quarter past noon. Kindergarten only meets for half a day, and you'll probably find her at Exit 2. Okay?"

"Thank you," replied Mrs. Zirner in a slow, deep voice, looking up for the first time, knowing no other way to acknowledge her gratitude.

"You're welcome. I'm sure Arlene will be happy here."

A week later Arlene's schedule nearly doubled in length. The point of kindergarten was some combination of socialization and regimentation, with the emphasis usually on that latter element. Arlene's teacher recognized immediately that this child simply did not need an empty year to learn how to sit still and follow instructions. Since her student's birthday was just a month or two short of having her start school the previous year, she recommended to her principal that the child be placed in first grade before losing any significant ground. Thus, Arlene came home with a note addressed to Mrs. Zirner asking permission to move her to the first grade and, with that, a full-day schedule. Mrs. Zirner signed her agreement, and Arlene joined a new class with distinctly fewer crayons and beads. At the time, she did not know what was happening, and the other members of her class simply assumed she had just moved into the neighborhood.

Fortunately, this was not the same first-grade class that Miranda was enrolled in, so neither Arlene nor Miranda had reason to be, respectively, either frightened or tempted by that pointy hammer.

Most of elementary school was a kind of plateau for Arlene. She grew in basic skills and knowledge of the world, but emotionally little changed. She learned to navigate the social context of school, but never actively engaged in it. Her classmates gave her the respectful distance that she seemed to want, and while they thought she was funny looking—as she grew, her limbs looked something like those of a balloon animal and her skin and hair soon had the rough texture of someone much older—but she never became the target of harassment. A kind of reciprocity operated with respect to her remote demeanor; moreover, even at a distance, the other children sensed that she was too harmless and innocent for teasing.

This emotional stasis was the result of the extraordinary sameness of her life at home. Julia and Albert Zirner had seen enough instability in their early lives to want nothing more than the safety of absolute stability. Arlene's father was older than her mother by more than ten years, and her mother was herself older than the average parent of an elementary school attendee. Her father spoke so little that Arlene barely knew his voice. He sat on the sofa of their living room day by day, dressed in shabby clothes, half turned to stare out of the living room window of their second-story flat. Mrs. Zirner often served him his meals there on a shiny tin tray painted with bright flowers against a black background. When they did eat together at the kitchen table, he remained quiet, often staring down at a newspaper beside his plate. He had no job, but rather a small income from a small inheritance that he had brought with him to his new country. This was enough, and while he had worked as a carpenter in his youth, he never thought about getting another job. That would mean going back out into the world.

Julia Zirner supplemented their small stipend by working the middle hours of the day cleaning the lavatories and canteen area of a department store not four blocks from where she lived. She worked mostly alone and only saw someone in personnel once a week to collect her wages. These were paid in cash in a small yellow envelope containing bills and coin. She did not know it, but the job was completely secure: the store supervisor had never seen these menial tasks performed so well or so reliably. She was in fact a valued member of the staff, and might have known that, except that her evident desire *not* to be seen discouraged contact, an aspect of her character that she had silently transmitted to her daughter.

Arlene was just over nine years old. She came home after school to find her father in his usual place on the sofa. She entered the living room just long enough to be sure that he had registered her presence in the flat and then went into her bedroom, a place that was smaller and more austere than that of Van Gogh's painting. She took off her light, pale rose jacket and set her textbooks and notebook on a wooden table just large enough to serve as a desk. Her school clothes, a yellow cotton blouse and a gray, faintly checkered skirt, were too plain to require changing. She stood for a few moments staring at the wallpaper: a faded, but somehow compelling arrangement of color-spattered shapes separated by much more organically conceived burgundy curves. No words intervened. She pulled her wooden chair up to the table and in twenty minutes had completed her homework. Her mother had not yet returned from work.

She looked up from the table, again into the wallpaper, scraped the chair backwards and put on her jacket to go outside. She left the flat, closing the door to the second-floor hallway just sharply enough to be sure that her father would know she had gone out. When she got to the sidewalk, she looked both ways to check that Miranda—whom she had never forgiven—was nowhere to be seen. There were no parks or playgrounds in the area to attract her interest, and so, as usual, she walked to the bus stop bench about fifty yards away and sat down. From where she sat, she could see a few shops with whatever foot traffic they might attract. She watched the people and wondered about them, especially when she could see a face clearly. She did not think of herself as an oddly solitary little girl in an oddly solitary family—she was who she was, and her mother and father were normal by virtue of being the only mother and father she would ever know—and so this quiet fascination with others at a distance did not seem at all strange to her. She simply enjoyed being outside under the protection of her rose jacket and the limited sense of community this brought her.

A blond woman in a green, belted coat caught Arlene's eye. She was walking on the same side of the street as the bus bench. Arlene thought that the distance between them, her small size, and large glasses gave her license to stare. The woman was definitely younger than her mother, but not too young to be married and have children of her own. She walked with a fluidity that Arlene admired at once, and as she got closer, Arlene became fascinated by her beautifully symmetric face and hazel eyes. She wondered what it would be like to be so pretty and was trying to take a step into that world when all at once she noticed that the distance between them was much too close and the woman was looking back through Arlene's glasses and right into her own eyes. Her simple smile transformed her face from pretty to beautiful, but Arlene was now too startled by her sudden attention to notice.

"Hello, little girl. That's a pretty jacket. Are you waiting for the bus all by yourself?"

Arlene's face froze except for her mouth, which made motions at first unrelated to speech. The woman in the green coat had stopped and was looking at her with no impatience whatsoever at her reticence. When she tilted her head forward to look more closely at the small figure who had been so openly observing her but had now become so awkward, her loose, blond hair shifted forward to the corners of her lips. She wore lipstick several shades deeper than the color of Arlene's jacket. At last, the movement of Arlene's own lips became coherent and aligned with language.

"I'm sorry, but my mother's coming home, and I have to go."

With that short statement the little girl hurried away from the bench in the direction from which she had come and away from the nice lady who knew shyness when she engaged it, even if she had never had any reason to be shy herself. Arlene looked back just once after a minute or two, to see a green coat receding from her. It was now well past the bench on which, just a few minutes before, she had been seated in such comfortable security.

The pale rose jacket was draped across the back of one of the kitchen chairs. Both dinner and the cleanup were done. Julia sat at the table—a rectangle with rounded edges and a nickel frame surrounding a scratched surface of regularly spaced yellow daisies on a forest green background—in the chair nearest the door leading to the rest of the flat. Arlene was at the sink, looking absently out the window above it, when she heard her mother.

"Come, Lena. Sit and tell me about your day."

She spoke the name as if it were spelled LAY-nuh, an odd derivative of "Arlene," but one that her daughter had become accustomed to from her first memories, just as she was accustomed to her father pronouncing "Julia" not as their doctor or any other respected adult might normally do, but rather as YOO-lee-ah.

"Okay, Mutti," replied Arlene in a tone that split the difference between cheerful and neutral. She was happy to talk to her mother, but this invitation was hardly surprising: it followed most of their dinners, especially on weekdays. Arlene had been born into the world alone, except for her mother, but Julia had lived, in distant times, in a far more social environment. These conversations with her child were all that was left to her, especially since her husband had no inclination whatsoever to make friends.

Arlene slid onto the adjacent chair facing the wall and looked at her mother. Julia looked back at the small girl who had never been and would never be pretty or cute; the large glasses, which she knew Arlene needed from almost the moment that she began to learn the alphabet, still made her unhappy, but that unhappiness was overwhelmed with a flood of affection and a will to protect this child beyond any strength she had remaining in her sorrowfully weakened life. She made sure always not to crush Arlene with this love, and so her expression and her words remained quiet and placid.

"So, what happened today?"

"The lessons were like any other day. We spent an hour in arithmetic multiplying numbers that had two digits. But we did that yesterday, too. Anyway, I think I can do it now."

"Lessons hardly seem to move at all from day to day at your age. It was the same for me. Did you learn *anything* new today?"

"I must have, but I can't remember," said Arlene, softly biting her lip.

"And did anything interesting happen with your friends?" Julia knew she was abusing the term; she knew only too well that her daughter had no friends; but neither did she or her husband.

"I sat on the wall against the fence during lunch and watched Louise and Charlotte pretending they were getting married."

"Are they nice to you, Lena?"

"Well, they say hello and know my name. Also, Kenny always says hello to me. The other boys do not seem to like him and make fun."

"You mean they make fun because he says hello to you?"

"No, for other things. He will not play games with them—or they do not want him to—and when he reads something he holds if far away from his eyes. Things like that."

A year or so ago, Julia had nearly met Kenny when she and Arlene had been out walking on their way to a store. He lived nearby and was on the sidewalk in front of his house, fully absorbed in digging between two concrete slabs of pavement with a popsicle stick. After identifying him to her mother, Arlene softly called out his name. He stopped his excavations at once, looked up, and gave Arlene the kind of sunny smile that little boys on general principles do not often give to little girls. He started to say something, but an old woman tending a window box called him away sharply, and when he got back to his worksite, Arlene was at too great a distance to exchange words.

"Kenny is being raised by his grandparents, isn't he?" asked Julia, now staring at one of the daisies on the kitchen table. This one was somehow not quite of the same hue as the others and had always caught her eye.

"I don't know…" The sentence had clearly ended with another thought entirely. Julia waited for her daughter to continue.

"Someone else said hello, too," she muttered.

"Another one of your school friends?"

"No," replied Arlene, knowing fully that she had given the answer before the question was asked. She didn't understand her own discomfort.

"I went out after school just to be outside and sit on the bench at the corner. A lady in a green coat was walking toward me, but when she was far away, I started watching her. She was so pretty that I wondered... Anyway, she saw me watching her and said hello and that she liked my jacket and asked if I was waiting for the bus. She seemed nice, but I just ran away."

In the year in which this story takes place, it would never have occurred to Julia to be afraid or even suspicious of an adult stranger talking to her daughter, but she could see by the almost spasmatic twisting of Arlene's lips that something disturbing had happened to her.

"If you thought she was nice, why were you afraid, Lena?" she asked gently.

"I don't know. I felt like I was caught doing something wrong."

Julia smiled a little at that. She had never known a human being as unlikely as her daughter to do something wrong.

"Staring at someone *is* wrong, if you make them feel uncomfortable. But I don't think that's what happened."

"No, Mutti. Her face was so pretty. I cannot believe she ever worried at all."

"I'm sure that's not true. Everybody worries about something. But why were you staring at her?"

"I do not know. I like to look at people and imagine their insides." She stopped for a moment and then added in a puzzled tone, "But I do not like it at all when somebody outside looks at *me*."

"Do *you* like to look at you, Lena?"

"No," answered Arlene immediately. "I am just me."

"I understand," said Julia. "That seems like a good way to live."

Arlene got up and stood next to her chair, waiting to be sure that her mother was done with their conversation. Her lips pulled down and out, but she gave no further voice to her thoughts.

Perhaps Julia's assertion was too simplistic, or perhaps it was flat out wrong, but neither of them knew that yet.

Arlene stood still for many years.

Reading Five

"Fusion -- Part Two" by Marla Kraft

[That same Caribbean island, but now on a bench in dark shade at a botanical garden. A centuries-old one-room structure made of rock with a few gaps for windows and a tile roof stands in bright sunlight. The light varies in intensity from dazzling full sun to vague darkness in the shadows; plants and flowers of both spectacular size and nearly microscopic delicacy fill the warm, tangible space. Alina and Scott are alone, turned toward each other. She is wearing a white blouse and a short yellow skirt. He is dressed in an open shirt with a muted floral pattern and simple tan shorts.]

Scott: I told you it was beautiful.

Alina: I feel like I am breathing pure oxygen, Scott. I have never been anywhere like this. How is it that after walking for an hour we have seen no one else? Why isn't everybody here?

Scott: I suppose if you lived on this island, you would have no reason to come and if you didn't, you would almost certainly not know about it, since the beaches and the town shops command all the attention.

Alina: But then how did <u>you</u> find it?

Scott: There are only two towns of any size on this island. One of them is within walking distance of our hotel. The other you can get to by bus, and when I took that bus once before, we passed by the sign, which is barely visible. The next day I asked the driver if I could be let off and picked up here. He said of course, and the day after I walked past that sign and into this deserted place of every hue and texture of green and of every searing color I never imagined. I've been back on every trip. But I didn't think I would ever share it with anyone. Yet here we are.

[Alina continues to look off in one direction then another. Scott can only watch her face.]

Alina: I don't know when I have ever been so happy just to be part of the world. You were right, Scott: this is not just an exquisite display of life in the moment. There is something timeless about this place.

[The sentence is spoken in a kind of rapture, but then the look on her face suddenly decays into something beyond tragedy.]

Scott: Alina, what's wrong? Alina?

Alina: Timeless. This place is timeless. But we're not. Scott, I met you two days ago. Since then, we have had dinner together and a swim about twenty times further than I have ever been from shore. Just floating on our backs with the sun, as you said, going right through our bodies and right through the ages of life that passed below us in that gentle water. In two days, we have spent a thousand hours together, and that fusion you saw in me when we first met has now happened to us. But it's not really a thousand hours, is it?

[Her lower lip disappears, and she takes several deep and audible breaths trying to control her face.]

Alina: This place is timeless, but we are not! In just a tiny march of days--and we've never even dared speak about that--we are each going to go back to that arid little airport and take different planes, going to different places, a thousand miles apart. Scott, time is what we <u>don't</u> have, and here I am ruining the most beautiful place I have ever been, with the most wonderful person I have ever known, crying about an ending that hasn't happened yet.

[She buries her face in her hands. Scott pulls her hands away and down.]

Scott: Let's fix this right now.

Alina: What do you mean?

Scott: I'm not sure yet. I don't know what either of us is about to say, but I am sure I want to fix this right now and that we can. And that I never want to see you in such pain again.

Alina: Okay.

Scott: You're right, of course. Back home we do live a thousand miles apart, and I hadn't thought about that. But that doesn't mean I ever thought of this--or of us--ending when we went back. If we want to stay together, we can and we will. Our lives are ours.

Alina: But how?

Scott: There are three ways, Alina. Both of us can work almost anywhere. I could come to you, or you could come to me. Those are two ways. But there's a third one...

[Scott is quiet for a few seconds as if trying to absorb and focus all of the vibrant, unending life and beauty that surround them. He is speaking to Alina, he is speaking to himself, he is speaking to the world.]

Scott: We are here, both in this garden and on this island, alone. We could do that. We could both leave where we are and what we know and start over with each other and for each other. Beginning again with only each other. We could decide on someplace new and wonderful, live there, be married, have a family. I know you have your sister, and you love her, but you won't have to let go of her; we can manage that. And you and I simply continue this, what we have here, in another new place.

[Alina's eyes grow wide with understanding. She smiles slightly and nods.]

Alina: Let's do that.

At six-fifteen in the afternoon in late September the sun had lost its harshness but still retained that special equinoctial effervescence. The whole room seemed to glow from its walls. This time, Katie and Jill sat shoulder-to-shoulder, left to right, against the west wall, just to the left of the window that admitted this suffusion of light through a simple, sheer curtain. The tan and gold "beach sofa" they had used for their prior reading was unoccupied.

They had been sharing some papers which were now set down on the floor. Katie was crying silently, just one or two tracks of tears. Jill held her right hand in both of her own which rested on her left thigh. Katie wore a simple blue top with a black skirt; Jill had on the green floral dress that she had worn to work that morning. Her hands, with Katies' enclosed, fell right at the hemline of her dress.

"I'm glad we made time for this, Katie. It's been weeks and weeks since we read the first part." Jill could not take her eyes off those quiet tears.

"Me, too," said Katie. "I hate to ask you for something that I know will drain us both so much after you've been away working all day."

Jill smiled. "You've been working, too."

"I have, but I know it's not the same. I have my assignments, and I make my sketches and detailed drawings, but I am alone and in my own world while doing it. You can be interrupted at any second, and sometimes twice at the same time. You have to keep your public face and alert system on. I don't, except for maybe once every two weeks or so when I have to hand in what I've done and get the next set of assignments. It's all so different."

"Well, I like working with people and you like working alone, and we both like being together, so what's the problem?" Jill's eyes were bright and playful. "I have more than enough energy to be Alina, no matter what sort of state she gets herself into."

The skin around Katie's eyes tightened and then relaxed; her expression became serious—almost grave—but Jill recognized this as the preamble to a complicated thought.

"Jill, when we did the first part of this last month, you asked me why it was so special to me. I told you something about how much I liked Alina and Scott, but I have only just now realized why I like them so much.

It goes beyond the mutual recognition of each other's value. Alina is so much in love with him that she's terrified that she won't be able to draw breath without him, so she breaks down like that. And Scott *doesn't* for the exact same reason: he can't draw a breath without her, and so he never even considers it, even though a feather's brush with reality would have knocked him off that bench and right through the walls of that stone building."

"But that was a good thing, wasn't it?" interrupted Jill.

"Yes, honey, and that's my point and why I was crying and why I am starting to again. That kind of all-in love isn't only for special people. It's for plain people like Alina and Scott. And even if Marla Kraft, whoever she is, did set it in a beautiful, exotic place, it's for plain people in plain places. That kind of love becomes the center of everything, has its own inescapable gravity, and the overwhelming wonder of it is that it's possible for anyone lucky enough to grow up in a place that allows self-expression and self-definition, even if those things are often devalued by becoming ordinary and are still not without unnecessary and hurtful limits.

"That kind of all-in love happened to us in the plainest of circumstances. It's happening right now, and I am so grateful for you. That's why I can't stop crying."

Jill could only answer with her own sudden rush of tears, and they held each other in that lovely September light that never seemed to fade.

Chapter Six

The evening that Arlene forever remembered as Typewriter Day was, in contrast to her early-morning near euphoria and midday distress, comparatively ordinary—at least it began that way. Charlie had come home at his usual time, between seven and seven-thirty, and Arlene, expecting no engagement from him, set out a dinner that had been left warming for over an hour. His "usual time" was an odd construction. He finished work at five and could easily have been home by five-thirty. Their conventional dinner time was six, and that is the time for which Arlene prepared and when Arlene took her meal. But within months of their marriage, Charlie was invariably late. Arlene began to understand what was expected: he no longer wanted to share meals with her, and so, without ever acknowledging that, he simply came home too late. At first, she waited for him but then understood his intention without understanding his motive: he wanted her to finish dinner before he got home so that he could be served but otherwise responsible for no interaction with her. This hurt enormously at first—as did his corresponding disdain for her in their bedroom—but she was used to a lifetime of being alone and well-taught by her mother's example and words, and so she simply let these insupportable conditions devolve into the norm. When she allowed herself to think about it, she was sad to realize that this armed neutrality on his part was preferable to verbal interactions that had become increasingly more caustic, with no reason that she could divine. Her discipline of inner silence with respect to Charlie, an implicit worldview inherited from her mother, and the prevailing ethos of the times kept her from any consideration of the obvious course of action: to leave him. To live was to survive, and almost invisibly.

Charlie finished his dinner without a word while Arlene remained at the sink with her back to him. He arose, went into the bedroom. She heard a small click and thirty seconds later, after its internal components had warmed up, the sound of their modest television. Its move from the living room to the bedroom was the last of their brief sex-life.

Arlene's afternoon nap on the church bench had left her with far too much energy to think about sleep, and yet it was too late to slip out for a walk. She thought for a second that if Charlie weren't there she would have enjoyed a walk, or better yet, a ride on one of the city buses, with no particular destination except for the bus itself; it would be near empty at this hour. With a quick movement of her neck and brief widening of her eyes, she made her decision. It would cost her some ugly words tomorrow morning, but she had to get out, and suddenly a solitary bus ride in the darkness became irresistible. She got her purse and a light coat and was gone within seconds. The last thing she noticed as she closed the door was the sound of a swelling laugh track coming from the bedroom.

❁ ❁ ❁ ❁ ❁ ❁ ❁ ❁ ❁

Arlene dropped a dime and a nickel into the glass box at the front of the bus. The coins lay there long enough for the driver to verify the fare before being somehow digested by the device. She asked politely how late the buses ran, only to hear the most disinterested of replies:

"Until about twelve-thirty."

"Thank you," she answered. She needed no further details. That was more than enough time.

Before the bus began to move, she looked down the aisle. There were only two other passengers, and neither was reading. The dim, yellowish safety light that ringed the ceiling of the vehicle provided just enough light for her to move toward the back. About halfway, the driver moved back out into traffic, causing her to adjust her posture abruptly but gracefully. She took the seat in the back left corner and looked out of the window. The lighting caused only the slightest reflection of the interior of the bus, leaving her free to see the deserted city streets. Only one or two convenience shops were still open.

"Twenty-three," she said to herself—or perhaps out loud but too softly to attract any attention. She realized that she was repeating the bus route number, something that played no role in her getting onboard since the destination had been of no consideration.

Twenty-three. Papi liked that number, but why? It had something to do with being two eights and seven ones, but I cannot think what is special about that. I think Papi liked math…

Arlene had had two years of algebra in high school, in which she got B's without much effort—because she had not been willing to *expend* much effort. Geometry was different, it was pretty and seemed to be about something direct and beautiful. But algebra seemed utterly dead. Three years of math was already unusual for a girl, which is to say, for someone with almost no prospects of going on to college, but her counselors had never quite figured out what to do with her, so these multi-section math courses were always available.

What am I doing thinking about the number twenty-three when I have two much more important things to figure out. What is Charlie going to do when he notices that I have left the apartment? And to ride a bus to nowhere in particular? I tried so hard to make this day look normal, and now this. But I haven't done anything wrong—not wrong like how he treats me.

Arlene saw something then in the gossamer reflection of her own half face on the window. It was an almost microscopic wince. She had never thought that before, about how Charlie treated her. What was, was. She had lived her life that way, so much so that the very notion of self-effacement was invisible to her.

You can't think about Charlie or the number twenty-three now. You have more important things to worry about.

"Last stop!" Arlene could not be sure if the aggressive edge was just a matter of volume needed to make the announcement or if was directed at her. At her or no one, since she was the only passenger remaining. She promptly got up and stepped out through the back through the folding door on the right, midway along the length of the bus. She started to say thank you as she stepped off, but the words suffocated in her throat. The driver's tone seemed to forbid any sort of polite conventionality. She hoped someone else would be taking over the route for the return trip.

She crossed the street and noted the times posted on the glass kiosk where she would later board the bus back and then moved a few yards away to get some feeling for her surroundings. A breeze moved her hair and pressed her coat against her body. She realized that she had not noticed where the bus had gone, which puzzled her because this was the terminus of the route, but there was no evident waiting loop; it had simply driven away. The area was not as urban as her own neighborhood, but certainly not suburban. No stores could be seen, but an array of middle-aged single-family houses dominated the space.

Arlene looked up the street to the left of where she had alighted and was happy to see a break in the houses: there was a modest green space far too small for a park. Nonetheless, she walked in that direction, and as her angle improved, she saw a gazebo of some twenty feet in diameter set back from the street. A path of small stones led to a hexagonal platform paved with smooth, gray hexagonal brick tiles. The cover rested on six poles, one at every vertex, and was made of wood. Whether the construction was tight enough to serve as shelter from a rainstorm was impossible to say. On each edge, midway between the poles, there was a two-foot cube; the surface was a hard ceramic, lightly patterned to resemble marble. Evidently one was invited to sit, but not to linger. Arlene sat down facing away from the structure on the cube furthest from the street. The green area only extended the width of two residential lots. Likewise, the area where two houses might have stood on the next block over had been supplanted by open grass except for one squat tree opposite the gazebo. It seemed older than the neighborhood and perhaps the whole point of the space was to preserve this single tree. Arlene stared at the vague, dark form of the trunk and lower branches, admitting that speculation was pointless but mutely congratulating herself on having chosen the right bus. She raised her line of vision to a sky made featureless by a misty cloud cover, closed her eyes, and inhaled deeply through her nose.

This was the second time on Typewriter Day that she had escaped the apartment to find isolation outside, but this time she would not fall asleep: there was too much to think through. She opened her eyes, continued to inhale, and began her work.

The apartment was quiet when Arlene returned some hours later. A light was on in the living room, but none in the bedroom. Charlie was asleep. She saw that the curtain that divided her alcove from the main space was drawn. She could think of but two options, and neither seemed promising: she could go behind the curtain and fall asleep until morning, or she could quietly change into her nightclothes and slip into bed. Both had the same problem. If he had noticed she was out before he turned out the lights in the bedroom, there would be snarling questions—that for all her innocence—she could not answer.

She again chose solitude. Closing the curtain behind her, she made a pillow of her coat on the table. Taking off her glasses and sitting forward on the loveseat, she fell asleep.

Charlie swept the curtain aside in a violent motion, and screamed, *"Where were you?"*

Arlene was instantly awake, deeply frightened, and required no time at all to come to terms with where she was and what was happening.

"Dammit, where *were* you? Did you think I wouldn't notice? That I would think you just fell asleep in your little, stinking hole?"

She had left the light on last night in the vain attempt that he might think she had merely nodded off here, but it added nothing to the broad light that was streaming through the window. She had raised her head no more than a few inches from her folded coat and dared look nowhere else but down. She knew her glasses were just to her right on the table but could not reach for them. Her hands were lying, right over left, a few inches forward. Her body was numb, her mouth dry, and she had no physical sensation of the world beyond the sound of his voice.

"Tell me! Were you with somebody?" His throat and vocal cords were not equal to the intended volume. His voice was distorted beyond anything human and small blood vessels burst in the whites of his eyes.

Arlene tried to raise her head, the totally present adult woman watching the helpless child who could not speak.

"Charlie, I..."

His frustration with his own inability to damage her with his voice alone broke through. He struck her neck with the side of his right hand, stunning her, and with the same motion swept out of the alcove and the apartment.

Arlene remained paralyzed. For the moment, there was nothing to do except to allow her mind and body to absorb the sudden quietness of the space. She had a flash of memory, of the nurse stroking her when she had been so afraid of that immunization shot on the first day of school. It was exactly the place where Charlie had struck her.

Charlie and Arlene did not see each other again until that evening. Their days could not have been more divergent, but each wanted the same thing, at least in the immediate future: to draw back from such open hostility; to retreat to some kind of normalcy, no matter how ugly it had felt or where it had brought them.

Charlie walked to work, found Bruce in his usual place. Bruce glanced up from his workbench, and Charlie nodded to him.

"What happened to you, man? You look terrible! You get drunk last night?"

"Why would you think that?" Charlie responded indignantly. He could not understand for the life of him what Bruce could be reacting to. He still felt shaky, but he couldn't imagine that he was showing it.

"Your bloodshot eyes are screaming bourbon, and your voice sounds like it's been blowtorched."

"Oh. Well, maybe." Charlie's eyes dropped to a desk covered with disordered papers. He pretended to have some interest in them, while Bruce returned to his own investigations of a worn belt on one of the heavier sewing machines. When Charlie was sure that Bruce had lost any further interest in talking, he headed for the door.

"Have to hit the head," he said over his shoulder as he left the workroom.

With some evident haste Charlie did indeed head for the bathroom. He and Bruce shared a small toilet with a door that locked, while the women who worked at the factory used a larger more communal set up. Charlie entered, turned on the light, and immediately secured the door. He turned to the mirror without knowing what to expect. His eyes were full of red splotches, but these were already beginning to diffuse. He moved back a bit from the mirror and was soon looking at his own reflection as if it bore no connection to him.

I don't know what I'm doing. She was a sweet, quiet kid, and I don't know why I hate her so much.

His fists were clenched. Those thoughts were not new, but the violence was, and if any part of this morning's altercation surprised Charlie, it was how naturally the violence flowed out of him. And how good it felt when the flat of his hand made contact with her neck. He knew that must never happen again, and yet…

For a moment two Charlies stood in the same space, one who lived within the expression of anger that had engulfed his life, and another who could reflect on what he had become. They fused, and the reflective part evaporated. What was left to consider was only a matter of tactics, a way to get through the day and the evening that would follow. He disappeared into the background of the factory for the rest of the morning.

Arlene left the alcove and walked directly to their bathroom. With no thought for anything else, she took off her clothes and undergarments, stepped into a chipped, cream-colored tub, pulled around the vinyl curtain, and stood for a long time in a lukewarm shower. She took shallow breaths as if refusing to engage fully in the moment, and she let the feel of the water over her naked skin distract her into a well-controlled trance. Finally, almost as an afterthought, she washed herself with unscented white soap, rinsed, and stepped out.

Although she was quite alone in the apartment, she dressed quickly, not liking the feel of being unclothed in her bedroom. She stepped into a simple, light blue, A-line dress that just covered her knees and reached around to zip it up. It was patterned in a regular lattice with pale white and yellow flowers separated by a few inches of plain cotton. She put on a pair of matt black shoes, flat with rubber soles, which she wore over low white socks that hardly rose above the line of the shoes. Finally, she pulled on a white sweater with blue-gray buttons, took her purse and immediately left.

Her sister-in-law Mary lived five miles away. She could walk that easily in under two hours, and the walking would give her time, mostly to reinhabit her body and her life. The minute spent in the alcove with Charlie had driven her out of herself and had, moreover, made her afraid to return within. She knew that was only a metaphor, but there was truth in it. She needed time and a simple goal to recover from the bruising of her neck and the far worse bruising of her psyche. The sky had become slightly unsettled, but enough sun broke through that the exertion and the sweater kept her comfortable in the almost chilly morning air.

Arlene had to get to Mary's house and hoped that she would be there. She might have called ahead from a payphone, but then she would have had to explain herself before she was ready. Worse yet, if Mary wasn't home, she would have been left with nothing. No temporizing goal. A trip to see her mother might have offered a more direct sense of comfort, but Arlene could not think about organizing a complex trip involving two buses and a train in each direction. The immediacy of walking to Mary's house with no plan beyond getting there was by far the better choice. And Arlene knew that just being outside on an early morning in late spring suffused the world with hope, even if one hadn't yet consciously acknowledged the need for some.

Mary, her husband, and two children rented a two-bedroom house separated by less than four feet on either side from their neighbors. The children, Annie and David, had, since the time they could safely be left outside to play on their own, been fascinated by the space between the north side of the house and fence. It was only fifteen inches wide, and so a one-way thoroughfare when more than one child was in it. From time to time, Mary's husband, Hank, might try to store something there, but the children always displaced it to leave this skinny way clear for their own explorations. Vines growing on the dark, splintered wooden fence that separated the properties added to its narrow charm.

Their house could not have been less exceptional. It was one story with off-white wooden siding and army green trim. Since Mary and Hank did not own it, there was no motivation to repaint it in more attractive colors. The front yard consisted of two oblongs of scraggly grass separated by a flagstone walkway to the front door. Weeds grew between the flags, and, apart from the grass, the only other flora was an unprepossessing fig tree that produced inedible fruit in early autumn. The figs fell, rotted, and drew an unwelcome swarm of biting flies.

Arlene looked at the tree as she walked carefully on the flagstones toward the door. It was midmorning, still cool, and the now full sunlight penetrated the large leaves to give them the green glow of waves on the ocean. Her eyes turned back to the door. She had no idea what she was going to say if Mary was indeed at home, but she had met her primary objective in reaching the house.

She rang the bell and waited.

After a few seconds the doorknob rattled, and two eyes peered around the partially opened door. The evident surprise on Mary's face was almost instantly superseded by a look of welcome recognition.

"Arlene…" There was really no way to punctuate that one-word sentence without something of a hybrid drawn from a question mark, an exclamation mark, and a period.

"Arlene," she repeated, opening the door fully.

"Hello, Mary. I hope this is not too inconvenient," said Arlene softly.

"No, not at all." Mary stood to the right of the door and gestured Arlene in with her left hand. In the instant that Arlene crossed the threshold, her puzzled delight turned to alarm, both from an intuitive sense that all could not be well and the red-blue mark on Arlene's neck.

"Sit down anywhere. Shall I make us some coffee or tea?"

Arlene's eyes took a moment to readjust from full daylight to the relative darkness of Mary's living room. She had only been here a few times before, with Charlie, and she remembered the slightly irregular, soft cream sofa with sparse green stripes that anchored the room. The upholstery was plush, if a bit worn, and the fabric had been partially ripped through near one of the legs by their cat. Arlene looked around for their pet and found its coiled, striped-gray form in one of the two other large chairs, upholstered in a similar material, but in deep brown with a grid of red diamonds. The floor was unpolished wood, and a multicolored, fringed rug of a vaguely Turkish design covered most of the room.

Arlene sat down in the far corner of the sofa, unconsciously forcing herself as deeply as possible into the pocket. Mary sat on the empty chair closest to the door, across from the one occupied by the sleeping cat, thereby giving Arlene the distance she seemed to want.

"Where is Annie?" asked Arlene.

"Asleep, for a miracle. She had a bad night with her stomach." Mary smiled. "I know I shouldn't say this, but I am delighted for the quiet. A three-year-old is not the easiest thing to keep up with, even for a mother still in her twenties."

Mary's kind smile meant the world to Arlene, and she relaxed for the first time since she had been awakened this morning by the threatening roar of Charlie's voice.

Mary was a beautiful plain woman. (Here the comma is omitted with full intention.) Her eyes were an intense green, her skin was clear, her features were striking in their regularity and symmetry. Her forehead seemed a bit wide, but that was perhaps just the effect of the framing by her curly, mid-length hair. The curls were natural—not tight but certainly more definite than waves—and their shifting directions showed off the highlights of her auburn hair. She wore no makeup whatsoever, and strangers often had to look a second time as it registered just how striking her face was. Her clothes matched her face: she wore a simple dress with an unremarkable belt that effortlessly set off her figure. With the right clothes, hair style and cosmetic accents, she could have been stunning, but there was no indication that she knew this.

Arlene began to ask about David and Hank, but Mary cut her off, looking at her with such intensity that Arlene could not keep her eyes down. Her question seemed to come right through and be focused by Arlene's glasses:

"What's wrong, honey?"

Arlene stared for a few seconds, knowing that the time for temporizing was over, both with Mary and more so with herself. But that is why she had come.

"Your brother…"

"That mark on your neck: did he hit you?"

"Yes," said Arlene, feeling herself beginning to cry. "But that is nothing."

"It's *not* nothing. But tell me."

"Mary, I do not know what happened, especially over the last few days or weeks. Yesterday I bought something, and I was going to tell you about that before Charlie and I fought—to ask you to help me—but I guess I need to talk about this first."

"Okay, deep breath. Let's go back a little. I have never understood this: why did you marry Charlie? You are so nice, and he just—well, he's not. I'm his sister, but I have to admit that. If you only knew…" She stopped, thinking about the mud on her communion dress.

It was Arlene's turn to feel concern and sympathy, and this finally lifted her emotionally back into her own person. Her lips trembled.

"Mary, I cannot know what you are thinking, but I did not come to make you sad."

"I know. Forget about me. I'm fine. Tell me about you and Charlie. Why did you marry him?"

Arlene drew a deep breath through her nose. Her lips stopped trembling and pulled down into a shallow, tight inverted *u* shape, but she could not yet take hold of herself. Her eyes grew watery, and droplets of tears adhered to her glasses. Her face began to distort itself with emotional tension. She bent her head down, pulled up her knees, and closed her eyes.

Reading Six

"Rebellion" by Marla Kraft

[Late afternoon, in fall, with a chill, darkness, and wetness in the air, but no rain. Two young women are walking on a residential street filled with green lawns and trees, in coats just heavy enough to protect them from the chill and possible shower. One wears lavender, the other yellow with light green accents. From time to time, they feel the cold wetness of a drop on their cheeks and foreheads. They keep their hands in their pockets, walk with no space between them and are happy about having brought the umbrella, not yet in use.]

Marilyn: I don't understand. He really liked you, but you stopped seeing him after two dates?

Danielle: Yes--exactly right.

Marilyn: But why? I am sorry, Danielle--you know I love you--but I think those are the only two dates you've had in your whole life. No one would expect that you were going to marry the guy, and unless you really didn't like him, what was the harm?

Danielle: He was falling in love with me.

Marilyn: <u>That</u> was the harm? This makes less and less sense!

Danielle: I know.

[Danielle stops, turns to face Marilyn, who likewise turns. Their eyes lock, and Danielle swallows.]

Danielle: I was falling in love with him, too.

Marilyn: I don't know what else to ask; you have to explain. How could you break up like that?

Danielle: I didn't really, or honestly--or, I mean, honorably. I would no longer take his phone calls. When finally he started writing, I never wrote back. I let it end by doing nothing. God knows what he thinks.

Marilyn: If he loved you, why didn't he just come to your house. He did know where you lived, didn't he?

Danielle: Yes, he had come to pick me up there for our second date. We were living in that tiny duplex. Of course, I had to introduce him to my mother. That's probably why he never came back.

Marilyn: What happened with your mother? Didn't she like him? From everything you've told me, he seems like the last person in the world she would object to for you.

Danielle: All true: he had a job and was going to college. But that was completely beside the point. Since I was four, I have been the only family my mother has had, and she wasn't going to risk that. That night he came, she said all the right words, but it was as if they were coming from someplace far away and frozen. She hated the idea that he might like me, and there was no way to hide that.

Marilyn: Did he say anything?

Danielle: When we left, he just looked at me with his mouth open slightly. It was as if he had been slapped, but he didn't know why. I did know, but I never told him. It's as if we weren't together on that date, even though it was perfectly lovely. He took me to a concert in which a woman sang the most beautiful song I have ever heard. But I wasn't really there with him. It was at the last part of an exquisite symphony. I will never forget it.

Marilyn: Those things he gave you... Did you give them back?

Danielle: How opposite they were! A folded rectangle of wrapping paper in a green and gold foil alligator pattern, just because he thought it was too pretty to use. A little music box that played a tiny bit of Mozart, but it sounded as big as a stereo.

[The darkness and raindrops thicken; lights begin to come on. The umbrella is raised, and the pair are further squeezed into the same isolated space as they continue walking. They find themselves sharing the shank of the umbrella held between them.]

Danielle: Of course, I still have them. They are all I have.

Marilyn: So, you gave up this chance for your mother--who doesn't sound all that nice?

Danielle: Think, Marilyn, why did you put it that way? "Who doesn't sound all that nice?" We have known each other since fourth grade. Why don't you know her the way your mother knows me?

Marilyn: I don't know. I've never thought about it.

Danielle: Did she once ask you about yourself? Did she once ask you to stay for dinner? Did she once ask to meet your mother?

Marilyn: No, but that doesn't make her terrible.

Danielle: No, it doesn't make her anything, but it's been like this because of what she is: the person who chooses to be my owner instead of my mother. She doesn't know you and you don't know her because she didn't want either of those things.

Marilyn: But if you feel that way, Danielle, then why...?

Danielle: Why did I let her chase off the only boy who ever loved me?

[Marilyn nods silently. The wind whips the rain into such random turbulence that they stop, huddling under the suddenly insufficient umbrella.]

Danielle: Because she's so frightened of losing me that being nice to you or him or anybody else doesn't matter. Only holding on to me matters.

[The wind abates, and they are slowly moving forward again.]

Marilyn: So where does that leave you?

Danielle: Being held, with no choice, until she decides to let me go.

[Marilyn's hand, for an instant, is bound more tightly to Danielle's than to the umbrella. She releases, and the two walk on through the wetness and occasionally sparkling night.]

Valerie came home from work late that afternoon and walked straight to her bedroom. Everything in it was either white or a shade of green: walls, lacquered bed tables, the velvet chair, bedspread and pillows. She had no thought at first except to get out of her trim but stifling work clothes. She had worked as a bank teller for the last three years—four years since she had graduated from high school. The bank was spacious and airy, but the dress code and make-up code were strict. She stood for eight hours in uncomfortable shoes (although no customer could see her feet) while her face rigidly maintained an expression of studied politeness, with just the hint of a smile. She was in every way a model low-level employee.

She kicked off her shoes as she removed her business jacket. Then she removed her skirt, blouse, tight stockings, and all of her undergarments except for her lavender cotton panties. Immediately she threw a long flannel nightgown over her body and began to relax. The nightgown matched her room décor; it was mostly white with a delicate spring green diaper pattern printed onto the flannel and came down just above her ankles. Her eyes closed for a second in relief—she felt as if she could feel both the texture and color of the garment—and then she began to clear away the debris of the day. The clothes that could be worn again were hung neatly in her closet with the rest folded and deposited into a wash hamper. Within a few minutes of entering her room, she left it, barefoot and carrying a light green pamphlet that was not at all current. It had a seascape on the cover, was clean and free of wrinkles, but nonetheless showed some wear in its stapled binding and would no longer lie completely flat when closed.

Valerie went into another bedroom and opened a window. She enjoyed seeing, hearing, and smelling the light rain in progress, and the chill that immediately seeped into the room transformed her nightgown into a warm blanket. She dragged a soft medium-sized chair across the floor to the window, sat down, and drew her legs up onto the cushion. She took a breath and opened her magazine to the pages offered by the worn binding.

It was almost too dark to read, but she wanted only the weather-shrouded illumination of the remaining daylight. This exactly served her purpose. Besides, she needed very little prompting from the pages she would turn.

She read "Rebellion" out loud, feeling every word. There was no one outside to hear her, and in fact she paid no attention to the sound of her own voice. But reading aloud made it a physical experience, and she could better follow every thought and feeling of Danielle and Marilyn as they walked on *their* path and *their* falling darkness.

When she finished, she sat quietly, still held by the rain and the words she had just spoken to no one.

I have no lost love like Danielle's to remember and regret. I have no friend like Marilyn to listen to me, to talk to me, to hold me. I have only this tiny script and the comfort that somewhere there is someone who could understand my loneliness. But Marla Kraft is only a name; her physical and psychical reality are nothing to me.

Valerie was too exhausted to read the script aloud a second time. Besides, she did not want to kill it by repetition. She didn't know when she would have the chance to read it again. Certainly not tomorrow, when her mother would be returning home, eager to hear the latest news from the bank and to make sure that her daughter was getting close to no one.

Valerie moved the chair back to its former place in her mother's bedroom, closed the window, and took the magazine back to her own room, restoring it to the bottom of her dresser, under some folded blouses. She had eaten nothing since breakfast, but still had no thought of supper. Instead, she went into the living room and pulled a long-playing record out from a small library stored in their modest console phonograph. She loaded the record onto the turntable and carefully placed the needle into one of the narrow channels that separated the tracks. A few seconds later the third movement of Mahler's Fourth Symphony filled the room much as the pleasant chill of the air had filled her mother's bedroom less than half an hour ago. She lay down on the sofa and curled herself deeply into her nightgown, in the darkness that had now fallen completely. Marla's script had somehow given voice to the acute discomforts of her life; Mahler's peaceful music now anesthetized them.

Chapter Seven

Arlene left home on her first day of high school wearing a bright blue dress that her parents had bought her for her eighth-grade graduation. It was a simple design that was fitted to the waist with a dark blue patent leather belt and flared out considerably at the hips, falling just below the knee. Arlene worried that it might be too fancy for high school, but she did not object when her mother suggested that she wear it. She also wore black shoes with white socks. Her coarse blond hair was confined at the crown of her head by a yellow and white tortoise band, but then left to expand laterally down to her shoulder blades. She had a canvas bag that served as a purse and was large enough to hold a notebook and some pens and pencils. She imagined she would be assigned a locker to hold most of her books.

The day was brilliantly bright and clear, with just a hint of the melancholy that always marked the end of summer. She had some idea of what to expect by way of procedures from the guidance counselor that had visited her elementary school in spring. As she walked, her mouth twitched in anticipation, but this was anticipation with no object. She smiled a little, remembering the terror of her first day of kindergarten, feeling a small degree of enchantment that on this day she must manage on her own, without her mother; this slightly outweighed her usual discomfort at being an introvert in unavoidable social environments.

As she neared the school, she noticed other students on the sidewalks all headed in the same direction. She paid some attention to the girls and concluded that her dress would do—although more wore skirts—but her socks might be a bit unusual: almost all of them seemed to be wearing sheer stockings. She owned none, and so this could not count as a bad decision.

Arlene had spent much of her life on crowded city streets, so the increasing density of all these young people should not have brought her into an indefinable, elevated—perhaps excited—state. She frowned at her own lack of self-understanding but did not hesitate when she reached the main concrete walkway from the sidewalk to the front door of the high school. She was some ten feet ahead of three nattering boys and somewhat closer behind two much less chatty girls as she reached the door. Signs unambiguously directed freshmen to the right into a hall and then into a well-lighted auditorium that held a few hundred creaking wooden seats that folded up, as in a movie theater, for ease of access. The seating was divided into three sections, with two interior and two exterior aisles running from the stage to the back. The stage was empty as Arlene entered.

There were considerably more seats than new students, and so Arlene found a row toward the back on the left side with three vacant seats adjacent to the aisle. She sat down in the middle seat and looked around. While no one was yet on the stage, she could see some teachers or administrators gathering in the wings to the right. Students continued to enter and to seat themselves, as Arlene watched with more and more excitement.

Suddenly she understood what was happening to her. She had known for years how much she enjoyed looking into other people, but outside of school, that had been an experience limited by the small number of people she encountered, like that stylish lady who had tried to talk to her at the bus stop. Her elementary school was, of course, filled with children, but their way of being in school was per force, almost entirely regimented. What was different here, even among these other freshmen, whatever their diffidence on this first day, was the lack of regimentation. They found their own seats, they chatted openly with their friends, and their souls illuminated the space for her more so than the auditorium lighting. She was not transformed by this in any way; she would continue to be shy and, she expected, mostly alone. But here was a festival of new people to look into in a place where they were free to be more expressive than they had ever before been in school. Arlene smiled at the thought of the four years that lie before her. Her lips formed a rare smile.

Something abruptly broke into her reverie. Her name was Linda, and she sat down to Arlene's right and introduced herself. Arlene had noticed many students from her own elementary school, yet she knew none of them well enough to expect any sort of greeting. She had never seen Linda before, but she felt a touch on her arm.

"Hi, I'm Linda."

"I am Arlene." Those words were produced automatically; Arlene was too surprised by the contact—in both senses—to say more.

"Isn't this exciting?"

"I was also thinking that, Linda."

That sentence was long enough for both of them to make some assessment of the other.

Linda at once detected the absolutely correct but unmistakably strange way that Arlene spoke. She got closer than most in characterizing it: *It's as if she wants to leave little spaces between words, like she was typing*. As she got to know her better, she would also become more aware of the way Arlene accented longer words in longer sentences, but for now she forgot about elocution and looked more at Arlene's face—especially the artificially enlarged pale eyes behind her large glasses, her comparatively ungroomed hair, and the simplicity of her clothes. She decided, then and there, that she liked this girl.

Arlene, for her part, saw a girl who was much shorter and plumper than she. She wore a yellow blouse, whose buttons were strained just a little by her seated posture, a textured tan skirt, brown kitten heels, and—Arlene frowned inwardly—sheer beige stockings. Her brown-eyed face was pleasantly round, with skin that was somewhat less than smooth, although Linda did not use any makeup to cover the flaws. Arlene took in all of this in an instant, but then found herself completely captivated by something else. She could not help staring.

"Why is your hair two colors?"

"Oh, have you never seen that before? It's called streaking, and I do it myself at home with foil…?" The second sentence had not started as a question, but it ended that way when Linda noticed the confusion in Arlene's eyes and lips.

"Well, never mind how I do it, but this mousey brown hair of mine needs something, don't you think?"

"It is interesting," said Arlene. "There would, of course, be no point with mine."

Linda stopped her smile from becoming a laugh before Arlene could mistake her mirth at her new friend's self-deprecation for even the tiniest hint of meanness. No, Arlene was not blessed with attractive hair, and Linda knew of no treatment that would transfigure it from its native chaotic state into the soft, lustrous waves she saw on shampoo bottles and hair-dye kits.

Linda turned her eyes to the stage for a few seconds to see if anything was about to happen yet. In the gap, Arlene had time for her second epiphany since she had entered the auditorium. *I don't have to look into Linda—I can talk to her*. A simple thought, indeed, but such a new and marvelous possibility!

Linda turned back. In her excitement she held out her hands as if holding a beach ball.

"This is the first day, and I have no idea what is going to happen! You must have gone to a different grammar school."

"Mount Vernon," murmured Arlene.

"I went to Lincoln. I guess they both have something to do with presidents. Anyway…"

Her next thought was cut off by the sound of hard-tipped high heels making their way onto the stage. A bespectacled, angular woman of medium height in a checkered suit stopped in the center and faced the students. She was holding quite a few typed pages in her left hand. The auditorium lights dimmed to bring attention to the stage.

"I am Mrs. McCarthy, the head guidance counselor. Welcome to high school. I'm not sure you'll meet again like this until graduation—for those of you who make it that far."

Arlene and Linda frowned at each other: this was an odd beginning.

"In any case, I have only one duty to perform today, and that is to give you your homeroom assignments. All high school administration is done via your homeroom, and you will report there every school day at 8:30 for attendance and announcements prior to your first class. So, listen carefully, and I will announce your homeroom designation, its teacher, and the students assigned to the group in alphabetical order, last name first. When each list is complete, I will give you the room number and you should proceed directly there, where your teacher will be waiting with further instructions. I cannot imagine that there could be any questions at this point."

She looked sharply over her audience and then raised the sheaf of pages and began reading.

"Homeroom 9-1, Mrs. Vikaris: Adler, Kirk; Chudoba, Michael; Franklin, George…"

Linda listened carefully until her last name was passed and then waited for the next group. (Arlene Zirner assumed correctly that hers would be the final name called for any homeroom.)

"...Winkelmann, Henry. All of you report to Room 206. Homeroom 9-2, Miss Martin: Beech, Helen; Donaldson, Arthur..."

Not much was needed to crack the homeroom code, if one were interested, and not many were. The first number designated the grade and would be incremented by one each year. The second number was not so straightforward, but hardly obscure. The 9-1 group included students with an interest or aptitude for math and science, with the expectation that they would continue on to college. (In a few years, after the USSR space program became a perceived threat, this group would become somewhat elite.) Naturally, at the time of this story, they were virtually all boys. Homeroom 9-2 included the literature, art and history types; again there was an expectation of college, although far more girls were in this group. Then came a few more college-preparatory sections, but with no anticipated orientation. These were followed by homerooms for "general studies," which was the high school administration's way of saying that they had little idea where these students would land, but it might be college. Beyond that were the business studies homerooms, where young women decidedly *not* going to college were housed, and one last one designated—with a truly glorious circumlocution--as industrial arts. To this were assigned all of the boys with no academic promise whatsoever who were almost certainly headed for the drudgery of manual labor—or so their college-educated teachers and administrators assumed. These descriptors were never used publicly, but one only had to look at who was where to decode the architecture of homeroom assignments.

"...Homeroom 9-7: ...Lassman, Linda..."

"Well, that's that," said Linda to Arlene as she waited for Mrs. McCarthy to complete the 9-7 roster. When the room number was announced (310), she arose and added, "Maybe we'll be in gym class together or have nearby lockers. Bye!"

Arlene's lips shrugged at the loss of Linda's company, and she returned to her usual engagement with the world, while still, of course, listening for her name.

"Homeroom 9-9, Mrs. Moloney: Abruzzi, Antony,...

The auditorium was now more than half empty, but Arlene once again felt the thrill of all this burgeoning self-expression and self-definition, now somewhat recolored and enhanced by her brief exchanges with Linda. Her eyes sparkled from behind her glasses.

"..., Zirner, Arlene. Room 311."

High school days ended a full half hour earlier than elementary school. Arlene walked home slowly; the sun was brighter and warmer than when she had left in the morning. The homeroom session, which except for the first day of school would be limited to ten minutes, extended to most of an hour. Mrs. Moloney had given her and her classmates their schedules, locker assignments, and some advice—some of it perfunctory and some of it sincere and well-intended. When the bell rang for first period, Arlene filed out with the others and found about half of her homeroom cohorts on their way to General Science, taught by Mr. Boonton. The classroom periods for the day were abridged for the entire school to accommodate freshman administration, and so the business of each class was limited to roll call, book distribution, and the vaguest of introductions. Thus it went through English I, a typing class, Algebra I, a lunch period, World History, gym and health, and an eighth-period study hall, which brought her back to the auditorium in which she had begun the day. The students were expected to sit quietly and not to talk, with no expectation at all that they might study. Arlene found no difficulty in this, but two or three older boys were vehemently hushed for whispering.

Almost all of the freshman had fourth-period lunch, which was a thoroughly hybridized affair: one could bring or buy lunch, eat it in a basement cafeteria, or at one of the few tables in the large high-fenced asphalt yard that was used for sports. Arlene took the first few minutes of the lunch period to find and learn to open her locker, into which she deposited the three books she had been assigned during the morning. She went to the cafeteria only to realize that she had no money and had entirely forgotten about bringing lunch in the excitement of her first day. No matter, she wasn't hungry. She peeked into the cafeteria where the students were eating but found it too crowded and noisy. Despite her continuing excitement at this new social environment, she realized she needed space to be alone. This led her out into the playground, where she walked to the far corner and sat as well as she could on the low concrete wall that anchored the chain-link fencing. It was a good place to rest and to survey, and only slightly spoiled by little groups of more sophisticated students migrating there later in the lunch period; it was, with the tacit compliance of the faculty, the one place at school where they could smoke without harassment.

As she made her way home, Arlene regretted her decision—although at the time it had felt more like meeting an intuitive need—to isolate herself during lunch period. With little difficulty she might have found Linda and continued their nascent acquaintance. Perhaps tomorrow.

Letting herself into her home, Arlene found her father, as always, on the living room sofa, staring out the window. His progression throughout all their years in this place had been monotonic: each year he undertook to move less, to speak less, to stare more. A twitch of an eyebrow was all that acknowledged her return, and she knew he would ask her nothing about her day. This silence held without the least bit of antagonism from either father or daughter. Arlene saw a man she loved, who had never spoken a harsh word to her, a man who, almost too many years ago to remember, took her up on his lap and held her as a small child; and yet a man who seemed to be passively reflecting on a life draining away. By her present age, Arlene knew that his behavior was abnormal, even pathological in a way, although that is not a term she would ever have used. But his whole life could not have been lived in such a way. *He married Mutti. He had a child. He could not always have been like this, or even on his way to this.* Something that preceded anything she could remember must be responsible for all these wasted days, but she dared not to ask him, or her mother, about it. Such a question must imply a caustic disapproval that she had no right to express.

Albert Zirner likewise loved his little girl. He did not know her well enough to be proud of her, and besides pride would have required more energy than he could summon. He knew she didn't understand what was happening to him and was enormously grateful that she didn't ask, and that she still loved him. Julia understood and was the only person in the world who could interact with Albert without destroying what was left. It was as if he were made of filaments of dust, and whatever structure that still held on would dissipate at the slightest contact. Except for Julia.

Arlene went to her room and did not come out. She needed to think. She knew that Mutti would want to hear everything about her day, and she needed to work out what to say.

Arlene's father no longer sat with his wife and daughter at dinner. Instead, Julia brought a small tray into the living room, which Albert held on his lap. He sometimes watched television, sometimes listened to the radio, and sometimes just sat in silence. The television and radio were always turned down to the lowest perceptible volume. Julia did not resent his isolation at meals and even understood it in a weird, metaphorical way: it was as if he were withdrawing what was left of himself to make room for his growing daughter. The progression seemed entirely natural.

As a side effect, Julia's conversations with Arlene now occurred during dinner, often extending the meal to twice the time it took to consume whatever had been prepared. On this evening, as a small celebration of

Arlene's academic advancement to high school, Julia had presented one of her favorite dishes: lambchops and red cabbage, served with lima beans and fresh bread. Very little remained on their plates.

"Lena, if you liked her so much and she was so nice to you, why didn't you try to find her at lunch?"

"I couldn't. I mean, I might have, but it was so crowded that I just wanted to get outside and be alone for a little while."

Her mother nodded in complete understanding. Arlene seemed to squint with her whole face and then continued:

"There was so much that was so different. And if I had found Linda, I know she would have already made other friends or been in the middle of old ones, and I just didn't think there would be space for me."

Julia was more aware than anyone of just how much time Arlene spent alone. She knew that her daughter managed well enough—and that she often enjoyed her solitude—but the thought of a friend like Linda was a delicious possibility that surprised her. She was sometimes afraid that, by her own example, she had taught Arlene to expect far too little from life. And yet, Julia knew herself to be who she was with more than sufficient reason.

"Well, I suppose you'll have many other chances," Julia responded. She took a small bit of bread and used it to wipe some of the liquid from the red cabbage from her plate. She looked evenly at Arlene.

"I don't suppose you actually learned anything today." The question might have been cynical, but the smile in Julia's eyes did not allow for any misinterpretation. Still, this was the question Arlene had been waiting for.

"Well, not in the sense that the teachers actually taught us anything—no." Her lower lip disappeared under her front teeth.

"In what sense, then?"

"From the first moment I got there, there was something new, something different from elementary school. I know that every student in high school is not yet an adult, but there was such a sense of freedom compared to all the years I spent at Mount Vernon. I don't think I can explain very well. We all sat at desks and mostly kept quiet when asked, but it's like some kind of *anti-regimentation* signal had been given."

"Anti-regimentation?" Julia certainly understood 'regimentation,' but was unprepared to hear her daughter use the word, and especially in this context. While Arlene was by no means verbally slow, she also wasn't—the only word she could think of came from her previous life—*schlagfertig*. Witty? Always ready with a response? No matter. She waited for her daughter to explain. By now both Arlene's lips were completely engaged in finding the right words.

"Oh, Mutti, in my old school, I looked at the other students all the time and there was nothing trying to get out. Everything was coming in from the teachers and how we were taught to act. But suddenly there is this kind of reversal. So many things want to get out, and the teachers and the rest of the people who work there have to somehow hold it in. It's like all of us doing the same thing has gone from normal to something that's hard to control. How could that happen in one summer?"

"I don't know," murmured Julia, shaking her head unemphatically.

Arlene continued: "High school is so much less *stationary* than grammar school. I mean, you change classes and move about far more than you did a few months ago. Maybe that was the signal?"

Julia frowned. All of this was new to her. "But, Lena, why is this all so important? Are there things you want to do now that you couldn't do before?"

Even as she spoke these words, Julia felt that they were not right. Arlene's behavior had never caused her any concern, and she did not mean to imply that this small manifesto had somehow changed that. But as a consequence of Arlene's epiphany, she felt that Arlene was less safe—although Julia knew all too well that regimentation and safety were far from synonymous.

"Oh, no!" exclaimed Arlene. "I shall do what I have always done in school. You know that. But I have so much more to watch and listen for! That's what I learned today."

Julia's lips tightened and drooped at the corners, but not in a frown, an affectation she realized she had picked up from Arlene. She was looking for the right words.

"I trust you, Lena—completely. I didn't mean what I said to sound otherwise. I just want you to be safe, and that means staying in the middle, not calling attention to yourself. That's all I meant to say. I know how much you can be fascinated by other people, that you wonder what the world looks like from another place. And here you have so many people showing so much more of themselves than you ever saw in school before. Isn't that right?"

"That is exactly right, Mutti. That is exactly what I was trying to say."

"And I only wanted to make sure that you could see all of this without changing too much from the steady young woman you have become. From someone who finds it easy to do good and disappear."

Arlene was pleased and stunned by this reference to adulthood, something she had never considered before. Julia realized how close she had come to saying "steady, *invisible* young woman you have become." She was ashamed at having thought that and yet certain that her gentle nudging of her daughter in the direction of invisibility was right, especially in view of her own and her husband's life. She had often told Arlene to "do good and disappear." But she knew that this advice wasn't entirely given in the spirit of the convent of Belgian nuns from which it derived.

"I will never forget that, Mutti. Never."

At this point in her life, Arlene took this aphorism as one might accept an axiom of geometry: it was something true and not to be questioned. Sometime later she would begin to understand it otherwise—and on more than one level.

Over the next few years Arlene continued to watch the swirling personalities that surrounded her in high school. One girl, Monica, seemed perfect. She had dark, luscious hair, deep green eyes, a smile always at the edge of laughter. She was bright and showed the gift of physical coordination—as well as her exquisite proportions—in her spot as lead twirler. Arlene never shared a class or even a word with Monica, but this twirler was center stage at pep rallies and indeed created the illusion of being center stage wherever she stood. Arlene watched her as she might watch a celebrity that showed up at a bookstore, never daring to get too close, to intrude on a life that was already overcrowded, especially by boys who fell in love with her and girls who simply wanted to be part of her world. The shy invisible girl could see from the beginning that despite expectations developed from watching other attractive people, this spectacularly attractive person was essentially good and kind. Monica clearly understood her own allure but did not exploit it, as many might have without a second thought. Arlene appreciated that, but her real interest in her wasn't Monica's goodness, but to ask herself what it might feel like to be *that* attractive. Her curiosity was such that she imagined that if she ever found Monica alone, she might just put the question to her directly. *What does it feel like to be you? To be always seen and always admired?* It was so far from her own world that she had to remind herself constantly not to stare; to use the lesson she had learned as a little girl at that bus stop where she had run from a well-intentioned woman who had surprised her by speaking to her: not to lose her composure in the presence of everything she was not.

In her third year, Arlene was placed in a biology class. This course was usually reserved for students preparing for college, but it worked out as an administrative convenience in scheduling her courses, and she had done fine in General Science. She immediately noticed a group of freshman boys in the class, but this was easily understood. By now her homeroom was designated 11-9, but these boys would have come from the newly minted homeroom 9-1, the math-science sequence. Such students were given biology in their first year so that they could complete two years of chemistry and one of physics before graduation, and thereby be acceptable to a better range of colleges. One of these boys was Herman Leitz, and Arlene picked him out for special attention immediately.

Herman was in some ways the opposite of Monica. He was more of a boy than a teenager, visibly—absolutely *not* invisibly—one of the shyest people she had ever encountered. He was uncomfortable even in responding to roll call; the word "here" seemed to catch in his throat. And yet, every now and then he would ask a question in a voice so saturated with curiosity and insight that his self-consciousness evaporated. After a few such questions, Arlene knew that she was seeing someone with such a tremendous grasp of science that her own understanding of the material seemed insignificant. Their teacher, Mr. Ewe, took on a stance of annoyance whenever Herman spoke up, and in some cases, it was clear even to Arlene that Mr. Ewe could not respond adequately. Herman never pressed this as any sort of intellectual victory and simply nodded his head and retreated into silence. As with Monica, Arlene found in Herman someone to explore. *What does it feel like to have this depth of understanding of the physical world? To grasp abstraction and detail so effortlessly, and then to want to go deeper?* But unlike Monica, Herman was approachable, and she tried speaking a few words to him before or after class to get a sense of his interiority. This, of course, was not to succeed. Herman's natural, nearly paralytic reticence was dwarfed by this tall girl, two years older than he was, addressing him. Arlene could not inflict such pain and left off with her attempts, but she felt an ambiguous satisfaction in sensing that the extremity of his discomfort in part owed to her gender. It was perhaps the first time that she felt being a teenage girl mattered as such—that she was not invisible as a girl.

Academically, Arlene heeded her mother's advice and performed respectably but never stood out. That was easy enough in the business, math, and science courses in which she had either little interest or no special talent, but in literature and history, she definitely held back. In Senior English, her teacher, Miss Julienne—that was, of course, her first name, but that is how she instructed the students to address her—locked eyes with her more than once to ask silently, "What are you hiding? There's a bright light under that bushel, isn't there?" Still, Miss Julienne respected her students too much to intrude, and Arlene respected her mother too much to accept the offer implicit in those looks to share something of herself with one of her most respected mentors. Moreover, without understanding why, she felt that her delicious sense of entering the lives of others would be compromised if she let them into her own life by in any way calling attention to herself. This included not telling Miss Julienne what she really thought of *The Red Badge of Courage* or *The Great Gatsby*.

So, she watched and did well enough, but not too well, and disappeared.

When high school ended, Arlene's greatest regret was the failure to thrive of her friendship with Linda. In mid-October of her first year, Arlene saw her standing alone in the corner of the playground early in their lunch period. She did not hesitate to approach.

"Hi. Remember me?"

"Ahm…Arlene, right? We met on our first day. When I ran off to homeroom, I never imagined it would be so long until we met again. I guess this place is bigger than it seems at first."

"Yes. I enjoyed talking to you and was hoping we could be friends."

Linda looked down for an instant. The sun was wan that day, but the blond streak in Linda's hair sparkled nonetheless. A light breeze lifted a few strands without introducing any disarray. When she looked up, Arlene again felt the warmth of those brown eyes and felt something of an ache: she had never wanted a friend before as she wanted Linda to be her friend now.

"Well, of course, we can! I guess we don't live nearby, or we would have gone to the same elementary school, but these little legs can walk—and so, I should think, can your much longer ones." These words were framed by a placid smile, and Arlene imagined that they might really become friends. But then Linda's eyes shifted just slightly and refocused; Arlene saw a group of three girls, two of them definitely older than she, moving toward them.

"Hey!' cried Linda, moving away from her, with no hint that Arlene should follow. The group of four coalesced about ten feet from Arlene, who stood there awkwardly for ten seconds or so, and then quietly walked away. Linda's neck made a small movement, just enough to take in Arlene's retreat. She turned back to her friends, smiled, and chatted, but inside her she knew that she had just chosen to lose something valuable, although that was all too easily hidden, even from herself.

Arlene only spoke to Linda two more times: once when they found themselves next to each other in a short line to check out and return books from the high school's one-room library, and then when Linda sought her out at lunch, late in Junior year, to tell her that her family was moving out of state. In that last exchange, someone with far less empathy than Arlene could have read the message in Linda's eyes: *We could have been friends, we should have been friends, and I'm sorry*. Arlene replied to the unspoken words simply enough.

"I shall miss you."

Linda heard that correctly as, "I shall miss the possibility of our friendship," in a voice that exactly matched that affectation of speech she had discovered with Arlene's first words to her. She turned away to lose herself in the crowded, between-class hallways. Arlene tried, without success, to catch one last sight of the girl whose hair was two colors, and silently mouthed a final goodbye.

Arlene completed high school in a ceremony held outdoors in early evening with a vast number of benches set up to accommodate the students and parents. A few benches were placed behind a make-shift podium for those who were graduating with honors. The single positive distinction that might have been noted was that the valedictorian did *not* begin her speech with, "It was the best of times, it was the worst of times…"

Afterward, Arlene walked home with her mother. Her father had remained at home in his ever-growing inertness. Julia did not ask Arlene about her plans, but was clearly proud of her daughter. In the 1950s, dropping out of school was not so uncommon, especially when one had no clear use for even a high school education. Indeed, Julia found herself swelling with affection for her daughter. Her own education had not been much, but she had always listened for great ideas. She remembered something said millennia ago about the virtue of the child whose parents' only worry was for her health. Arlene was just such a child, and for Julia, acting so long as a single parent, raising her had been almost effortless. She took Arlene's hand, stopped walking, turned her toward her, hugged her and stroked her hair.

"Thank you, Mutti," murmured Arlene.

"Thank you, Lena," whispered Julia through tears, her forehead resting on Arlene's shoulder.

Reading Seven

"The Golden Monster" by Marla Kraft

[Early afternoon in late spring. A woman in her mid-twenties, both delicately and blatantly beautiful, sits at a corner table of a sparsely populated outside restaurant along a wide urban boulevard. The foot traffic has diminished with the resumption of work following lunchtime. A handsome man who had been walking on the broad sidewalk stops dead in his tracks and then hurries over to her, bypassing the restaurant's hostess.]

Harry: Monique? Where have you been? It's been six days! You don't answer your phone or a knock on your door or a note slipped underneath. I was worried sick. What happened? Where were you?

Monique: I wasn't anywhere special. I just didn't want to see you.

Harry: I understand if something was wrong, if you were worried about something, or if you were sick, but--

Monique: I didn't want to see you anymore. I still don't. Almost.

Harry: What do you mean? We love each other. We <u>have</u> loved each other. There were times when I couldn't believe someone like you would choose someone like me, but you did. And then you disappeared for almost a week. I tell you, I was sick with worry. I missed you. I longed for you. And here you are, but it's like it's not you.

Monique: It's exactly me, Harry. It was the other one that was wrong.

Harry: What are you talking about?

Monique: The one you fell in love with. Oh, she is beautiful, with all that blond hair and that perfect face of artful innocence. And that body. Don't think I am unaware of what her figure and a few inches of leg above the knee can do to a man. But she's so nice, for someone with those looks, isn't she? It's a miracle that someone who is that attractive could be so nice, wouldn't exploit those looks. That's right, isn't it Harry? That's the woman you fell in love with.

Harry: Yes, but that's you! What is going on? Please tell me! Monique, I am sick in love with you, you cannot take that away and...

Monique: And expect you to survive? And not hurt so much that you can see no end to the hurting and to the longing? Is that what I can't take away?

[Harry's face loses any organization. He has no template for dealing with what is happening and so no way to express the chaos inside.]

Monique: It makes no sense whatsoever, does it? Unless...

Harry: Unless what?

Monique: Well, I have already told you--you can believe me or don't--that the one you fell in love with was the wrong one. This is the right one. What if she is deliberately hateful and hurtful and has known since she stopped being a little girl what pain she could inflict? What if her goal is to inflict that pain and drive it to an unbearable intensity. What if she let a man fall in love with her, have her, cherish her, only to take herself away from him? She'd want to watch that destruction, and to see that pain doing the destroying. I'll tell you what she would do. She would let that man into her life and into her body and make sure that he felt safe and blessed. Then she would take herself away but, after just enough time had passed, allow herself to be rediscovered. And then she would reveal herself to this sad buffoon, hiding nothing, blowing oxygen into his burning humiliation and suffering. She would sit in the open, in a pleasant, sunny, normal space and wait for him to find her so that his emotional state would be so incoherent with the circumstances that his sense of unreality could only add to his disintegration. That is exactly what she would do.

Harry: I... But why like this? Why even start? You don't talk like this. You have never spoken like this.

Monique: Don't think I don't know what "like this" means, Harry. It's not just what I am saying but how I am saying it. Where is the little girl in the sexy woman's body who couldn't think such thoughts and couldn't express them this way, even if she could? Where is she? I told you she was never the real one. This one is.

Harry: You're a monster, and I am just the fool who will suffer for having met you! But Monique,...

Monique: I know, you'll accept it all, if only you could have me back. You want me even as the monster. The golden monster.

[She smiles, offering a hint of kindness. Harry looks at her, his face again a face, organized by the smallest touch of hope.]

Monique: Well, Harry: no.

"My God! What was that about? Has Marla Kraft lost her mind? Why would she write something like this?"

Chris looked up at Robin, who had been reading one of the parts, to see a face that looked sickened by what they had just experienced.

"I don't know," said Robin. "I mean, yeah, it's crazy and ugly, but it sure does pull you in. It's so ugly you can't look away."

"God, we waited weeks for this to come out in the magazine, and now I wish I had never seen it. Why did she do it? Hasn't there been enough evil in the world for this century?"

"I don't know, but imagine that power, even if it was the power to destroy. I guess she wanted us to be able to imagine that."

"Or to imagine it for herself."

They fell silent until their emotional states had recovered enough to go on with the small events of their evening. But for days, their eyes would go dark for a few moments, and they would remember the monster.

Chapter Eight

A deep quiet filled Mary's living room. The darkness inside the house in contrast with the bright sunlight brought an eerie sense of isolation. They were the only two people in the world. The cat had leapt off the chair cushion and taken its graceful, ghostly body into the bedroom, where it nestled with the sleeping Annie. Mary looked earnestly at Arlene, who had tucked up into an almost fetal position in the corner of the sofa. The bruising of Arlene's neck and shoulder was completely exposed, but her head was down. In a single motion Mary moved from her armchair to the sofa and bent herself into an uncomfortable posture, as if to see Arlene's face from below. She asked for the third time:

"Arlene, why did you marry my brother?"

Arlene looked up and their eyes locked. She straightened and turned away. Mary shifted about a foot back, feeling that her sister-in-law was now able to take control of herself. Arlene's first response when she looked back at Mary was to smile at her kindness. Mary smiled in return and nodded, both as an acknowledgement and as a gentle prompt to proceed.

"Right after I graduated from high school, there were a few weeks when I just stayed home with my father. My mother went to work as usual, but we could both see that he could not continue on the path he was on. He barely ate or moved from the sofa in the living room. I asked Mutti why she did not insist on taking him to a doctor, but she said that would not help. She knew what was wrong and that it was not medical—and she could not explain it to me.

"After these weeks I took a job in an office building around the corner and half a block down from where my mother worked. We often walked in together, and so many times I was there long before the people I worked with were, and often even before my manager arrived. I think the woman may have mistaken this for ambition that I did not have, but since I was there, I worked.

"The work was very bland. I do not think I had one interesting day there—we'll maybe one. I had a big gray desk, one that sat in the fourth row and second column of similar stations staffed by other girls doing more or less the same jobs. On each desk there was a stack of incoming documents and two machines. Some of the papers were already typed, and we checked them over for mistakes. The company did some sort of technical auditing of insurance, so we didn't really know what we were reading, but we could find obvious errors before these documents went wherever they were going. Other things in the in-baskets had tables with simple calculations imbedded, usually sums or products or averages. We were expected to check these with the adding machine on our desk. We called them adding machines, but with the right trick you could use them to multiply and check division, too. So, this was a whole other kind of proofreading, and we understood even less what we were checking. The third kind of thing in the in-basket was just typing, which we did on old, dull gray machines with the most irregular letters. You could not type as fast as we did in school because the machines would jam, but I think most of the girls, like me fell into a slow rhythm to avoid this. Sometimes the rhythms would synchronize across a few of us, and that was one of the few interactions we had. We were not allowed to talk to each other, but you had to grin whenever the thumping of the typewriters fell into step.

"That was it, Mary. A desk, two machines and work that needed attention but was still tedious and repetitive, with virtually no social interactions. At least I didn't feel singled out as an outsider. There were no insiders, except maybe Mrs. Raymond, who gave permission to use the restroom or shushed the girls if they were whispering, and certainly let you know if you were late and never allowed anyone to leave early. I don't mean to say it was a harsh place, and I was grateful that I could be paid regularly for such a small skill, but I did not like it, and it was not really about the work and certainly not about the isolation—I was used to that. When I finally realized what it was that made me so uncomfortable, I could not help but wonder why it had taken me so long for me to see it."

Mary nodded in understanding and was not the least inclined to rush Arlene toward an answer to her question. She knew her sister-in-law was by no means a stupid young woman and that all of this was part of her answer. Arlene continued:

"Whatever our company did, it must have been doing well, and the number of girls grew, and soon there was a second room. I do not know whose idea it was, but one day Mrs. Raymond signaled us to stop by tapping her pencil against an empty glass pitcher and said that while she would still be in charge, we would be divided up into four sections, two in each room. Four girls were to be chosen to lead these sections, and the name Arlene Zirner was mentioned along with three others. This was the interesting day. Mrs. Raymond apparently felt that my early starts showed initiative that should be rewarded. That was, of course, not true in either sense. But none of us was given any choice or warning that this was about to happen."

"Whatever the reason, that sounds like a good thing," said Mary. "I guess I am going to hear that it wasn't. But first, would you like some coffee or tea or juice?"

"Maybe some tea with lots of sugar."

"I'll be right back, hon."

And so, Arlene had a few minutes to herself to consider where she was going with this story, although that was intuitively clear to her from her first words. The cat reappeared from the bedroom and jumped into her lap. She responded absently with the lightest of touches. Mary came back from the kitchen with two cups and handed one to Arlene. The cat, apparently disdainful of Arlene's attention being split, immediately jumped down and walked out of the room.

Mary sipped her coffee, looked into Arlene's glasses and raised her eyelashes and eyebrows a trifle.

"That announcement was made right before our lunch break. When we came back the desks had been moved. Instead of the usual array, each room now had a definite separation between the middle rows, to make four equal groups. But in each group the desk at the right column of the first row was separated from the array in both the forward and outward directions, and turned around so that it faced the other desks in the group. Mrs. Raymond visited both rooms to show the girls where their new assignments were. The leaders were, of course, assigned to one of the four separated desks, and that included me. I sat in the middle of the second room but not really as part of the second grouping.

"I know you think I should have been happy at this tiny promotion, but I was so embarrassed that I kept my head down all afternoon, and I could feel how red my face was. One girl, who had only been there a few days, came up to me with a question that she would normally have asked Mrs. Raymond. I answered her, barely looking up, in as few words as possible. She must have thought me very rude and went back to her desk. When the afternoon ended, I stayed at my desk until everyone else had left the room because I was so ashamed. But that just called more attention to me. I didn't know what else to do."

Mary let Arlene catch her breath and said, "Arlene, you know I like you, so I am not asking this with any edge. I even understand the discomfort you might have felt that some of the other girls would resent your being chosen above them, but so much anxiety? What was that *really* about?"

"Oh, I don't know. I mean, I do, but I don't know why it has to matter. My mother taught me my whole life to stay invisible. 'Do good and disappear,' she told me over and over again. I've thought about that a lot—how it makes sense—and being singled out just seemed to be wrong. Especially when I hadn't done anything to deserve it. And there was another reason, Mary, that made it even worse.

"When I was in high school, it was like so many lights had turned on. Before that, students just sat at their desks and mostly did what they were told. Almost nobody was interesting, and that was because of teachers. Not that they were bad people, but their first job seemed to be *to keep order*. To keep everyone in such good order that they didn't even know that there was another way to be. I was comfortable with that for me because of my mother: it left no danger of standing out. But I love watching other people and wondering who they are and what they feel like, and elementary school was a kind of endless desert. Then came high school. I could keep to myself, but there were so many people to watch. I remember a girl named Linda who had two-color hair. And some of the boys were so vulgar and uncontrolled, but they seemed real. In that first job, I was back in elementary school, and worse I was almost one of the teachers expected to impose order. It was impossible for me not to feel crushed from both directions."

"So you already hated that job?"

"I suppose I did, although that is such a terrible word. But yes, after a few days, I knew I could never be happy there."

"What happened next?"

"I went home that night and talked to my mother. She seemed startled at first that I had been chosen to lead a section, and I had to explain that it was probably about me coming in early. In any case, I knew she shared my discomfort, but she did not want me to leave the job. My father was in the last weeks of his life, and we needed our two small incomes to replace the little annuity that he derived from his inheritance—which has still never been explained to me. Mutti hated to see me so upset but there was nothing to be done. Mrs. Raymond was so haughty that it was useless to ask her to choose another section leader. I just had to go back.

"I stayed, my father died a few weeks later, and I have never felt worse in my life—until today. It would be easy to say that my father had made a graceful, gradual exit from life, which was somehow easier on us than the alternatives might have been. But there was that gaping emptiness in my life at the same time that I had to walk into a room five days a week, placed in a role in which I could not blend in and from which I could not disappear. The other girls thought I was mean or sick, and it did not help that a few had found out about my father's passing and tried to be nice."

Mary saw a few tears spill out behind Arlene's glasses. They both sipped their tea. Mary had no model, no point of reference, for how Arlene saw the world, and saw herself in the world, but she was certain that this young woman was neither crazy nor mean.

"But you weren't working there when you met Charlie, were you? At least you got out." This worked: Arlene's eyes brightened, and she smiled.

"Oh, yes. A week later, on a Saturday, I went to buy some groceries for my mother. We shopped together every Saturday, and wheeled this big shopping basket to a new supermarket to get everything we needed for the week. But that day, Mutti had a terrible ache in her knee, so I went alone. On the way back, I was just looking across the street at nothing in particular when I saw a sign on the door of Mr. Potter's hardware store. I had only been in it twice, but it was such a big store full of such unlikely things! I always wondered how he could afford to keep so many things that he could sell maybe once every year or two. And the whole place had such an odd smell. But the sign said he wanted help, so I walked to the next corner, bounced my shopping basket down one curb, pulled it up the opposite one, and soon found myself in the store asking about the job."

"Pretty different from an insurance audit office, wasn't it?" said Mary. Her face showed a deep, placid contentment. She was happy to give Arlene this respite.

"Exactly! It was nothing like that office. It was the difference between elementary school and high school, even though I am sure an office job is considered more respectable. The clerks and the customers were all moving in their own way; there were no grids of desks, and the things Mr. Potter sold were themselves in a beautiful state of disarray.

"Mr. Potter was funny, but nice. It was easy to read his mind. He could see how young I was for working in a less supervised place like this, but, of course, the work did not need someone either smart or experienced. The most amazing thing was that I could tell he was glad that I am not pretty. He did not want customers or other staff flirting with me—which is really ironic, given how things turned out. He asked me straight out if I was working someplace else and how soon I could start. I asked him how much notice he'd want from one of his own employees and said I would give that much myself. Mr. Potter laughed, and we agreed that I would start in no more than two weeks. Sooner if I could arrange it.

"Monday, I spoke to Mrs. Raymond. It was early, and we were the only two there. I thanked her for the promotion and told her that I really didn't want it and that it would be best for everyone if I gave notice. Well, I tried to tell her that, but I didn't get past saying that I didn't want the promotion. She turned white—really not much of a change in color, but still a definite change—and told me to pack my things. There would be only two days of severance pay since I had only worked there for a few months. I was to leave at once. She turned away and those were the last words said.

"I had almost nothing to gather and so left before the workday had even started. On the way home, I stopped by the hardware store and told Mr. Potter that I could start tomorrow if that suited him. He grinned, and then his eyebrows shifted as if he were going to ask me about my sooner than expected availability, but he didn't. 'Tomorrow will be fine, see you then," was all he said and that's how my work at his store came about. I told my mother that afternoon when she got home from work, and she asked a few questions. When I explained to her that the office work was too much like elementary school, the questions stopped. She understood."

"But did she seem happy or disappointed?" asked Mary. "I mean, changing jobs is not too big, but not too small either."

"Oh, Mary, you have to remember that this all happened right before my father died. I know Mutti still cared a lot about my situation and my happiness, but she was also saying goodbye to the most important person she would ever have in her life. There wasn't that much emotional energy left for me. For that matter, I probably would never have looked up from my desk to even think about other possibilities if it hadn't been for Mrs. Raymond's reorganization. That and Mr. Potter's kindness made losing my father easier, although nothing could help with seeing my mother in so much unexpressed pain. Nonetheless, I had a new job and the sense of freedom I felt on that first day of high school, even if that job was plainer and I was about to lose a parent.

"And so I did. On Thursday of the following week, when I came home, I found only my mother. She had been coming home for lunch—which left her almost no time to eat—to check on my father. On this day she found him as usual lying flat on the couch, but not breathing. An ambulance came and took him away, so that by the time I got home, it was as if only two people had ever lived in that house. Mutti held me, and we both cried silently, sitting on the couch where he had spent so much of his last months. We didn't move and didn't speak. We shared the loss, of course, but also something else. For years, as I got bigger, my father got smaller. When I started the job in the hardware store, it was like the final stamp that I was full-grown. I never knew why my life seemed to crowd out his—I think Mutti understood but would never talk about it—but now there were just two of us."

Arlene was now streaming with tears. Mary got a washcloth from the bathroom and cleaned and dried her face. She wanted to hold Arlene but did not. This would have been too close to the tableau on the afternoon of her father's death. So, she just waited.

"I feel like I have been talking for hours," said Arlene. "I never meant to take over your morning, and I still haven't answered your question."

"I understand that these are things I have to know to understand your answer, Arlene. Take as much time as you need. It hasn't been all that long. Anyway, Annie is still sleeping, so I have no place else to be." Again, her kind smile almost made Arlene's heart burst.

"Well, apart from my father's death, I was happy in the hardware store. I learned where everything was, the names of the regular customers, and Mr. Potter even allowed me to do some of the paperwork and accounting. That was fun as long as it didn't take me away from the customers. It was so strange. You would think that they would come into the store knowing what they wanted—at least the *kind* of thing they wanted—but more often they just wandered around like bees in a garden. I think it was the smell of the place and the incredible range of items packed into that space. I would watch until they finally chose something and came up to the counter to pay, and almost all of them would have something inconsequential to talk about as I tallied their bill. There was so much to see! Or feel! Just like high school again. Anyway, it was only a few weeks later that—"

There was a soft sound from the wood flooring in the hall that led out of the living room. Both young women turned expecting to find the cat. Instead, their eyes met something much bigger than a cat but smaller than either of them. Annie stood there in her footie pajamas of white flannel strewn with read hearts; she blinked once. Her sleep-disarrayed hair had the texture of satin and was mostly gold with a hint of orange. Her eyes were light brown, with slightly rounded, perfectly symmetric eyebrows that matched her hair. She had a smallish nose, with nearly circular nostrils, and her lips were straight and pink. She had her mother's natural beauty, but her features were uniquely hers.

"Auntie Arlene, what are you doing here?"

Reading Eight

"The Unknown Celebrity" by Marla Kraft

[Late morning in a midsized park; sweater weather. A woman is sitting on a bench. An older man approaches on the path, slows his pace, frowns, and sits down next to her.]

Man: I recognize you, don't I? You're an actress.

Woman: You must be kid-- No, you're not. I am an actress of sorts, but how in God's name would you know that? I've done nearly nothing. Certainly nothing for credit.

Man: I see. No, it wasn't a painfully uninspired pick-up line. I'm too old and too happily married to make a pass at you.

Woman: Well, I'm too young and too happily married to let you. But you mean it? You really recognize me? From what?

Man: The movie about the six people that work in that two-story office building in the suburbs. You get out of a car at the beginning of the workday and then reach back in for your bag or some papers or something.

Woman: My God, that's right, but how could you know? You can't even see my face in that shot.

Man: I love that movie. I think I saw it ten times at least. I'm just a substitute teacher now, and I don't work every day. My wife loves me, but there are times, like now, when one of us has to leave the house entirely to the other one. We saw that movie together, and I fell in love with its cheerful silliness. I never told her that I went back time after time over the next few months until it disappeared from all the theaters. It was the second or third time that I noticed you.

Woman: But still, my face?

Man: Oh. Well, I thought since you were in that car scene you might be in other scenes, and I started looking for you. You were in the cafeteria, too, right?

Woman: Yes! But why were you looking for me?

Man: Yeah, it does sound strange, even creepy, doesn't it?

Woman: It sure does. And it leaves me with two choices: One, get away from this weirdo immediately, or, two, ask for the explanation that I will otherwise never get. Alright, that same harmless look that got me past the pick-up line decides it: I choose option two.

Man: My guess is that after my explanation, you'll continue to think of me as weird but harmless. Okay, ready?

Woman: I think so.

Man: When I first noticed you in the car scene it was exactly your anonymity that caught my attention. I thought, there is a full-grown woman. I cannot see her face, but I bet she's pretty, and I will never know her, or even know her name. But still, she is the center of her own world, and, more than that, she is more than likely someone's love. And that absolutely fascinated me. That we can be nothing and still be everything, not just to ourselves, but to someone else. That for the most part we exist in and for such relationships. And this applies also to this woman in a green skirt just arriving for work in this movie. I don't know why this occurred to me for the first time in connection with you, but every time I saw the movie I noticed you more and tried to recognize you by your figure or by the color of your hair or by something in the way you move. I just wanted to see your face. And I finally did in the cafeteria scene. And I just did it again, five minutes ago, in this park scene.

Woman: But this has to be one of the most incredible coincidences in human history! I mean, really!

Man: Maybe. But I suppose you had to be somewhere, so... Oh, God, I hope you don't think I somehow arranged this!

Woman: No, I don't. How could you? Anyhow, you seem nice enough and just as surprised as I am. And yet I don't know what to make of it at all. Is there some meaning here that we should be seeing. It's not as if we are going to fall in love and go off to some backward Pacific island together. I love those stories, but that's not going to be our story. Still, it makes no sense to me that our meeting could mean nothing.

Man: You could say that about life, too, couldn't you? It ends with nothing, but, nonetheless, does it make any sense that it's <u>all</u> for nothing. I could never quite accept that, even though I am at best an agnostic. I try never to think about death.

[They remain silent for a minute, as if neither of them has any will to leave the bench or has any other place to be.]

Woman: I don't know your name.

Man: Nor I yours.

Woman: Do you want to?

Man: No, I don't think so. When I walk away there will be no chance of reconnecting, and that makes this more special, doesn't it?

Woman: Glittering fish?

Man: Excuse me?

Woman: It's something I read somewhere once. A story. The narrator spoke of a human life as a fish that comes to the surface, glitters for an instant in the sunshine, and then sinks back into the water. This was our one moment to glitter, wasn't it?

Man: I like that. And while it is, as you said, almost unimaginable that this meeting ever happened, I thank you for not spoiling it for me with who you are for real.

Woman: Of course. And I thank you for not being the kook that anyone would have thought you'd be.

[They both smile broadly. The man rises and walks away. A few moments later the woman departs in the other direction.]

"Harry, our lives together couldn't have been more different, could they?"

Sammie was seated a couple of feet from him on the bed, their usual place for reading these scripts, when she could persuade him to.

Harry's eyes narrowed. "Samantha Evans, you say that like it's a bad thing! You wish we had spent only five minutes together instead of these twenty years, fifteen of them married?"

"You know I didn't mean that. But isn't this a kind of tragedy? The fatefulness of these two souls meeting but in such a way that their relationship could only last five minutes?"

"Relationship, Sammie? This dialog—if it is interesting at all—is only interesting because they did meet."

"No, you're wrong. That two people could understand each other under such circumstances means to me that under other circumstances they might have fallen in love and stayed together. I mean, he was obviously attracted to her, or he wouldn't have paid any attention to a silent extra in a movie, and that she talked to him after that first line he gave her—"I recognize you"—doesn't that tell you that deep down she accepted him as, well, somebody special? I know that's what I was feeling when I read her role."

"I don't know, but I will tell you what *I* felt: this is too silly to take seriously."

"Too silly or too unlikely?"

"Okay, unlikely. When have you ever heard of someone recognizing and then meeting a less than minor player in a show?"

"Never, but almost everything that happens in our individual worlds is incredibly unlikely. Maybe science or religion makes us think that there is some sort of necessity to the direction of the world, but certainly not to the fate of individuals. Well, I'm not sure about that for religion. I guess it does speak to individual times and places. Still, a lot is intended as somehow universal. In any case, all I'm saying is that we shouldn't ignore their encounter because its design seems so far-fetched. So are *our* lives, if you want to look at it that way, Harry."

"Okay. So, what should I take away from this? A very unlikely nothing happened."

Sammie smiled so broadly and honestly that her words went right into Harry's psyche almost without the need to process her language:

"Yes, Harry, very nice nothings happen sometimes, but they are never nothing."

Her face suddenly went crooked and serious, and her lips moved as Marla's might have, had Marla been Marla.

"Sammie, what is it?"

She opened her mouth, froze for a fraction of a second, shook her head slightly and said, "Nothing. I was just thinking about Jane Austen."

Harry shook his head in turn, but to a very different effect. (Scene.)

Chapter Nine

Arlene blinked. Her sister-in-law still sat close to her on the sofa, and Annie's pale face was framed by her shoulders and neck.

"Hello, Annie," she said. "I have just come by to see your mother."

Annie smiled. She liked her Aunt Arlene on many counts. Arlene was always kind and attentive and the youngest adult in her life, which made vaguely for some sort of pleasant proximity. Annie also liked the way her aunt spoke, both her funny cadence and that she didn't speak to her the way other adults did. Mary's sister, her only other aunt, would have said, "Auntie has just come by to see your mummy," as if Annie could not understand the use of words like "I" and "we" and "mother." And, maybe best of all, Auntie Arlene's lips made Annie's eyes open wide as she took in the wonderful, twitchy movements.

For her part, Arlene loved her niece, but something in their relationship always felt strange—inverted. Arlene was senior to no one else in her life. She was her mother's daughter, her husband's wife, Mr. Potter's new shopgirl, her sister-in-law's younger, much less experienced sister-in-law. It always felt odd to her that this little girl both figuratively and literally looked up to her.

Before the aunt and the niece could have any further exchange, Mary cut in, so that she and Arlene could continue their conversation.

"Are you done being sick, sweetie? Is your tummy better?"

"Not so much," replied Annie, still watching Arlene, "but I was thirsty and had to go to the bathroom."

"Don't those cancel out?" asked Mary.

Annie got the sense of the question and frowned adorably.

"No, I don't think so."

"So, I suppose I could get you a glass of water while you use the bathroom and then tuck you back in?"

"Okay."

Mary got up and walked to the kitchen. Annie hesitated for a second and said, "Goodbye, Auntie Arlene. I hope you will come back soon."

"And I hope that you will feel better after you finish your nap, Annie."

Annie smiled, turned and walked out of the living room. She loved the way Arlene said her name with just a delicious hint of an "ah" and both *n*'s audible.

"I think you'll be able to finish your story now," said Mary after Annie's water and bathroom needs were sorted, and the child was safely tucked up again.

"There's not much left… A few weeks later Charlie came into the store for something he needed for his shop. He came to the register to pay for it, and at first, he acted like any other customer. But then he seemed to take a second first look at me—if that makes any sense—

and somehow I had his attention in a way that I had only seen once before, with a younger boy in high school, a boy who liked me but was afraid of me. Charlie liked me, too, but there was no way that he would be afraid. And so…"

Arlene stopped; her face was strained, and her lips twisted, leaving her unable to speak. Mary knew that Arlene was about to revisit and for the first time put into words the greatest mistake of her short, kind life.

"Take a breath and go on when you're ready."

Arlene inhaled—and then again—but only her lips had relaxed, and just enough to allow her to speak. Her face remained taught.

"I'm ready." She closed her eyes and continued.

"Charlie came back twice more, and when he asked me to go to a movie with him, he was smiling and acting as if we were old friends. I did not quite trust him, not that I thought he was in any way a bad person, but because I was uncomfortable with his familiarity and that he liked me at all as a girl. But I thought those reasons reflected more poorly on me than on him. Still, I changed his plans and asked if he would instead have dinner at home with Mutti and me. And so, on a Saturday, between afternoon and evening, he rang the bell at our house, and I introduced him to my mother. He talked to her more than he did to me throughout dinner but was still very attentive in a way that Mutti couldn't miss. He was very polite and even offered to help with the dishes. Mutti said that was out of the question and he left shortly after we finished eating. He must have thought he needed my mother's approval before I would go out with him, and he looked confident that he would have it."

"I guess he was right," said Mary.

"Yes, but Mutti trusted me enough that I really didn't need to do that for her as much as for me. It is like with the doctor when you want a second opinion."

"So, what did your mother tell you?"

"Much more than I expected! I mean, I could see why she would be excited that any boy would want to date me, but it was more than that. She told me that with my father gone, she had been thinking of moving in with her cousin, who lived alone about forty miles from here in an undeveloped area. It was inexpensive and made a lot of sense if she was going to retire from cleaning, but she did not want to bring me there both because she did not care to take me to such an isolated place where I would never find a job—or a boyfriend—and while she did want to make her cousin less lonely, not at the expense of forcing a third person into her small place."

"She was practically telling you to get married?"

"She never said a word about that or about Charlie, except to say that he seemed nice. I remember that at one point I looked at her in such a way that she could not miss how puzzled I was that she had just jumped over anything important about him, and all at once she stopped talking, looked down, and bit her lip. 'I understand,' she said, and then we did talk about him, although there wasn't much to say because nothing much had been said during dinner. But she looked at me very seriously and maybe a little embarrassed from going on about retirement and living with her cousin and told me she was sorry that she had acted 'as if you had just announced your engagement.' She mumbled something—I could hardly hear her and don't know if she meant it more for herself or for me—but I understood the thought: we should only expect a little happiness."

Mary sat up straight and looked right through Arlene's glasses. Her normally kind face took on an angular expression of contempt.

"That's so depressing! What a thing to say to you!"

"Mary, you must not think badly of Mutti. She had led a small life and taught me to expect the same, and I think in her world, to see me married and herself move beyond decades of hard work were pleasures she had never considered. And the first time she did consider them was maybe the first time since I had been born that she had not put me first. And she was not really putting me second. She thought that Charlie was finally the answer to getting me settled on my own and that was a good thing for me."

"Okay, I understand, Arlene. I'm sorry that at that moment I had such bad thoughts about your mother, but I don't think you had anyone else to turn to, and today, right now, as I look at the bruise on your neck and shoulder, I don't think she gave you good advice. I wish I had known you well enough to—"

"But don't you see? She didn't give me any advice really, just reminded me of what should be enough."

"Okay," said Mary for the second time, looking away toward the hall and Annie's room. "So that's why you married Charlie."

"Yes. We dated for a few months and then he asked me and I agreed. I never saw the whole person who is your brother. I did it because I could see nothing wrong with the part I did see. I did it because I thought that was what my mother wanted. I did it because I was raised to be happy with what I had and never to expect more."

"You didn't love him, Arlene?"

"I'm not sure I know even now what that kind of love is. I love my mother, and I loved my father. I don't know what it is to love a husband."

And suddenly Arlene was crying again. She took off her glasses, making a fist of her right hand.

"But the worst part is that I never saw the whole person who is your brother, or even thought to ask why *he* married me."

They both needed a break from the emotional overload, and Annie's quiet return gave them the chance for one.

"Mommy, I don't think I can sleep anymore. Can I play with Auntie Arlene?" She was carrying a half dozen stuffed animals, including a floppy giraffe. She had brought the giraffe because it reminded her of her aunt.

Mary looked at Arlene. Her face was still red and ravaged by pain, but she put her glasses back on and gave Mary a slight nod, her lips tightening in resolution.

"Indeed, you can, honey, and I think your aunt would like that very much. I'll go make us some lunch while you two are playing."

There are more than enough ways to arrange six stuffed animals and more than enough pretend conversations to be had that Arlene really did feel better fifteen minutes later when Mary called them to lunch. The two young women sat along adjacent sides of the kitchen table while Annie took the chair opposite her mother; she was propped up on two throw cushions so that she could manage well enough at the table.

Mary chose her words carefully to keep them safely beyond her daughter's interest or comprehension.

"What are you going to do next, Arlene?"

Arlene looked sideways at Annie before speaking and answered in an unstressed tone.

"Oh, I suppose I'll go home and just see what happens. Besides, there is this other thing I want to talk to you about, but not today. It's just an idea I have had that has nothing to do with what we were saying before."

Abruptly Annie decided this was too good a chance to waste to tell her aunt about some new cartoons she was enchanted by. There were talking animals of so many kinds that she couldn't count them, but her favorite was a dog that talked slowly and funny. (It was a southern accent, Mary explained.)

Lunch ended. Arlene used the bathroom, and when she came back, she hugged both mother and daughter and thanked Mary with her words and with her eyes.

At the open front door, Mary said, "I'm sorry I don't have an answer to that last question you asked, but I know it's the right one to ask. And whatever the answer, you can't let this"—she touched her own neck—"happen again."

"I know."

Arlene closed her eyes for distinctly longer than a blink, smiled a little, turned away. She then began her long walk home.

Reading Nine

"The Diamond Pool" by Marla Kraft

[Early afternoon at the seashore. A middle-aged couple stands at an old, crevassed wood railing, with only the scantiest traces of white paint remaining. He wears an open white shirt and white pants; she has a lemon sun dress on that gives the sun ample exposure to warm her shoulders and an inch or so of her breasts. Below, between the shore and ocean, is a saltwater pool, sparkling frantically in the brilliant light. It's a large pool, with about forty occupants. They have each paid one dollar for the privilege of bathing in it.]

George: I have never understood attaching a pool like this to the ocean.

Mora: Is that what you are staring at? I don't think so, George.

George: I didn't say I was. Just that I have never understood why someone would come to the beach to use a pool.

Mora: You mean like those two? The ones you are staring at.

George: I wasn't staring, but, yes, I noticed them.

Mora: So did I. She's lovely, isn't she? Especially in that dark blue bathing suit. That little skirt does no good at all in covering her bottom, does it? What do you suppose, about seventeen-years-old? I bet he's the same.

George: Well, there is something hypnotic about them. Look at how he cradles her in his arms and just rocks her around and around in the water.

Mora: Why not? They are clearly in love.

George: Or maybe just enjoying the contact of each other's bare skin in one of the few places where they would not be noticed.

Mora: Except by you, George.

George: Mora, I am hardly obsessed with them. It's just that they are so young and happy. There is no responsibility for them, no death for them. Just this sun and the warm, salty embrace of the water and of each other. And they expect that it will go on forever. Imagine that.

Mora: That's easy enough: we were them once.

George: Just "once," Mora?

Mora: Oh, sweetie, I didn't mean it that way. You know that!

George: But I do know what you meant. Every moment once carried the excitement of reaching across to make fresh contact. You were my girlfriend. That word is magical.

[George frowns, looks at Mora, looks back at the couple in the pool, then looks at Mora again, his face relaxing but his eyes slightly crinkled with astonishment.]

George: ...You still are my girlfriend.

Mora: Yes. Yes, I am.

[He holds her full on and kisses her. A second later, four eyes look up from the pool and smile.]

✽ ✽ ✽ ✽ ✽ ✽ ✽ ✽ ✽

Laura: I feel like we have been here for hours and I want this to go on forever.

Paul: What's it like for you?

Laura: Sometimes I close my eyes for a little while, sometimes I open them a little. The sun is so bright. But not harsh bright. And the same things come and go when my eyes are open. There is just that, and the rocking, and the slow turning, and the feel of you holding me and me hanging on with my arms around your neck.

Paul: It's the salt water. You feel so light, my arms have so little weight on them. Holding your legs behind your knees...it's almost as if...

Laura: I know. And we'll be married soon.

Paul: Yes.

[They continue to rock and twirl silently; the ambient sounds are diminished to the point of vanishing. Suddenly...]

Paul: Did you see that? Were your eyes open then?

Laura: The white and yellow couple kissing? Yes, I saw that.

Paul: They look like they have been married for about twenty years. I hope we are still kissing after twenty years.

Laura: Well, why wouldn't we be?

Paul: Our parents.

Laura: That's true, but both your parents and mine are older than those two. Most people our age have younger parents, don't they?

Paul: I'm not sure with the war and all. But even so, what about thirty years?

Laura: I see. I won't pretend not to know what you're talking about, even if I do want to marry you more than anything else in the world.

[For an instant he tightens his arms about her body, she responds by tightening hers about his neck.]

Laura: I have the silliest idea, Paul, but it helps when I think about being as old as those two and then older.

Paul: And what is that?

Laura: Let me close my eyes, and I will tell you. Don't you dare drop me in the water because it's silly.

Paul: I promise.

Laura: It's like this. Right now we are almost as close as two people can get. I have to believe we are not the only ones to feel this way about each other, and that includes our parents. Nobody made them get married. So, imagine we are old, so old that even in this salty water you couldn't hold me, or maybe we would be too embarrassed to even come here in swimsuits. Just imagine. But the people we are now can still talk to each other.

Paul: How? Time travel? Because when I look at people who have been together for a long time, I see--I don't know--a kind of habit or inertia or something, but not love.

Laura: If that's how you feel about the future, then you must love me a lot right now to want to marry me. But the future doesn't have to be like that. I suppose there <u>is</u> a sort of time travel involved that makes it possible.

Paul: I'm utterly lost.

Laura: Okay, Paul. We're old and we're together, and it's gray and wintry and we are nothing but wrinkles. We look at each other, and we don't see what we see now. But here's how it works. The me in me that's here right here can talk to the wrinkled old lady. No one else can, but I can; that is called memory. And the old wrinkly you can talk to the you in you that's here right here. No one else can, but you can. Again, memory. And all of this goes both ways. So, the two of us now, if we want to, will always be able to talk to each other through the people we become. Does that make sense?

[Paul looks up to find the white-clad man and the yellow-clad woman on the boardwalk. He looks at them looking at each other.]

Paul: Yes, Laura, it makes sense.

"Gloria, why the hell are you crying? You spend weeks getting me to agree to read this stupid thing with you, and now you're crying in misery? I read my part as well as I could. What did you expect? Gregory Peck?"

Herb and Gloria sat on an uncomfortable little piece of lawn furniture built for two, but it was not on a lawn. A sliding door from their living room led out to a six-by-ten concrete slab of a terrace bordered by a wrought iron railing that came up to their waists. The only ornament on the terrace was an unprepossessing rubber plant in a terra cotta planter. They looked out from their spacious ninth-floor apartment across an uncongested city with a surprising amount of green space. There was just enough room on the cloth seat for them to be separated by a few inches. Gloria used this space to turn slightly toward her husband, but he sat perfectly parallel to the arm of the loveseat.

"For God's sake, Gloria, 'The Diamond Pool?' Yeah, I get it: two couples mutually past and future. We get old. We know that by the time we are teenagers, and we certainly know it in our forties. What's to cry about?"

She looked at him for a second, eyes and mouth tightening in anger. When she spoke the anger and tension were gone, replaced by a monotonic resignation. Her words were unstressed and evenly spaced.

"You think that I don't know and appreciate everything we have—everything you have given me—don't you? That's wrong. I know how lucky we are to be living in this apartment and in this city. I know how much is open to us, available to us, particularly because we don't have children. I never wanted to be a mother, and you never wanted to be a father, and that suits us both. We are quite well off."

"So what are you crying about?" he repeated, more insistently, offended by her placid resignation.

Her voice rose a bit, and the tension was back.

"I am crying"—and she was—"because what Laura said is right. The people we are when we fall in love *can* always talk to each other. And many times they do, just like George and Mora. But we don't... Does it ever occur to you, Herb, that we *chose* each other to marry. That we once *were* in love. Why doesn't that Herb ever talk to that Gloria?"

"Why doesn't that Gloria ever talk to that Herb? Is this my fault?"

Gloria looked terrified at that. She swallowed hard, and the tears continued to stream.

"You're right, but I think there is a reason that the other Gloria doesn't talk, even when she wants to. What happens when two people fall in love but then one slowly—day by day, year by year—has to accept that who she fell in love with was never there? That where she saw bright flowers there were only brownish weeds? It's not easy to admit that kind of mistake, to change the incredibly strong narrative of love into... what? Just a mistake in perception? Young Gloria doesn't talk because she has no one to talk to. That's why I wanted you to read this with me, both parts. But all I got from it was a confirmation that I had nothing. That I never did and never would. I wanted us to read and revive something that was never real. What *was* real could only sit there and ask in obvious annoyance, 'Why the hell are you crying?' Now you know."

"And what do you want *me* to do about that? What do you want *us* to do about that? What are *you* going to do about that?"

"Why nothing, of course."

They continued sitting on their sterile little terrace in the ninth-floor breeze. He wondered how long he would have to sit there and how long before her goring words would no longer cause such discomfort and frustration. She wondered about living alone in this nice place among all the nice things they had amassed in twenty-five years of marriage. But she had no more energy for discomfort or frustration, and that, she thought, should make things easier on Herb, in the long run.

Chapter Ten

Charlie kept to himself that morning, avoiding Bruce as much as he could. He inspected things that needed no inspection, scowled at the seamstresses to keep them off balance and in line, and spent a lot of time in the farthest, darkest corners of the factory.

Just before noon, he walked into the workroom, stood behind Bruce's back and asked, "How about I take you to lunch?"

Bruce jumped for two reasons: first, because he didn't know Charlie had come in; second, because the offer was, no matter how casual Charlie's tone, unprecedented.

"Sure," he said uncertainly. "Just give me a couple minutes more with this." He gestured vaguely at the parts of some disassembled device that had held his attention for well over an hour.

Fifteen minutes later, they sat across from each other at an unprepossessing diner on a busy street. The big glass windows at the front and the ubiquitous chrome were not comfortable on the eyes, but the customers didn't seem to mind. The food was mostly digestible and agreeably priced.

A young woman in a short, mint-green smock with a narrow dark green belt came to their table and looked at them inquiringly, pencil and tiny pad at the ready. Charlie noted a small gap in the buttons of her smock through which the tiniest glint of her flesh could be seen. She was a pretty girl, he thought. Bruce never even looked up.

"Egg salad and an orange soda," said Bruce.

"Grilled cheese, fries, and ginger ale," said Charlie.

Bruce looked placidly but alertly at Charlie. They didn't have much time, so he knew that Charlie would have to get to the point soon enough.

"Why don't you seem all that interested in women?" asked Charlie.

"Oh, I think I had the same interest that every other boy in my high school had, but you live and learn. Eventually I realized that they were more trouble than they were worth. So, my time is my own, my life is my own, and I don't mind being alone. Maybe someday."

"What about her?" Charlie gestured toward their green-clad waitress who was reaching for something on the shelf behind the counter. Her hemline lifted slightly to show the dimples of her knees, but Bruce barely moved his head to follow Charlie's glance.

"Maybe someday," Bruce repeated, adding, "but not today." He then looked right into Charlie's eyes. "So, what's this about?"

Charlie looked toward the counter to see if maybe their meals were about to arrive, but no luck: he had to answer. He blew out his cheeks.

"I hit Arlene this morning, Not a playful slap or anything like that. I hit her and hurt her, and I wanted to, and it felt good."

"Charlie! *Why would you do that?* She is as defenseless as she is attractive." He suddenly straightened his fingers, with the heels of his hands resting on the table. "I'm sorry. I shouldn't have said that. But for God's sake, why would you hit her?"

"I can almost tell you, and I thought if I started, I could maybe figure it out. Our marriage never worked, but lately…"

His voice trailed off. He was remembering the incoherent feelings he had had right after she agreed to marry him. A kind of conventional excitement, the kind that everybody was happy to share with him, and another, darker feeling that he had to acknowledge. *Once we're married, I can do whatever I want to her.*

"But lately…" And then he didn't want to say that she had somehow changed because he knew it didn't matter. That was not what this morning was about.

Bruce just sat quietly, watching the uncertainty and conflict on Charlie's face. Then Charlie got a break. The waitress was back with their orders. She put the tray down on the table and then began to transfer the plates, glasses, and flatware. Charlie saw her name tag: Amber. Neither of them thanked her, and she turned away. Charlie arranged the things in front of him, searching for words.

"It's not really about anything lately," he said, not touching his sandwich but rubbing the knuckles of his right hand against his right eyebrow, half speaking to himself. "But she's been different, like she has something new on her mind. And last night, she just went out."

"To see another guy? I can't believe that."

"Neither can I. But she went out for hours. Except for things like cooking and cleaning, I have no idea what she's doing most of the time, so it doesn't matter, does it? But she went out, and when I got up this morning, she was in that little space of hers and I just got so mad that I hit her and walked out and came here. I have no idea what state she's in."

"Do you think you really hurt her?"

"No—not like an injury, at least. She might have a bruise. But I never know what she's thinking even when things are quiet between us. Now..."

Bruce took a couple bites from his egg salad and chewed thoughtfully. He put down the sandwich and scratched his head.

"I don't get it. If it's not about 'lately' and you don't think she did anything wrong last night, why did you hit her?" Bruce knew that wasn't true and that he did get most of it. He had seen Charlie's unprovoked meanness many times at work; he had even seen that Charlie enjoyed it in a strange way. Hitting Arlene was probably just another part of this, but he still wondered why Charlie did it and, even more, why he enjoyed it.

Charlie made fists and relaxed them several times. His words explained nothing, and he just accepted that in this moment he would be incoherent.

"Bruce, sometimes you get a headache, and you can still do whatever you're doing, but the light hurts your eyes and it still hurts when you close them. You can't get away. That's pretty much me except that it makes me want to get away by hurting people. I once—to my sister..." he never completed the thought. "For no better reason than she didn't seem to have the headache, and when I did it, just for a little while, I didn't either. It's the same with Arlene."

Bruce thought that Charlie might as well have been drunk for all the literal sense he made, but he got some part of his question answered.

"Eat your sandwich, Charlie."

Bruce waited until Charlie finally began to eat, maybe so that he wouldn't be interrupted.

"Charlie, I have never wanted or expected much from life. I like fixing things. I didn't like school. My family didn't care about me one way or the other. I live a small life, and I know it. But the thing about being so small is that it is safe. I am mostly alone in the world, but I feel safe. There's nothing I want that I am not getting, and there is nothing forced into my life that I don't want. Just small and safe."

Charlie stopped eating and his face broke out in anger.

"So, you think I am small *but not safe*?"

"Whoa! Not in the sense you just meant. You put that there yourself. But as you mention it, no, you are not safe in either sense, as far as I can tell. You are not safe from the things around you, and you are not safe to be around, to be close to."

"I thought we were friends."

Bruce squinted, then looked out the big window. It was his turn to speak without knowing what he was going to say. He didn't want to make things worse for Charlie, but he didn't want to accede to a friendship he didn't feel, even if he knew that Charlie didn't feel it either. He would have to listen to his own words as he spoke.

"We know each other, of course. We know what we look like, how we dress, how we expect each other to behave. But, to be honest, if either of us disappeared from the other's life, how much would we notice it? Not much at all, I imagine. So, we are something less than friends. But that doesn't mean I won't listen to you or try to help you if I can. Right now, I don't know what you want help with, unless it's just to listen."

Charlie drew a deep breath, with his eyes focused on nothing. He shook his head a little.

"I wanted to hit Arlene, and I like hitting Arlene, but I know that can't go on. So, I just want to put things back the way they were, as little as that was."

Just then Amber returned to the table with a perfunctory "Is everything alright?" Bruce and Charlie put on matter-of-fact expressions and nodded. Bruce felt some special need to hide from her what they were talking about, even though she had paid them no attention. "That's a pretty green uniform," he said in a way that could not be misread as flirting. She smiled slightly and turned away. Bruce looked back at Charlie.

"But you aren't really sorry about this morning?"

"No."

"And you aren't sorry about this weird marriage you have."

Charlie hesitated. "No. And I want it to continue. It took about a month to go from pretending to be happy to where we are now, but I still want it to continue."

"Okay. I just wondered. I guess it doesn't change anything about what you might do, except that the flowers-and-candy routine becomes silly. I guess you could say, 'Sorry, I was just not myself this morning,' and even if Arlene thinks you were *completely* yourself, it might give her time to cool off… But do you even think she's angry?

"It's hard to imagine her angry, but something must be going on in there after what happened."

"Whatever it is, maybe she'll just go back to whatever's normal for her. Still, you can't hit her again. You do understand that much, don't you?"

Charlie only tightened his lips in response, and they finished their lunch. He paid the check, Bruce left the tip, and they walked back to the factory.

Arlene began her walk from Mary's house back to her apartment just after one o'clock. She wished she could enjoy how pretty the day was, but she couldn't get past the extent to which time had become her enemy that day. She imagined walking home to empty rooms and then just waiting for Charlie to return. That's where the terrifying blank spot was. It never crossed her mind that Charlie might be having something of the same problem.

It is useless to try to figure out that if he says or does this then I will say or do that, like some kind of chess game. So, I should plan nothing? But it is not about making moves; it is about knowing how I feel with this bruise and with knowing that I did everything Mutti wanted and now I am here. I wish Mary could have helped more, even though she helped so much by just listening and asking that one question over and over. Mutti, you never wanted me to be unhappy and every day of your life was an example of being happy with very little. I understand that and I love you, but…

She stopped herself right there. She knew she was about to say to herself, "…but nobody ever wanted to hurt you," but even though they had never spoken of it, she knew that they brought their uncomprehending little girl out of someplace incomprehensibly dark and dangerous. She had no right to think that she suffered in a way her mother could not understand. It was quite the other way around.

How can I face him—not in the sense that I have done anything wrong—but how do we talk to each other, be in the same room, sleep in the same bed? I cannot just leave; I have nothing. I cannot go to Mutti and bring her two new burdens: me and why I am there. She and Aunt Carlotta are barely getting by. They manage to be happy, but they are both old and have no more energy than they need to survive. Yes, I could visit. No, I cannot ask to live with them.

She kept walking, knowing that every step brought her closer in space and time to somewhere she dared not go, but she had no alternative. She stopped to take off her sweater, draped it over her forearm and then continued, looking as far ahead as she could and to either side for something to pull her attention away from her emotional confusion. But she was in a residential part of the city, school was still in session for a few more weeks, and there was nothing but the usual houses and yards deployed over a small range of styles: hedges, lawns, hydrangea, roses; yellow, pink, white and blue paint on wood or stucco. A pleasant enough vista, but nothing to distract her from her acute emotional and cognitive paralysis.

Arlene got home just after three o'clock. She opened the windows to the living room and in her alcove. She frowned and decided that to stay in her private space would be too much like hiding. Fleetingly she remembered the precious thing stored in the low cabinet, but she could take no pleasure in that. She sat on the living room sofa and waited. There was nothing else to do. She had made no plans or resolutions. She sat without moving, adjusting her glasses from time to time when their constant weight on her nose began to cause a slight ache.

At five-thirty the door rattled and opened only about a foot. Charlie's head entered the apartment and looked to the right to find Arlene, who still sat without expression. His face had an odd sort of smile, and for a moment Arlene thought that—contrary to Bruce's advice—Charlie might have brought flowers and candy that he was still concealing to heighten the surprise. His expression was so inappropriate to this morning's events that even her lips remained still in wondering what was about to happen.

Charlie opened the door fully and she saw that he was holding a small animal—in fact, a somewhat frightened puppy. The foolish smile held as he revealed his surprise and peace offering.

"It was only two bucks. It's just a mutt. But I thought maybe—"

"TAKE IT BACK!"

She was on her feet, shaking with her whole body.

"TAKE IT BACK!" she screamed again, while Charlie's face dissolved itself of any coherent expression.

"NO! You will not bring this little creature into your world! Not for one night! If you want things to go back to how they were for us, you will take it back right now, before the store closes!" She knew exactly where he had bought the animal, in a small, nearby store that she had passed countless times.

He had never seen her like this—nor had she. He opened his mouth to say something, to explain, to defend himself, but no sound came forth. The puppy closed its eyes against the world. He opened his mouth again.

She spoke first. "I don't care if they will or will not give you your two dollars back. Take him back. Do you understand? When you come home, things will be what they were, as much as I can make that happen. That's the price."

He didn't know what she was talking about. Price paid by whom and for what? But clearly his inspired gambit was not going to work. For once, Charlie was too confused and too overwhelmed to respond with his reflexive anger. He simply turned his back, left the room, and closed the door behind him.

Arlene was still shaking when he left, but at least now she knew what she was about. This was easier than the walk home from Mary's. Finally, she sat back down and waited for the door to rattle again.

Charlie came back forty minutes later without the dog. He could not get a refund, but the pet store owner was agreeable to taking back the animal with hopes for another sale.

Charlie generally avoided introspection, and he certainly was in no mood for it now. Just over an hour ago he had hit on what he thought was the perfect solution for getting through this evening without the discomfort that this morning's events deserved. Now he was immersed in eager anticipation of something even more explosive and satisfying. His eyes grew smaller as he approached the door of his apartment, which he threw open and then threw closed. Arlene sat quietly on their sofa, but again she drew first:

"Shall I fix you something for dinner, Charlie?"

She got up. There was no shaking. Her voice was unstressed and natural, without any hint of an effort to control it.

"No." He had intended to fling this word at her in scathing retribution for her unendurable delinquencies, but it was just a simple "no." Her unexpected question in its unexpected tone had utterly disarmed him. Not that his feelings toward her were in any way affectionate. In that instant, he hated her. He hated that he could make sense of her reaction to the dog, of her reaction to him. All of that flooded his psyche, but there was nothing to fight about and nothing to fight with.

Arlene stood up and looked right at him. She was still wearing the same light blue dress that she had put on that morning. Her face, like her voice, was completely normal. She nodded an acknowledgement of his declining dinner and waited for his next move. Charlie went off to their bedroom and closed the door, but not emphatically. About a minute later she began to hear unclassifiable sounds from the used television set that sat across from the foot of their bed. Arlene did not like television, and Charlie liked to lie back as he watched.

Arlene was finally ready to move to her alcove. She raised the window about a foot and opened the curtains, which then moved slowly in the breeze. She sat on her loveseat and looked outside. The open window made the space seem contiguous with the open air. The day was still bright, with only the first lessening of the intensity of the sun becoming ever so slowly apparent. On this day she had known surprise, pain, helplessness, closeness, apprehension—and anger. All of that merged and dissolved into an open, thoughtful connection with the world she could see through her window. She sat for hours, thinking, not presuming to plan. The sky lost its light and its blueness to become a noncolor. A few wispy clouds moved in over the city, picking up the faintest orange cream reflection of a half-moon, just rising. Her peace, such as it was, was interrupted by the sound of the bedroom door opening partially. It was, of course, Charlie.

"Arlene, are you coming to bed?" It was less than a bark but certainly without any of the false overtones with which he had introduced that terrified puppy just a few hours ago. She appreciated the relative honesty.

"No," she said, but the words did not seem to originate from within her consciousness. "Tomorrow," her voice continued. "Everything will go back to the way it was tomorrow."

He closed the door, she closed her eyes, and the day was finally over.

Chapter Eleven

Arlene awakened on the living room sofa. She had slept on her back, with her head resting at a not entirely comfortable angle on the arm closest to the door, so that the illumination of the new day came from under her chin. She reached over to the coffee table for her glasses and put them on. She lay quietly for a few seconds longer, her lips twitching slightly as she took in her immediate surroundings. She could hear Charlie in the bedroom, probably just about to leave for work. At that thought, she sat up abruptly, walked over to the kitchen area and quickly assembled a salami and cheese sandwich for him, with a bit of mustard. She wrapped it in wax paper and placed it in a small white paper bag, just as the bedroom door opened.

"Good morning, Charlie. Here is your lunch."

He looked at her sideways with hooded eyes, attempting to mask his heightened anger with his more usual air of impatient annoyance. He grunted, took the bag, and left.

"See you tonight," she called after him.

She inhaled deeply, looking at the empty apartment, held her breath while listening to the sharp hum of their old refrigerator, and then exhaled in some relief. Twenty-four hours had now passed since he had struck her neck with the back of his hand, and she had a stable way forward.

Her first movement was toward the bedroom to shed the clothes she had been wearing since her walk to Mary's house yesterday. She showered quickly, dressed in something yellow, and went out, taking only her small purse. While it was barely half past seven, the air had already lost some of its morning coolness. In fifteen minutes, she was sitting on the same bench in the park that she had shared with Mrs. Forney a few weeks back, the same bench where she had overheard a little snippet of a child's conversation—a child pretending for a few moments to mimic an adult in her family—that had set so much in motion. She sat there now in consequence of that, on a bench that seemed much larger and stronger in Mrs. Forney's absence. Arlene permitted herself a small, but genuine smile.

Children began appearing across the street, drawn to one of the last days of school for the year. Their lightness at this impending liberation was perceptible, and their numbers grew and then suddenly died away. There was a bell, and she was alone in the park, with the street running in front of the school nearly deserted of any pedestrians.

Now I can think. But there is nothing more to be decided. I know what I want to do—what I have to do—and all that remains is to do it. That is entirely in my control, and Charlie makes no difference, as long as I can manage his anger.

She realized that she was using the word "manage" in both a reflexive and transitive sense. She would need both in order to remain in control of herself for as long as it took.

When Charlie got to work that morning, he knew that it would be useless to try to avoid Bruce. He walked into their space, and immediately Bruce turned in his chair to look at him. He spoke no words, but his eyes said, "Well?" in a clear voice. Charlie likewise spoke only with his eyes: "Not now, not ever." But the mere thought of describing the evening that had passed made him resolve, irrevocably, never to think of that puppy again.

Two weeks and a few days had passed. During that time, Arlene and Charlie carried on much as before. He spoke little in the morning, taking the lunch she had prepared for him on the way out. She worked almost the entire time at her typewriter in her alcove, stopping only for a brief lunch, which she occasionally took outside. There was nothing else. The machine and her papers were always safely stowed well before the earliest she could imagine Charlie's return, but she sometimes continued working while staring out the window, or making a dinner that as often as not Charlie ignored. Their evenings were spent in a silence that was at most a trifle more tense than before, with the television serving as a welcome diversion for both of them, although she never watched. Once or twice, she announced quietly that she might go out for a short walk, and he grunted his indifference. She never stayed out long or rode the bus. Usually he was first in bed, and she joined him, making as little disturbance as possible. There was no question of intimacy, but this had already been true after the first few weeks of their marriage. Arlene was grateful that she need not extend herself in this way as part of the peacekeeping operation. After all, Charlie's loss of physical interest in her had never been a surprise; the surprise was that he had ever shown any interest at all.

Finally, Arlene was ready to speak to Mary again, and early one afternoon she went out to a pay phone to see if she could come over tomorrow morning. Mary agreed at once, but then suggested that they meet for lunch someplace halfway between Mary's house and Arlene's apartment. Both her children were out of school for the summer, and she saw no problem leaving Annie's brother in charge for a couple hours with some discrete oversight from a neighbor who was also a mother. Arlene was a little disappointed at not having this chance to see her niece and nephew, but this small regret was overwhelmed entirely by her relief at being able to see Mary at all. She knew well enough how much she needed another pair of eyes and ears, and Mary's sympathetic ways.

Arlene set off a little after eleven o'clock the next morning wearing a softly lime-colored frock adorned only by deep green cloth-covered buttons that were evenly spaced from her collar bone down to her waist, and a shiny narrow belt that matched the buttons. She carried her small purse inside of a wide tote bag woven of flexible bamboo strips, with large brown looping handles. Her shoes were tan, not quite flats, with heels no more than an inch and a half high.

While high clouds provided a brief dimming of the harsh summer sun, it was hot outside, and Arlene controlled her pace so not to reach her luncheon with Mary in a state of soggy perspiration. When, after nearly an hour, she reached the restaurant that her sister-in-law had chosen, she was relieved by the dark coolness of its interior. She ate out infrequently, and then usually in a diner or coffee shop. As her eyes adjusted to the light, Arlene recognized that this was something beyond that: the tables and booths were covered with white linens with ordered plates and flatware set out in advance of its patrons. There were only a couple of tables occupied—lunch would not begin its crescendo for at least another half an hour—and one of the uniformed waiters approached her.

"I am meeting a friend here, but she has not yet arrived."

"Then there will be two of you." Arlene nodded to the white shirt and black tie. "Well, we are not yet busy. Would you care for one of the booths?" The waiter nodded in the direction of the wall to the right of the entrance. She noticed that the deep maroon and jet black of the wallpaper had texture, like upholstery. Arlene mumbled her approval and soon found herself comfortably seated toward the back of the room with a clear view of the entrance. Her lips moved sidewise as she nudged the silverware into even stricter order and tried to acclimate herself to her surroundings. Her simple but neat attire was quite appropriate for the place, but still she felt uncomfortable that Mary had picked a venue so much fancier than she had expected.

I cannot let this place distract me. It is going to be difficult enough to have this conversation without worrying about the fine china and textured wallpaper.

Her resolve was sensible and seemed manageable—until Mary walked through the door.

Even in the ill-defined silhouette resulting from the flood of backlit illumination when she first opened the door, Mary was instantly recognizable by her full loose curls. As she walked toward Arlene and her full person came into focus, Arlene's lungs, eyes, and lips all froze simultaneously. She had known since their first acquaintance what a pretty girl Mary was, but she had never seen her outside the setting of her or someone else's house. Mary had dressed in a red suit with the skirt cut just above the knee and a short jacket worn over a white blouse with a frilly ruff below the neck. Her shoes were stylish black pumps with short heels and ornamented buckles, perfectly adapted to her suit and sandalwood stockings. The stockings brought back a flash of Arlene's first day in high school, and Linda, but she was in the main simply overcome by what a beautiful woman Mary was.

It's not how she is dressed—that is just an accent on her natural beauty and poise—and more than that, she acts as if she is unaware of it, or at least as if she would never think to exploit her looks the way some women do.

As Mary sat down across from Arlene, she could not help but read the admiration in Arlene's eyes.

"I hardly go anywhere or ever get to dress up," she said. "It's fun sometimes, even if I did have to waste money on a taxi because of these shoes. You look nice, too. That color really suits your hair," she added.

It was meant sincerely, but Arlene's first thought was that given the color of her hair, the implications for the color of her dress were not good. With that final self-conscious thought, she began simply to enjoy Mary and the nice restaurant in which she found herself. A waiter appeared with two menus and then withdrew; it was only his professional discipline and need for his job that kept him from staring into Mary's green eyes.

"Let's really have a good look at the menu and order something really good. Hank won ten dollars in some sort of pool at work, so I'm paying."

"Oh, no, I asked you and—"

"Never mind that. You can pay next time."

Mary eventually ordered fish fillet with a red sauce and vegetables, a side salad of tomatoes, small cubes of hard cheese and minute leaves of some species of dark green lettuce that Arlene did not recognize. Arlene, perhaps a little diffident about Mary's generosity, ordered what she thought would be a plain portion of chicken breast. She, too, had vegetables, but no salad. Mary ordered a glass of white wine; Arlene had only water.

After the wine and water had arrived, Mary looked squarely at Arlene, who knew exactly what was coming.

"I know you want to talk about something else, but the last time I saw you, you had a bruise on your neck. I must ask you first about how things are with you and my brother."

"Different…but not much worse. I mean that we have been living alone but together with so much tension for so long, and that hasn't changed. I suppose that what has changed is that tension now has a focus—although neither of us will speak about it—and that is the night I disappeared on a bus for a few hours and the morning that he hit me. As long as we don't mention that, nothing has changed."

"Did he ever apologize?"

Arlene's look was indecipherable, and her lips worked in every direction. She reached up at her face as if she were about to remove her glasses but stopped mi-gesture. Finally, she said, "He brought home a puppy, but I would not let us keep it."

"Oh… Oh, I think I understand."

"It really was not an apology, but a disguised bribe, and what was being disguised by it was an innocent, defenseless little creature that was going to be abused by Charlie's bad temper. It might have deflected some of his anger from me for a while, but I could not let that happen." She realized she was raising her voice and immediately retreated to almost a whisper. "I screamed at him to take it back. God, Mary, I never lost my temper like that, and when I think about it, it is as if another person were there playing my part."

Mary sighed, tilted her head sideways, and frowned. "I don't know how you manage. My life is so ordinary, but Hank would never try to hurt me. Never."

At that point, their drinks were served, and with a surprising flourish: "I have few chances to wait upon such elegant and attractive women," said the waiter, clearly addressing the one in the red suit with the short skirt. Mary murmured an indistinct thank-you in acknowledgement.

"I always wonder what it feels like to be attractive," said Arlene. "Not that I am jealous of you—you know I could not be that way."

"I guess I don't really know," answered Mary. "I won't pretend that I am unaware of the attention I get sometimes, but it's just never been—I don't know how to say it—part of how I act?"

"That," said Arlene, for once taking the stance of the more experienced of the two women, "is very much to your credit."

Their orders arrived. To her surprise, Arlene's dish came with a wine glaze and smelled faintly of rosemary and was not nearly so plain as she had anticipated.

Mary smiled both at Arlene's last words and the wonderful meals that lay before them. "Let's eat this before it gets cold, and then you can tell me all about whatever it is you want to tell me."

When they had finished, Mary ordered coffee for both of them, and Arlene excused herself to use the ladies' room, which was far too rococo for her taste but had an unusual floral scent that she would not have associated with any lavatory she had ever visited. She used the trip for her final moments of preparation, and when she returned to the table, it was her turn to look squarely at Mary. She took a breath, and really did not know what she was about to say. Just then, the door opened to admit some new patrons and the whole room was illuminated by the harsh outdoor light. As the door closed and the relative darkness of the restaurant returned, the whole space felt somewhat safer by contrast.

"Mary…" She reached into the tote bag that she had carried in and pulled out a large yellow envelope. "Would you read this?" She handed the envelope across the table. Mary opened it and pulled out several sheets of double-spaced, typewritten paper. Her eyes seemed extra wide in the dim light. She posed no questions but did as she was asked.

She finished, laid the pages on the envelope, to the right of her coffee. She looked at Arlene in unconcealed confusion.

"What is this? Part of some kind of play?"

"I suppose it is a kind of play, although I never thought of it so much that way."

"Did you write it?"

"Yes."

"And what did you think you were writing?" The question could have had an edge to it but didn't. Mary was simply overwhelmed by curiosity. She picked up the sheets again, as if to reread them, but Arlene gave her no time.

"About a month ago, I heard a little girl in the park across from the school say something and in such a way that I knew the words were not hers. It seemed that she was playing at being an adult by repeating someone else's words in someone else's tone. Later that night I tried it on Charlie. I don't even remember what I said, but I do remember two things: it was fun to do it, and his reaction to just a few seconds of me not being me was beyond anything I could have expected. And then I thought, what if someone were to write out little scripts for two or three people so that they could have someone else's words, be someone else. That is like a play, but not really: no sets or any kind of direction—just the words and the people. Maybe saying things they wanted to in places they wanted to be, or never would be, or saying things they never would say. It didn't seem to matter. But that's the idea."

Mary sighed and bit her lip. "So this could be something that me and Hank would read to each other, pretending we were there, even if we were just in the kitchen."

"Yes. Is it a good idea?"

"It *is* a good idea."

By now Arlene was past any embarrassment, but there was one question that still threatened to tear her chest open:

"But is that one good? What you just read?"

Mary looked down, and then looked up at Arlene. At that moment she was as close to another person as she had ever been, except for her husband. Arlene had chosen her to open her own heart with this undreamt idea. Mary knew that she had to be dead honest with Arlene. Indeed, her eyes were wet as she looked up, both from the experience of this unexpected closeness and the joy of communicating what she had to say.

"*Are you kidding?* I would love to play Laura, and to have Hank play Paul! It wasn't anything like *my* 'Graduation Night,' but I wish it were."

Arlene started to say something, but Mary interrupted: "Do you mind if I read it again?"

When Mary finished, she looked across their table to see that her sister-in-law was much more relaxed than before, but still anxious.

"Arlene, no one has ever asked me their opinion on anything like this before, and I am honored, confused, and happy that I really like this and your idea. But from the sense I got from when you were at my house, I feel like you want something more than just my opinion of your tiny play."

"Yes, I'm afraid I do." She looked down and away to her right, at the dark floor of the restaurant. It was made from large, square tiles of natural wood, sealed and waxed, that showed a deep pattern of natural contours, which were broken off abruptly at the edges of each piece. Arlene turned her head back to Mary, but still didn't look up.

"Mary, I have had school and two jobs. I have liked some places, not others, and sometimes people I have worked with have not liked me because I didn't quite fit in, and others—Mr. Potter at the hardware store, for instance—have liked me for the same reason. I have such a limited experience of the world except for watching people and sometimes finding secret places." She smiled a little at that and finally looked up.

"Arlene, I know I am older than you, but because of my marriage and kids, I'm not sure I have any more experience."

"Maybe, but you do fit, and you're confident of fitting and of being a wife and a mother. And you are so beautiful!" Arlene surprised herself with that last bit; she had not intended to say it, although it was not entirely irrelevant to where she was going.

"And so?" Mary still had no idea what Arlene was asking—or was about to ask.

"Mary, I loved writing that," she gestured toward the pages, "and I have written another, and I want to write more. But I want to do something with them. I want them to reach people, and I have no idea what to do with this, where to start, and I want you to help because whatever needs to be done, you'll do it better than I ever could."

"I get it," said Mary. "You want me to be your agent, don't you? Your housewife, sister-in-law agent?"

"I guess so," answered Arlene in obvious discomfort. *You need to be a real writer to have an agent.*

"I accept."

She reached her hand across the table, and Arlene took it, although it was not quite like a handshake.

"Just one question," said Mary, looking near the top of the first page of the typed manuscript. "Who is this 'Marla Kraft?' Where did *she* come from?"

"I don't know entirely. I mean, *Kraft* means strength in German. That's good. Marla just came out of nowhere."

Mutti, thinking of a famous German singer and film star, would have known differently, but there the matter rested.

Reading Ten

"The Frozen Sand--Part One" by Marla Kraft

[Two twenty-year-old women walking midday on a beach in early January. The clouds are dark and low; a relentless wind comes from the south. Bent forward, they walk into the wind, with the indifferent pale green ocean to their left. They both wear thick, woolly coats with hoods drawn so tightly that they have only a narrow cone of vision opening forward...]

Isla: I don't remember ever being this cold. My face went numb about five minutes after we got out of the car. Why don't our eyes freeze?

Sophie: I don't know, and I don't care. And I don't know why I ever let you talk me into this insanity. The beach in winter!

Isla: Because we have to think, it's easier to think together, and all this cold and wind and waves and desertion forces us inside ourselves, where the thinking is done best.

Sophie: Baah! You could have thought more efficiently on your own: I am just going to complain.

[Isla looks at the ocean; she has to turn her entire torso to manage it. Almost every muscle in her body is pulling inward. She stops and pulls her gloved right hand out of her pocket to stop Sophie, too. They both turn left, fully facing the ocean, moving their feet in several discrete pivots.]

Isla: The wind is not so bad when we are turned in this direction. Just look! Ocean and clouds and nothing else. But think of the immensity both above and below. And we are safe and tucked into these coats with every square inch of our skin covered except for the little bit around our eyes. I feel at the same time a sense of having no boundary between me and the world and yet being an almost entirely closed node of consciousness. Isn't that a good place to start thinking?

Sophie: I understand... But what did you want to think about?

[Just as carefully they turn back into the wind and begin walking again. Except for a few birds, they would seem to be the only living things within miles.]

Isla: I want to think about where we are going and why. School was like a conveyor belt; there were no decisions to make. Even the decision not to go to college was made for us and depended on nothing more than the length of our hair and the shapes of our faces and bodies. We are both smart enough to go to college, but we were too young to know that that option was being foreclosed before we were old enough to think about it. Well, I am not going to make that mistake again. One year out of school in a routine job that I never chose to be trained for is enough--and it should be for you, too. We've been friends since kindergarten; I know you know this as well as I do.

Sophie: If you could see my face now, you would see that I am frowning. I am like you in a lot of ways, and you know I do like you--you have been my best friend for most of my life--but I don't like these kinds of thoughts. You're right of course about how we got where we are, and the next step of my life will probably be defined by some appropriate young man that has my parents' approval, but I cannot imagine how to undo that, no matter how cold and dark and windy it gets or how frigid and far and deep and timeless the ocean looks. Please, Isla, let me go.

Isla: I know this seems cruel, but you sound like someone dying in pain who just wants to be left to die. I never meant for you to feel that way.

Sophie: I know. It just came out. I'm sorry to be so unhelpful. And it's because you are right. But I still can't think of the first thing to do about it.

Isla: I can't either, but it's in us to figure out what our lives mean. Won't that tell us something about what to do?

[It was now about as dark as midday could get without a tornado; the sky low enough to touch the ocean. It was Sophie who then took her left hand out of her pocket to stop Isla.]

Sophie: Do you see what's happening?

Isla: No. It seems to have gotten darker, but. Wait! I feel something on my nose. Something that's small, cold, soft, and sting-y.

Sophie: It's starting to snow!

Isla: It never snows at the beach, does it? I mean, it must snow sometimes because it is now.

[They turn toward the ocean again, this time only halfway. The snow thickens from something barely perceptible into a white wind.]

Sophie: Isla, are we safe?

Isla: I think so. It's not sticking, and we aren't going to get lost, are we? And anyway, it's perfect, isn't it?

[A few seconds pass without words, all motion, sound, and intent belonging to the wind and the sea. Then a single broad, blinding, fork of lightning connects the sky to the water. For an instant they watch the howling snowstorm in the dazzling light of summer.]

Isla: Oh, OH! I was wrong. I misjudged perfect. I underestimated it, and now I can't breathe.

[Isla is steady enough, but Sophie puts her arm around her, as if to support her. Even as the afterimage of the lightning strike fades, they continue to stare into the storm, paralyzed by its grandeur.]

Sophie: Isla, was <u>that</u> your meaning? Or at least some sign that there is meaning?

Isla: I don't know. If only I could at least make some kind of a start.

Professor Saghalia was fifty-five years old, distinctly graying, and a distinctly optimistic man. As usual, he wore a fine suit, dark grey with a tie in diagonal stripes of rich shades of green. His students were surprised to enjoy his introductory philosophy class as much as they did. He tried to make it relevant to their lives and was successful with about half of them. The rest, for the most part, did some of the reading, sat politely but quietly through his class, and, at times, tracked the occasional fly on the wall. In this section of the course, there were twenty-nine young men and two young women—although in his mind, never to be admitted, Prof. Saghalia thought of them as twenty-nine boys and two girls. One of the girls was an occasional fly-watcher. The other was signaling with her hand to ask a question.

"Molly?"

"Professor, I hate that part about his brother's death. I mean, I don't think the author really ever answers it. Even if you believe in God, and I know you don't, isn't Levin right that everything ends in death?"

They had been reading Tolstoy's *Anna Karenina*, and the professor was not surprised that Molly had zeroed in on this passage.

"Tolstoy wasn't the first to think this," he observed pitching his voice somewhere between a conversational response to Molly's question and the tone he took while lecturing, "You can find it in Shakespeare, too." He quoted from MacBeth:

> Tomorrow, and tomorrow, and tomorrow,
> Creeps in this petty pace from day to day,
> To the last syllable of recorded time;
> And all our yesterdays have lighted fools
> The way to dusty death…

Pleased with himself, he turned more seriously to the substance of her question.

"I have a theory, Molly." He noticed that almost at once he had lost the attention of most of the class. They rested their pens on their desks, setting aside any intention of taking notes. These colloquies with Molly were not all that rare and usually resulted in nothing memorable—certainly nothing they would be tested on. Prof. Saghalia became a bit too earnest and technical to be enjoyable, and Molly was not someone the boys much wanted to look at. First, she was a girl in college, which marked her by itself as just plain weird. Second, she was somewhat unkempt; not unhygienic, but the smart money was on her not owning a comb or brush or washing her hair more than once a month, and she wore not a trace of makeup. Third, her loose-fitting Bohemian clothes—sagging blouses and enormously long wraparound skirts—revealed nothing of interest, if indeed there was anything of interest to be revealed. One or two of the boys might have been intrigued by the intensity of her eyes, but since she generally sat in the front row, nothing ever germinated on this account.

"I have a theory, Molly. My father has been dead for many years, but his memory lives in me. I don't just mean that I remember him, but something of how he thought and acted is active in me, and so in that way he lives on, and his life has meaning. Does that make sense?" Prof. Saghalia knew that what he had said, however expanded, could never survive the carving knives of an academic peer review, but it might sound deep to a freshman. Aware of the social and professional asymmetry between himself and Molly, he had not suppressed an element of smugness in his short speech.

"I guess so, but…," Molly began, but then she hesitated. "I hardly knew my grandfather, and my father didn't know his at all, but still I have heard this story dozens of times," she paused and calculated for a second. "My great uncle lived in Sicily. Anyway, he was once in the park on a sunny day and saw this famously smart dog raise his leg and relieve himself on the head of a bald man dozing on the grass. I know this because my father told me, and now all of you know it." She looked around the classroom, "But someday when we are all dead, what is left of my great-uncle, or even of the smart dog for that matter? I mean, isn't Tolstoy still right because what you are talking about, Professor, fades? Even if you are famous. I mean, unless there is a God that holds on to all of our stories forever."

Prof. Saghalia looked away from Molly and then down at his watch. He no longer felt optimistic or sounded smug.

"Molly, I will think over what you have said, but that's all we have time for today. Class dismissed."

Chapter Twelve

On a Wednesday, about two weeks after Arlene and Mary had met for lunch, at about five-thirty, Arlene heard a knock at the door of her apartment door—an event so rare that she froze for the space of a few seconds. She opened the door a few inches and exhaled in relief.

"Mary!"

"Is Charlie home?"

"No, not yet—maybe not for quite a while."

"Good. You know we should have talked about how we were going to get in touch after that lunch. It's quite a nuisance that you don't have a phone."

"I know, but I thought you would write, or I would call you after a while."

"Write? I guess you just aren't used to having a phone. No, that's way too slow." She took a breath.

"Look, Hank is downstairs. He ran me over here with the kids, and I can only stay a few minutes."

"I understand, but why didn't you all come up?"

"Because Hank was worried Charlie might be here, and he's been spending the whole time we've been married avoiding him. Anyway, here's the thing.

"First, promise me you will call every day or two, okay?"

"I promise."

"Second, I have spent a lot of time at the library with the kids. You can find out lots of things there, or just be in a quiet space to hatch out your own thoughts. So, I know some things now that I didn't when we first talked and have some ideas. They aren't brilliant or sophisticated, but it's someplace to start."

"Thank you for taking this so seriously," said Arlene. The two women looked at each other in mutual appreciation. Arlene was wearing her pale blue dress. Mary was dressed nothing like at their lunch. She had on an enormous green and yellow, short-sleeved football jersey over rough gray jeans, and her hair was a vast tangle without form. Arlene noticed that her posture was not that of someone about to sit down.

"Two more things," said Mary in a quick almost staccato cadence. "Can we meet tomorrow at ten-thirty at that little bunch of picnic tables near the park on Wick Avenue? I can go over what I have in mind there. Call me if you can't come. Don't worry about me; I will be there."

Arlene nodded and then adjusted her glasses. Her lips were moving, but otherwise she was a soldier at attention, receiving orders. "Okay."

"Finally, have you been continuing with your little scripts?"

"Yes."

"Good!"

With that, Mary was out the door. She hurried downstairs and got into their car. With perfunctory instructions for the children, they pulled into traffic and effectively disappeared. Only then did Mary realize how nervous she had been both by way of contagion from her husband and the awkwardness that would have followed had Charlie in fact come home.

At a quarter to seven, Charlie came in. Arlene stood in the kitchen, tending an optional dinner that she had prepared for him. His eyes flicked in her direction, and his expression said, "Just leave it. Maybe later." He went off to the bedroom, took off his shoes, turned on the television, sat long ways on the bed, and picked up a newspaper she had left for him.

Arlene stood still at the kitchen sink.

This is about how it was before. It should be easy to bear, and I have the space I need for now. Still, I have done nothing to make him treat me like this, I never have, and I do not in the least deserve it.

Charlie let the newspaper fall into his lap and stared through the shifting monochromatic images on the television screen.

God, I still hate her. At least that morning I hit her doesn't seem to replay itself in her eyes every time I see her. I wanted to crush her skull and drench that thick, dead grass she calls her hair in blood. What can she be up to all day? Nothing she wasn't doing before, but still even though she acts just the same, something is different, but in a way I can't see and so can't do anything about.

And so, Charlie's anger and acute discomfort resumed a steady state with no thought of change, just a sense of familiarity tainted by some indefinable suspicion, while Arlene's sense of injustice, held under strictest control, quietly grew, its energy spilling out onto sheet after sheet of plain white, medium-quality paper. Contrary to her mother's wishes, she was in the nascent stages of un-disappearing, but she could not see that yet.

The next morning was cooler, but not the least bit chilly. Arlene wore a pink muslin blouse with white buttons and a simple tan skirt that came just to her knees, accented with a thin patent leather belt. She reached the picnic tables a few minutes before Mary, selected one that caught some shade, and sat down to think, and to wonder what Mary might have in mind. She hesitated a trifle before sitting because her skirt was such a solid, light color and the bench was thinly painted, unfinished wood. She did not like to soil her clothes, but there was nothing to be done for it.

Mary appeared from the opposite direction from which Arlene had come and wore green plaid shorts with wide-cut legs and a lavender sleeveless blouse that just met her shorts. Her hair had been brushed, but except for a single barrette, she had made no attempt to style or confine it. She carried a file folder, which she set between them when she sat down opposite Arlene. A slight breeze moved the leaves of the nearby trees to cause a slight shifting in shadows on the wooden table. The two looked at each other and smiled warmly, but neither said hello; it would have been redundant.

"So, let's see what might be done with Miss Marla Kraft," began Mary.

"Her expectations are not lavish, " answered Arlene.

"Let me tell you what I've learned and what I've been thinking.

"First, even if you wrote a hundred of these little scripts, a book is out of the question. If you were already famous, someone might want them for your name, but since you aren't, and you really don't expect anyone to sit with them and read them the way you would a book, it just makes no sense to waste any energy on that.

"So, what do other people pay to read? Magazines, of course, and I think your stuff makes a lot more sense there. The problem is—at least from what I found at the library—the two kinds of magazines that might make sense both don't. I mean, I can't imagine you getting past the person who opens the mail at both small literary magazines and big-advertising, big-circulation women's magazines. I looked through both kinds, and they both seem wrong. The literary ones don't want popular, accessible things—I sometimes think that being understandable is a disqualification—and the big ones are businesses. I can't imagine something creative fitting what they do or want."

Arlene looked down in disappointment, even though she had expected as much. Still, she was impressed and thankful.

"You did a really good job, Mary. You have such a clear head about these things. I knew the idea was a strange one, but I just had to try."

"Wait! I appreciate the appreciation, but I didn't mean for you to think that I've given up. I'm just getting started, but first I had to narrow the possibilities to something realistic."

Mary turned the file folder so that its contents faced Arlene and opened it. There was a single sheet of yellow paper on top, with four groupings of hand-written notes, four lines each. Underneath was a short stack of printed items, which Arlene could not yet make out.

"Let me say first that what each of these items has in common is that they are all local to the city. One of the things that I came away with from looking at bigger publications was that we would have to work by mail, and I just can't see us getting anywhere with that. It's too easy to ignore material you don't recognize and haven't asked for. So, I wanted places that we could go—both of us—and talk to the people who decide what gets printed in their stuff. I found four things, and on that yellow paper I have the name of the publication, its address, the name of someone we can at least talk to, and the phone number I used to get that information."

"Mary, that is wonderful. It is so much more than I hoped for."

"Not so fast, Ar. I should tell you that only one of these is anything close to a magazine, and it only comes out monthly, and it only sells less than a thousand copies. Its one virtue is that it's about things happening here, with an occasional article purchased when there is otherwise not enough material. It costs twenty cents. I guess if there's any money in it, it might be from local advertisers whose businesses sometimes get stories. Like restaurants and specialty stores.

"The rest of the items on my list cost little or nothing and are almost entirely cheap advertisements, with almost no other content. Still, they are published and distributed and homegrown."

Arlene looked puzzled. "Why would anything like that want to include one of my scripts?"

"Ah, there I have an answer: because your stuff will fit in very little space, it's going to cost almost nothing until you get some sort of regular following, and these rags seem to want to pretend they are something more than a big collection of ads. It's probably down to the publisher's ego, even though there's almost no content of any value. But if someone sees your work and likes your ideas, then at least we have a start."

Mary smiled, and Arlene looked down at the folder, looked up, and smiled back. She nodded thoughtfully and said, "It's a tiny start but beyond anything I would ever have thought of myself. I think I picked the right person to confide in."

"Not bad for what you're paying me!"

Mary saw Arlene's face fall and instantly regretted her little joke.

"Arlene, can't you see that I am having fun, too? I love Hank and the kids, and I love being a wife and a mother, but I haven't done anything else since I got married. This is fun! And I don't mean to embarrass you, but I love you, too, and I do want to help. So come on, no more of that face. Okay?"

"Okay."

"You keep at it, and I will make our first appointment. Call me soon so I can tell you where we're at." She got up and collected the file, explaining that she only had one copy. Arlene rose, too, stepped around the table and threw her arms around Mary. They didn't need to say goodbye any more than they had needed to say hello. Whether they ever got anywhere with Arlene's idea, Arlene knew that her life was better for having Mary in it. She was no longer her sister-and-law, but instead her first true friend.

"And you keep writing!" scolded Mary as she walked away. She knew Arlene didn't need the encouragement, but she had to say something to cover her own reciprocal feelings.

Two days later, Arlene called Mary from a pay phone outside a grocery market.

"Listen, Ar, next Tuesday morning at ten o'clock we have an appointment with someone at the ten-cent magazine. A Mr. Brandt."

"What are we going to say?"

"Leave that to me. You just bring some copies of your best scripts."

Light Breeze was not big enough to have the kinds of departments that a more ambitious publication would. The owner, Mr. Aloysius Brandt, had inherited enough money not to depend much on his modest business; he ran the place and was the only one to draw a living wage. Beyond him, there were only four full-time assistants, who were paid part-time wages. These were all women, who, for one reason or another, found the work agreeable. Their total workspace consisted of half of a floor of a modest downtown office building. Little of that was for offices; most was for layout tables, and records. The actual mechanics of the publication were hosted by contract, offsite, just as one might find for a high school yearbook. Nonetheless, most of its readers would not have thought—if they thought about it at all—that *Light Breeze* was such a low-budget operation. The final product was glossy and sleek. The advertising was standard, but the content, such as it was, was well edited and creatively formatted.

Arlene and Mary entered the main door of the offices to find themselves in a deserted room. There were three wooden chairs, none too comfortable-looking, and a receptionist's desk with a blotter, an open day planner-calendar, telephone, and typewriter. Behind the desk was an unoccupied swivel-chair. Neither the desk nor any of the walls had any trace of someone's personal space, but that was easily explained: the enterprise had no need for a full-time receptionist or secretary, so this place was only a buffer zone for the rare visitors and was therefore not a space that in any sense belonged to any of the employees. The key aspect that allowed it to function was that the wall opposite the door was glass from the top molding to some waist-high mahogany paneling, so that anyone in the working space behind would soon be aware that someone needed attention and could promptly step into the reception area. Today, Miss Pillsby, a plump thirty-something with red hair, gray and green striped dress, and narrow, oval-shaped glasses, assumed the duties. She came through a door behind and to the right of the desk and sat down, gesturing to the two visitors to do the same. She inhaled once and, on the exhale, transformed herself from copy and layout editor to her present role.

"Good morning, ladies. How may I help you?" Her voice was pleasant and polite, but somehow too perfunctory to be welcoming. As they sat down, Arlene placed the same tote bag she had carried for her meeting with Mary at the dark restaurant on the floor to her left. It was slightly heavier this time.

Mary spoke while Arlene, who was fascinated by a slight asymmetry in Miss Pillsby's jawline and a constellation of small moles on her left cheek, struggled to get some inner sense of the woman.

"We have an appointment with Mr. Brandt at ten o'clock. My name is Mrs. Mary Hudson, and this is Mrs. Arlene Zirner."

Mary had stuttered a bit on that last word because she was far less familiar with Arlene's maiden name than with her own. But Arlene had insisted on using Zirner, and Mary had not needed to ask for an explanation.

"Well, that's fine," said Miss Pillsby. She glanced down at the calendar. "Let me just go tell him that you are here."

With that, she was on her feet and through the door, closing it firmly behind her. Arlene and Mary looked at each other, wondering why she hadn't used the phone on the desk.

"That's a nice dress, Ar. Is it new?" This was a mere distraction from what Mary was sure must be a nervous interlude for Arlene. The dress was of standard cut, but the pattern was a rich plaid from the intersection of deep pastels of green, blue, and maroon.

"Thank you," said Arlene. "It isn't new, but I have never worn it before. When we got married, my mother gave me a little money that she said was just to be used for myself, and I bought this a few weeks later. It stayed in the back of the closet where Charlie wouldn't see it and wonder about it, until today. I wish I had something that looked more business-like, like you, but the clothes I used to wear to my first job, in the auditing pool, were too worn, I thought.

"This isn't business, but PTA," replied Mary with a broad smile. "I got it at a second-hand store." Her outfit was no more than a navy-blue rayon skirt, with a shallow slit on the right side, and a tan blouse with stitching accents to match the skirt. The business-like look came from a matching jacket, of the same material and color as the skirt, with large wooden buttons. She also wore brown stockings of the same hue as the buttons.

"Is this place what you expected, Mary?"

"I can't say I had any expectations. I mean, I knew it couldn't be a big outfit." She frowned and asked, "How would you like to work here?"

"Hmm... I suppose it would be better than the insurance auditors but maybe not as good as the hardware store. This space seems so isolated."

They sat quietly for a few minutes until the door opened again, and Miss Pillsby returned.

"If you ladies will follow me, Mr. Brandt will see you now."

Mary and Arlene crossed the magazine's general work area and came into a crowded and disorganized office. As Miss Pillsby announced "Mrs. Mary Hudson and Mrs. Arlene Zirner," then closed the door behind them they had time to notice stacks of books and papers that left just enough room for two visitors to be seated and Mr. Brandt's own desk and chair. What could be seen of the desktop showed wood grain sealed with a black stain—somewhat less antiseptic than the metal gray desks they had seen on their way from the reception room. The man himself stood up properly as they entered, causing his chair an acute squeak.

They looked at each other for just as long as would be polite.

Mary and Arlene saw a man in his fifties; he was thin and slightly above medium height. His face was narrow and wrinkled, with an unhealthy pallor, and marked by three heavy lines: two asymmetrical eyebrows and a mustache. All three were somehow unkempt, in keeping with his clothes, no item of which seemed to have been pressed. He wore a white shirt and plain black tie that nearly matched the color of his eyes and hair; the knot of the tie was relaxed just enough to show a jutting Adam's apple with a few scraggly gray hairs. Nothing about him seemed sympathetic.

Mr. Brandt first looked at Arlene. What could this neatly dressed scarecrow of a woman want with him? But he didn't dwell on her. Mary was much better to look at; he wished that the functional slit of her skirt were less conservative. He might have flirted with her twenty years ago, but he knew too well what he was, what he had become in his fifty-four years: a tired-looking man, with a tired-looking wife tucked away at home. Still, Mary brought some color into his gray life, and he might as well enjoy it. He gestured for them to be seated.

"So, why are we here?" he asked, looking at Mary. Arlene was not discomforted by this in the least, and while she was almost without guile, she knew that Mary could help not just in connection with Arlene's own shyness. She was, however, distinctly puzzled for a second or two, having at first taken his question in the metaphysical sense.

"What we want is simple enough, Mr. Brandt. We want you to consider publishing something—but what that is may be a bit harder to explain."

"I have a little time," answered Mr. Brandt. "But first, who wrote it?"

"That would be Arlene, here, who is married to my brother."

"Can't she speak for herself?" Mr. Brandt surprised himself with the sharpness of this question. He had really intended to prolong this interview just to keep Mary in his office a while longer, even though she had already said enough for him to know they would have no business together.

Arlene smiled awkwardly and spoke with her usual clear separation of words. "I can speak. But Mary can explain it all much better."

"I see," said Mr. Brandt. He tried to soften his expression as he turned back toward Mary. But he could see that his sharpness had put her off. *I should have held my tongue. It's not their fault this job is so awful. Well, nothing lost.*

Mary continued in a more formal mode. Her inclination was to walk out on such rudeness, but she and Arlene had taken the trouble to make and to appear at this appointment, and it was pointless to throw it away even if it seemed equally pointless for her to continue. This sour wreck of a man in this god-forsaken office would never have spoken in such a way if he was open to what she was about to suggest.

"Mrs. Zirner's idea is simple and will cost next to nothing to publish. She has written a series of short scripts. You can think of them as little plays that require no sets and are not intended to be performed in front of any audience."

Mr. Brandt had intended to just let her speak her piece, but again he could not hold his tongue: "Why would anyone be interested in something like that?" This was not an honest question; it was sarcasm.

Mary set her jaw and, if anything, became even more determined to explain. *You closed-minded nobody! You deserve to work in this horrible little office!*

"A good question, and one that might be asked about all of the sheet music sold at the store on Green street. Why would anyone want to buy a few sheets of paper and play the music when they could buy a record and hear a performance by a world-class musician. Doesn't that seem equally stupid?" She didn't wait for any response. "It's not. Even if you are not a good musician, when you play it yourself, you get inside the music, and people enjoy that."

"Couldn't they just buy real plays by real writers."

Arlene did not respond to the insult, but she answered for Mary. "No, real plays have many parts, and you would need a lot of people. Besides, the roles are often too big for ordinary people."

Mary continued for her. "Exactly. Arlene has written these little pieces so that two, at most three, ordinary people could climb out of their lives and into one that she has created. And they don't just 'watch' as they might in a movie or even reading a novel. They take part in it. They get inside it. And that's a kind of fun we never get to have."

Mr. Brandt paused for a few polite seconds, as if he had really heard what they were saying. He sighed as a kind of punctuation mark that would end the conversation.

"That's all very interesting, and I can see why you wanted to speak to me. But really, that has nothing to do with *Light Breeze*. And now if you will excuse me, I have other things to attend to." He got up, walked carefully around his desk, opened the door, and signaled to a tall red-headed woman. Mary and Arlene stood, making no eye contact with him or with each other.

"Patsy, will you show these ladies out?"

The tall woman nodded, and Mary and Arlene followed her back to the reception area and then left the office.

They were back on the street, walking in no particular direction. Arlene placed four fingers of her right hand against Mary's wrist. They slowed and looked at each other.

"I'm sorry, Mary. That was a waste of your time." Arlene's moral hesitations about using Mary at all to find someone to publish her scripts came rushing back. Mary's enthusiasm and clear satisfaction in helping her sister-in-law was not enough to overset her sense of guilt about exploiting Mary's natural generosity and attractiveness.

"Oh, not entirely, Arlene. I'm not sorry we went in, even if Mr. Brandt is a horrible old prat."

"But we got nowhere."

"Yes, and I'm sure that if my skirt had been two inches longer, we would have gotten nowhere sooner. But still it wasn't a waste of time because now we've tried once and that will make the second time less of a mystery."

"I suppose, but we have so few chances before there is no next time."

"Well, that's how it looks now, but who knows?"

The "next time" took them to the even smaller offices of *Town Chat*. This six-by-nine-inch local publication cost all of a nickel, had color only on the front and back covers, and was more than half advertisements. What remained were uninspired little descriptors of curiosity pieces, most of which did not have local origins but were purchased wholesale from other sources so that advertisements would have something to separate them. Mary, whose literary education ended with two high school English classes, was sadly amused to see pieces like "Having Three Cats and a Dog," "Bouquets from What's in the Yard," and "Inexpensive but Thoughtful Gifts for Mom." She thought Arlene's stuff was worlds beyond this sort of thing, but they had to start somewhere.

Town Chat was in the basement of a downtown office building and had a staff of three. One of the three typeset, printed, and collated the weekly publication. He benefitted enormously from the repetitive nature of the ads, generally contracted out for at least two months at a time, but on bad weeks, he was no stranger to late nights. A second employee did the copyediting—actually just proofreading—and generally took care of supplies, bills and distribution. The brains of the enterprise, and its owner, was Bernard Thompson, who had only bought the business because he hated working for anyone else; overseeing even so modest a publication seemed more appealing to him than a better paid office job. He had earned half of a college degree after serving in the Second World War, and then gone to work in a small advertising firm. Better educated than most men of his time, he in fact wrote copy on occasion—not all of it horrendous—and this he deemed sufficient experience to run *Town Chat* when he randomly heard it was for sale. But, as with his time at college, any original enthusiasm had dissipated into a sense of weak inertia. Occasionally he made suggestions to his advertisers without charge and was pleased when one of his ideas appeared in print. Nonetheless, he allowed his job to devolve into a great deal of routine administration with very little scope for creativity. Still, there was no one to whom he reported, and that perhaps was the only compensation for the utter grayness of the life he had chosen.

When Mary and Arlene appeared one afternoon, a few weeks after the aborted effort at *Light Breeze*, they saw a middle-aged rumple of a man, in a shabby suit, a white shirt that had never been ironed since its purchase, and a blue almost-silk tie that showed dull wear marks just below an asymmetric knot. Arlene wore a nondescript, but well-laundered and well-ironed blue dress, while Mary wore a fine yellow sweater, a white blouse with pearl buttons, and a lustrous green skirt. She had hesitated about the skirt. It was, give or take, as sexy as what she had worn to her last appointment, and she had decided that it was no bad thing to show just enough leg to keep a man interested for as long as she and Arlene needed to explain what they were about. Looking now at Mr. Thompson, she realized that any such thoughts were wasted in his case because it would have been a few decades—if ever—since he would have paid any attention to a pretty girl. He seemed to have gone dry inside. Nevertheless, they seated themselves in two folding chairs that he had graciously moved in front of his desk. There were no real boundaries to his office, which was just the corner of a larger room that he often shared with his proofreader-office manager-clerk.

After a few seconds to settle in, Mr. Thompson looked from one to the other with a tired glance that in no way invited them to introduce themselves or otherwise begin speaking. Arlene's face was polite enough, but her lips twitched, not so much out of discomfort as out of an instinctive and distressed empathy for such a forlorn sole. Mary began speaking, but nothing seemed natural about it. It was as if all of the usual conventions based on all of the usual feelings and expectations latent in her first words to another human being had been subverted by a man who seemed to take blandness and exhaustion to places she could not imagine. She would have enjoyed mere eccentricity—but this!

"Ah, thank you for your time, Mr. Thompson. I…my name is Mrs. Hudson, and this is Mrs. Zirner. As it happens, she is my sister-in-law, but that really has nothing to do with why we are here."

Mr. Thompson stared back at her, and he did seem to understand her words. But there was only a blink of acknowledgement where even the shyest of individuals might have at least nodded, if not spoken a word or two.

Arlene, hearing the strain in Mary's voice, looked over at her. An unlikely adventure had become scary and painful to her ever-cheerful friend. More empathy, and then she heard her own voice as if it belonged to someone else.

"Mary and I are here because we have an idea for your publication," she said, spacing her words even more carefully than usual. This at least got a reaction as Mr. Thompson needed to turn his head to look at this second speaker.

"Go on," he said.

"I write these little scripts, you see. My idea is that people will have fun reading them out loud."

And then, to Arlene's great relief, Mary was back.

"That's right, Mr. Thompson, but Arlene is much too modest. Her little scripts are like little plays and quite well done. I don't know where she gets the ideas for them, considering—" She stopped abruptly, not liking where that sentence was headed, although she knew that Arlene would not have been upset by it. "What I mean is that these scripts, as Mrs. Zirner calls them, are really wonderful vehicles for taking someone out of the most routine life and…" She stopped again and could only smile at what she was saying and to whom she was saying it. "The point is, we hoped you could use them in your little magazine just so that others could read them, too."

Bernard Thompson said nothing but tilted his head as if a sound from the floor above—the ground floor—had been more noteworthy than any information Mary might have provided. She waited until his head returned to its normal position, but still there was no response.

"And the wonderful thing is, Mr. Thompson, that they take up very little space and require no illustrations. So, they would dress up *Town Chat* with virtually no production costs. And, of course, since Mrs. Zirner is a new writer"—Arlene turned her head a full ninety degrees and virtually swallowed her bottom lip at hearing that—"we would only expect a small fee for her work."

Fortunately for Mary, since she could think of no way to continue, the mention of money finally got Mr. Thompson's attention.

"Fee? You expect me to pay for your friend to learn how to write?"

Mary began to swell as disappointment and frustration turned to anger. She locked eyes with Mr. Thompson as Arlene cast her eyes vaguely downward. After perhaps two seconds, Mary rose to her feet and gestured unambiguously to Arlene that she, too, should stand. The interview was over.

"Good day, Mr. Thompson," she said. They turned and walked away from his desk and into the hall that ran the length of the basement. Mary didn't want to wait for the elevator, so they climbed the stairs, exited into the building's lobby and then went out into the sunshine.

As they walked along the boulevard, neither spoke. Mary was managing her anger, and Arlene was managing her guilt. She knew her dream was over, but that wasn't of much concern. Mary was the happiest person she had ever known, and to have had a part in bringing her to this awful state of anger was mortifying. Mary read her mind.

"Arlene, anyone can see that you look worse than I feel. Yes, I'm angry and unhappy, but—"

"But I've never seen you angry or unhappy. Even the day I came with the bruise, I know you were concerned, but you were still so cheerful with Annie and so ready to help me. It was nothing like this! I didn't mean to do this to you!"

Mary reached out an arm to stop Arlene from walking. She looked around to find a concrete planter with a wide rim set back from the street in a small recess adjacent to the sidewalk. She took Arlene's hand to lead her to the planter and they sat down. Arlene's cheeks were wet.

"Look, Arlene, we are both adult women—neither of us is a child. I know that you feel some affection for me, as I do for you, but you don't have to cry and want to give up just because I got angry. I have a good life with Hank and David and Annie. I like where we live, and Hank is a good man. But do you really think that I never get angry with him or the children? Even Annie. I'm not made of thin glass; you don't have to worry about me breaking. That man, Mr. Thompson, was horrible. It wasn't just that he was going to say no to us, it was who he is, his—I don't know—his way of being in the world. Yes, going there to be nice to him, wanting something from him, that was awful! But it's over, and we learned something, and you are not to be upset about me. I meant what I said in there, your scripts are good, and people are going to find out about Marla Kraft."

Arlene's lips were still trembling, and her eyes were still wet. Her discomposed face with those big glasses, all framed with her course hair, made Mary want to smile at how someone who was so good inside could present such a sight to the world. But she suppressed that and pressed Arlene's hand in reassurance.

Arlene controlled her lips and breath well enough to ask, "What did we learn?"

"Nothing much," Mary said. "Just how to do this."

Reading Eleven

"The Frozen Sand--Part Two" by Marla Kraft

[...Isla is steady enough, but Sophie puts her arm around her waist, as if to support her. Even as the afterimage of the lightning strike fades, they continue to stare into the storm, paralyzed by its grandeur.]

Sophie: Isla, was that your meaning? Or at least some sign that there is meaning?

Isla: I don't know. If only I could at least make some kind of a start!

[The wind increases to the point that they have to lean into each other in order to hold their ground. The big lightening flash is not repeated but is followed by an irregular series of translucent illuminations, as if coming from well over the horizon. The snow continues and thickens.]

Sophie: Wait a minute! We are standing in a snowstorm at the beach on this frozen sand and have just seen the largest lightening flash of our lives--all while you're standing here, keeping me here, whining about finding yourself--and that doesn't count as a sign! What the hell would?

Isla: I'm sorry, Sophie, you must be right. That couldn't have been for nothing. I think it's because I would have expected something like that to fill me with an answer, and it didn't. For all its terrifying beauty it seemed to empty me more than to fill me. I came out here with you to concentrate myself and us, and then in that moment the concentration--the solidity I was trying to find in standing against the vastness and power of this place--just got shoved out of me. I am coming back. Please stay with me for a little while more.

Sophie: As much as I can stand, Isla.

Isla: Here's the thing: What are the possibilities?

Sophie: I have no idea what you're talking about.

Isla: You can go a long way with twenty questions--I mean that game.

Sophie: Okay. So, what's your first question?

Isla: God or no God?

Sophie: I don't know.

Isla: Well, we can do without that. This is more basic: Persistence or no persistence?

Sophie: Again, Isla, I have no--

Isla: I mean when you're dead and gone, is it really as if you never were? I don't mean whether you have changed the world. It would be hard not to. But the stuff on the inside, is it just gone?

Sophie: It looks like it's just gone. I mean, my grandmother, she's just gone.

Isla: Well, yes, from our point of view, from the outside. But is she <u>really</u> gone?

Sophie: How can we ever know that?

Isla: If you're right, and we can't...

[Isla begins to cry.]

Sophie: Oh, Isla, please don't. We only tried two questions and there are at least eighteen more to go.

[The wind, the snow, the waves, the hardness of the frozen sand, all of them seem to reach an intolerable crescendo. Isla and Sophie lock eyes, and the intensity of the soaring, swelling, twirling sights and sounds and feels push them into each other's arms, into the tightest embrace that either of them would ever feel. The left sides of their heads are pressed together with the same force as their bodies. They can no longer see each other. They could no longer see each other even if their eyes were open. Isla murmurs as if hypnotized.]

Isla. I love you, Sophie. Not like in the movies. But I love you.

[Sophie nods, and Isla, for all the effort she is making just to persist through that isolating, concentrating, and ultimately fusing storm, at last becomes peaceful.]

Samantha sat on a towel at the beach with her large, sagging bag to her left. She wore dark sunglasses, loose mint green shorts, and a white cotton blouse knotted above the waist to allow some sun on her back and belly. The towel was striped in tan and blue. Samantha held her knees close with her arms, and in her hands were a few wrinkled pages, which she had now read several times.

I wish there was someone to read Sophie's part so that I could concentrate more on Isla. It's also hard because it's summer, and I feel nothing but the open warmth of the sun and the horizontal peacefulness of the ocean. But I think I get it.

She leaned forward and drew her legs in to sit cross-legged, the papers cradled in her lap. As she stared straight out at the horizon, someone looking at her from the ocean would have seen two bright stars in her sunglasses reflecting the naked sun above. The corners of her mouth sank a trifle as she concentrated.

That book, a few years ago, about discovering some kind of creature that was and wasn't quite human. That all depended on us being scared because we are alone in our own private spaces. We try to communicate, but the essence of our souls is that aloneness. That's just who and what we are…but it's not what we want to be. We want to stretch across and into the space of another.

We can only approximate that, with language on commonalities of community and culture. That was the point of the book, the essential problem of being human. We look for acceptance, belonging, the good opinion of our peers. Sometimes honor. Sometimes it doesn't matter if we are noticed, but we still do what we do to belong to something bigger, to be less alone. We even fall in love sometimes.

Isla finally found some peace in a world that almost literally pushed her and Sophie into the same space. For whatever brief time, her experience for once became communicable. Isla called that love, and she was right.

Samantha put the papers into her bag and stood up. She stepped off the towel, turned away from the ocean and then back to it.

I am alone. Completely. I have no brothers or sisters or close friends or romance in my life. My parents took care of me, and I am grateful to them, but we are no closer for that. Not like Isla and Sophie.

She looked down at her bag, at the towel whose bright edges were being fluffed by the breeze. Then she looked at nothing and was aware of nothing but the omnipresence of the sun.

You know—she thought, knowing that there was no "you" but herself—*I am alone, but I am happy. I don't seem to care about everything that Isla cares about. I like things this way. Is that good or bad?*

Again, she wished there were someone to read Sophie's part.

Chapter Thirteen

Mary and Arlene were again carefully dressed, but this time on a bus rather than a sidewalk. Arlene didn't know where they were going—Mary wouldn't tell her—but that bothered her not at all. She knew they were going to try again to find a home for her writing, and that was sufficient. She would find out soon enough what the special mystery was this time.

It was midmorning, and had it been later in the day, they might have been uncomfortably warm on the faded brown textured plastic that covered their seats. Many of the windows were open in preparation for the heat that would accumulate later on. But at just after nine in the morning, the environment was pleasant enough. There was no crowding, and only five or six passengers shared the vehicle.

Their colors were impeccable, both singly and together. Arlene had on a full pale-yellow dress, with a necklace and a white sweater that she wore like a cape. Her stockings and shoes were white. Mary had the usual species of two-piece suit she wore for this kind of interview. The length of her skirt was significantly more reserved than on their previous outings. The color was a lavender just a shade or two darker than one might use to decorate easter eggs. Her blouse was more cream than white, and her only accessory was an enameled pineapple broach worn on the lapel; this meshed nicely with Arlene's colors. Her hosiery was a conservative tan and her shoes plain and brown, but well-polished.

"I didn't know you could ride so far on a city bus," said Arlene. It's all so green and flowery and pleasant. And I love how the houses are so much more spread out."

"Well, there are a few buses to the suburbs, and this one just happens to pass through a very pretty area. At the end of the line there is a gorgeous park with a small, artificial lake. I have taken the kids there when school's out—during the week—but it's still a bit crowded. We are not going so far."

Arlene looked a trifle disappointed; obviously she had not thought of swimming, but the bus ride was so pleasant. Mary read her mind.

"Unfortunately, the ride back won't be so nice, once it starts to get hot in here. Even your light sweater is going to be too much."

Arlene nodded but refused to become unhappy. She was born to enjoy moments like these. She looked shyly around the bus at the other passengers, wondering what their days and lives were like. There was one man in a three-piece pinstripe with a narrow-brimmed black hat. She tried to guess his story for a few minutes, but then Mary was talking again.

"Look, Arlene, I haven't told you where we are going because, as much as you seem to trust me, this seems an almost hopelessly unlikely idea. Somehow, I think that not preparing you for where we are headed is the best preparation. I just want you to be your lovely self."

“Okay, I will be me,” Arlene answered lightly. She smiled as if to say, “I don’t care how this comes out; I will still have had a wonderful time.”

They lapsed into silence, and the bus rolled along through the bright air and broad pastel neighborhoods.

While Mary and Arlene sat on that sunlit bus, Bruce had just stepped outside the door of his workshop office and frowned. The dirt on the windows did not transmit any of the radiance of the morning, and what he did notice was one of the working girls, Chelsea, coming out of a storage room, looking right and left, and then adjusting a skirt far too narrow for her sagging figure. The seams of her stockings were disarrayed, and her facial expression was a careful blank.

Bruce moved slowly across the factory floor, his eyes fixed on the storeroom. He reached a workstation and spoke in distraction to the operator of a heavy-duty sewing machine to which he had made adjustments late yesterday afternoon, inquiring about its performance. Just as he turned to go, the storeroom door opened, and Charlie walked out. He had no need to rearrange his clothes, but the lack of expression on his face matched Chelsea’s.

Charlie walked into the room he shared with Bruce, and a few seconds later Bruce followed. He stayed near the door, his back discouraging anyone from entering or listening.

“You must be kidding! With Chelsea? Why, for God’s sake? The only thing worse than her looks is her personality. And Arlene.”

Charlie faced him with his hands balled into fists. His face was stretched in anger and pain. His back was tense and slightly bent, as if he were about to be hit by a wave.

"Mind your own business," he growled.

"Charlie, it is not my business—and I know that—but we have been friends of a sort for years. You don't owe me any explanations, but you owe yourself one. Why would you do something as thoughtless and reckless and stupid as having your way with Chelsea? It doesn't matter if I know, or if the whole factory knows.

Charlie dropped the adversarial stance and sat down, as did Bruce. They both took some breaths to diffuse the confrontation, but Charlie knew that he had to explain. And that Bruce was right.

"I don't know where to start. I am seething. Arlene gives me nothing—not even anger—since I hit her for going out that night. I know she didn't do anything, but I couldn't stop myself. She wouldn't have that dog. She cleans the apartment, makes my meals, says the most meaningless, polite things, and lives her own life apart from me in the same space. I'd hit her again, except there's no one to hit."

Charlie's features became distorted with rage, as if something were pulling at the sides of his reddening face. He hissed out a breath, inhaled and went on:

"I might deserve it, but that doesn't make me less angry. Her indifference just makes me want to explode. It's as if she's telling me that she can keep this up forever, but she knows I can't keep up the anger, and then I will just go away. We hardly ever had sex before, and now I can't even think of it. It would be like raping a doll that wouldn't even feel you inside her. I don't know how she's managed this shield, and I know that something is going on. She spends so much time with my sister Mary, and, God, even that makes me jealous!"

"Charlie, I know Arlene isn't much to look at, but I also know she's a nice girl. Chelsea is not."

"Oh, screw Chelsea! It doesn't make any difference who she is or if she's nice or horrible. She's *not* Arlene! And even though Arlene doesn't know it yet, I am kicking crap in her face."

Bruce took a deep breath and held it. Finally, he let it out, shaking his head: "That's just garbage and you know it. If things are so bad with you and Arlene, just leave already. It's not like she's going to get something from you."

Charlie bared his teeth in a terrifying smile of hatred; his eyes virtually glowed. "Oh, yes, she is going to get something from me. Something that she'll never forget. I just need to figure out the right time and the right thing."

Bruce was an ordinary man with an ordinary range of feelings and experiences. He might say that he was friends with Charlie, although he well understood the other's faults. He knew Charlie could be short-tempered, inconsiderate, and at times downright mean. But now his eyes widened: he had no internal model for someone who could be so bent on giving so much undeserved pain. Bruce, of course, would never know how Charlie had contrived to cover his sister—a good and kind little girl, being fitted for a buoyant, white lacey dress, in preparation for a religious sacrament—with wads of mud flung up at her soul. Yet in that moment he shared something of the abject horror of Mary's incomprehension.

Bruce silently turned and walked back out onto the factory floor, with no idea of how he would ever again be able to face this man with whom he spent so many working hours. He reached the corner opposite their workroom and, as if by chance, stared in the direction of Chelsea. She paid no attention and thus served as a proxy for Charlie in Bruce's confused deliberations.

Mary pulled the cord and heard the buzz that alerted the driver of her intention to alight. She and Arlene climbed down from the bus, and for the first time, Arlene allowed herself a look of bewilderment. There was nothing there but a widening of the road to permit the bus to pull over, a bench and sign indicating that this was indeed a bus stop. On both sides of the street there were trees and bushes, with no sidewalk as such, just a narrow strip next to the road upon which the foliage did not encroach.

"This stop is actually a short distance beyond the street we wanted. It's not far," Mary explained.

With that they began walking back in the direction from which they had come. Arlene relaxed and smiled at Mary in a way that made Mary want to take her hand, but they were much too old for that. Mary could only smile back.

Across the street, about a hundred yards from where they had gotten off, there was the beginning of a cross street, but any automobile traffic would have had to reckon with two wrought iron gates, perhaps twelve feet wide and together forming an arch fifteen feet high. The gates were well-maintained, painted jet black, with very little accumulated rust. The trees arched and rustled above them in quiet consonance with the shape of the gates.

Mary released the latch to unlock the gates and pulled one of them forward. She let Arlene precede her and then stopped to reengage the latch. They continued on a blacktop road that narrowed to the width of one vehicle. The path curved to the right sharply, and the trees were high enough and dense enough that Arlene could form no idea of what they were approaching.

The path widened and split into a circuit. Directly ahead they saw a large building of irregular shape made from brown, rectangular stones. A good part of the walls was covered with a vine thick with small round leaves and even smaller lavender flowers with tiny vermillion centers. As they approached the entrance, a broad double door made of oak with an oval-shaped top, Arlene made out a modest placard of dark umber metal with embossed letters in tarnished bronze:

The Abbey of Saint Carta

Arlene looked at Mary, her head tilted to the side, and her lips, for once, frozen.

"Yes, Ar," said Mary, "this is where we're going. She gave three solid thuds with her small fist, and they waited.

Sister Camilla was both gracious and graceful. A novice had brough her to the door after admitting Mary and Alene. She led them silently through the intricacies of the abbey, and her silence—and that of the nuns they passed—was contagious. Neither visitor said a word but walked as quietly as possible behind her. Sister Camilla's hands were tucked under her brown habit, and she moved as if she were gliding rather than walking. The habit covered so much that Arlene could only guess that this was a slender woman of middle age, of plain features. Her eyes were an unremarkable brown, given prominence only by her strong eyebrows and look of natural empathy that was fully congruent with her calling. They were led past workrooms, a library, bedrooms, a chapel that could accommodate at most a few dozen congregants. Finally, they found themselves in a surprisingly spacious office. The air seemed colored in some unnamed hue: the effect of sunlight passing into the room through the green and lavender of the blinds and then through the stained glass.

Sister Camilla did not sit behind her desk, but placed three wooden chairs in an equilateral triangle so that all three could sit in the central space. Some subtle change in her posture suggested that they might now speak without inhibition. She looked attentively from one woman to the other. Mary spoke first.

"Thank you, Sister Camilla, for agreeing to see us."

"It is my pleasure, dear, although the message left for me offered no hint of how I might help you. Still," she continued as an afterthought, "whatever that might be, I am grateful for the belated Easter offering you've brought with you in the color of your outfits. Our habits, as you can see, allow no scope for such flamboyance."

The look on the sister's face and her cheerful tone assured Mary that no criticism was meant, that Sister Camilla was not obliquely taking issue with their attire. Thus, she began simply:

"I am Mary, and this is Arlene."

The space was so welcoming that she never thought to give their last names.

"Nice to meet you both, Mary and Arlene."

Sister Camilla nodded at each of them. Her gaze rested on Arlene, who was looking at the base of the wall across from the windows. A second later, Arlene shook her head as if to shake herself back into the office.

"I am so sorry, Sister. I did not mean to be inattentive, but—"

"Oh, don't give it a thought, my dear. It is easy to get lost in the spatters of color thrown by the stained glass in the morning. You would be amazed at what you see in spring before the leaves on the trees have matured."

"It's just that I have never seen that color before. I don't even know what to call it."

"Arlene, let me tell you something both sad and beautiful: you can never see it again. Nothing recurs." To judge from her expression, Sister Camilla seemed on balance to find that observation more beautiful than sad. "But now I am wandering," she added, turning back to Mary. "I think you were about to tell me why you are here."

Mary, reaching into her purse, pulled out a small booklet or pamphlet. It was only twenty or so pages, bound by two staples at the central fold. The paper was pale green, and the only other element of color was the front cover: a printed illustration of a richly hued watercolor of flowers, sea, and sky. Mary held it up just long enough for Sister Camilla to recognize it.

"Oh… Oh! A copy of *The Song of the Abbey.*"

"Yes," said Mary. "My husband mentioned something—well, I will get to that—to a friend at work, and his wife sent him back the next day with this."

Sister Camilla smiled softly. "It's so strange to see one of those just appear out of someone's bag. We make those—at least their content—but we never see them in the wild, so to speak. I suppose you want to know something about it?"

"Yes, very much!"

Mary stole a glance at Arlene, who by now was just beginning to figure out why they were here. The sister, knowing nothing of Arlene, did not herself yet know but seemed enormously pleased to talk about *The Song*.

"Where to start? I suppose with our history. This structure was built in 1888 and named after a far more important institution in eastern Europe. You know that nuns have orders of different stripes: teaching orders, nursing orders, midwifery, contemplative orders, and so on. This institution was the legacy of a very rich family that spent many years traveling abroad. They were so taken with the Abbey of Saint Carta in Romania that they bought this land, constructed our building, and left the founding sisters enough money to get things started. It was an odd start, and our first tenants came from all over the world by a kind of general invitation. There was no coherent function, which left us as something of a contemplative order for want of any other identity."

Just then a sister whose perfectly symmetric face had the color and texture of a light-brown chestnut appeared in the doorway. She spoke with an accent that neither Mary nor Arlene could identify.

"I am so sorry to interrupt, Sister Camilla, but this message seemed urgent." She crossed into the interior of the triangle of chairs and handed Sister Camilla a small slip of yellow paper.

"Thank you, Sister Rose," she said, glancing at the paper.

Sister Rose nodded, then turned to the visitors. "Again, I am very sorry, ladies. I will not bother you further." With that she walked smoothly out the door.

Arlene could not contain herself: "That was the most beautiful face I have ever seen! I suppose I should not be making such a personal comment, and yet—"

Sister Camilla cut her off mid-sentence, but somehow politely.

"I understand completely, my dear. She is exquisite, but, you know, I don't think she has seen her own face for the two years she has been here. There are simply no mirrors. We don't pay attention to our appearances or, in our actions, call attention to ourselves. Sister Rose comes to us from Nigeria, and she seems to have always wanted to be nothing other than what she is now."

Sister Camilla glanced down at the yellow slip she had been brought, shaking her head. "Nothing is ever urgent here. Shall I continue?"

"Yes, please," said Mary, who was not only interested in the story of the abbey but was reflecting upon the difference between this and their other interviews. Arlene pushed her glasses back against the bridge of her nose, as if this minute repositioning might aid her comprehension.

"Many of the usual things that nuns do were forced upon us as a matter of survival. We cultivated some of our own food and earned a bit by assisting local schools and churches. I was not here then, but some of the older sisters who were told me that these times were as peaceful as they were uncertain. We wrote to other orders all over the world for ideas, and then something wonderful happened. A convent in north England, taken by the style and sincerity of our letters asked us to review a request they were making of the Church of England for some material assistance. They were a nursing order, but the economics of the times left people suffering rather than paying for medical assistance, and soon they hadn't enough money to feed themselves and to heat the convent. Two of our sisters pored over their request and did a bit of rewriting. The English convent sent the new document to Westminster and received more than the assistance they were seeking. The surplus mostly went to the local poor, but they did send some to us, to assist us however we liked in finding our identity. But the truth is that in this serendipitous transaction we had found it. Technically, I suppose, we are still a contemplative order, but practically, we are a *writing order*. We help anyone, anywhere who asks for our assistance with the funding of charity. We charge nothing and expect nothing, and we remain entirely behind the scenes, but more than occasionally we do receive something for our work, and so this incarnation of the Abbey of Saint Carta continues.

"But what does that have to do with *The Song of the Abbey*?" asked Arlene artlessly. Sister Camilla recognized Arlene's total engagement in her story and did not take the question amiss.

"I think I know," said Mary, who was well acquainted with the copy she had brought along.

"That's right, dear," continued Sister Camilla, as if Mary had explained everything. "A writing order writes. So, about ten years ago, we thought a collection of short stories—or perhaps vignettes is more accurate—and words of praise organized into these little booklets might be worthwhile. They are offered for a small contribution to the congregants of corresponding churches, and the proceeds, meager though they be, are shared and further support us. I gather that at most half ever reach the hands of anyone but the trash collector, but as long as some are being read, we have no regrets."

Sister Camilla seemed to pause at that point, drawing a line under the history lesson. She tightened her lips, took a short breath, and exhaled.

"I suppose now, the only thing we need to complete the tale is for you to tell me why *The Song of the Abbey* has brought you here."

Mary knew it was her turn to speak, but she felt no nerves, only a relaxed sense of well-being. Whether she succeeded or not would not change the joy of this day, the joy of coming to this place, the joy of hearing this earnest and radiant woman speak with such loving affection of her home.

"We want to contribute something to *The Song*," she began plainly. "Arlene writes these tiny scripts that are to be staged without a stage, without props, by one or two people. The best way to describe them is to give you one."

She reached into her bag again and took out a copy of one of Arlene's plays. As she extended the pages to Sister Camilla, she felt the exact moment of transference out of her hands and into the sister's. She knew that moment would define Arlene's life. In that same instance, she knew how much she loved Arlene, and Mary had to look down to hide the possibility of tears. Sister Camilla could feel that something extraordinary was happening, but she would not know what for a few more minutes. Arlene looked on, as if frozen, except for her lips.

"'Graduation Night' by Marla Kraft." Sister Camilla stopped, look up, and frowned at Arlene. "Who's Marla Kraft? Your name is Arlene."

"I... I did not want to use my real name."

Arlene's speech was halting, far beyond her usual extra spacing between words. She looked into Sister Camilla's puzzled face.

She thinks this is some sort of stage fright about her reading my work, but she is wrong. Everything about this place overwhelms me: the silence, the sweetness of the air, the mystery of its spaces, its function. I feel like I was born here, and that's why I cannot speak.

Breathe and just tell the truth.

"That," she continued rather more evenly, "is because of something my mother taught me and repeated since I was a little girl. Just four words, but they feel so right, so beyond questioning, even though I cannot explain that rightness."

"And what words are those?" asked the nun.

Mary looked from one face to the other, her own having no expression whatsoever. She had no idea what Arlene was about to say.

Arlene drew a breath and even though she had only one short sentence to utter, she felt herself again losing the basic rhythm of speech.

"Do good..."

"...and disappear."

Sister Camilla completed the sentence with her eyes closed, as if in prayer. A few seconds later she opened them to see Arlene staring at her in naked wonder.

"Don't be so surprised, my dear! That saying is practically the motto of the original European inspiration for this place. We may have condensed it down to four words, but the sentiment is as old as the Bible. Or the *Bhagavad-Gita.*" Her eyes glittered from the depths of their sockets. "Like you, we have never found a good explanation for its 'rightness.' We just know it is right."

"I knew my mother was quoting something, but never in my life have I heard another person say it." She stopped there and thought for a second. "So, you understand about me not using my name?"

"Of course! Now, if you'll give me a few minutes to read this, we can let Mary continue."

"Yes, please do," replied Mary, but now her voice had a peculiar quality of its own, as if a second Mary had spoken the correct words automatically, while the real Mary tried to take in what was happening.

It was again a time for silence. Sister Camilla read the pages while Arlene tracked the imperceptible movement of light spatters across the walls and floors, spatters of intense colors that had no names. Mary sat rigidly as a well-behaved schoolgirl might. The older woman finished, let her hands, with the pages, fall to her lap, and looked directly at Arlene.

"You expect people to read these like little plays?"

"Yes," she replied. "I think people will enjoy experiencing something from someone else's life, but in a way deeper than they participate in reading a book, or even in watching others in a show."

"Are all of your scripts about love?"

"Yes, more or less. But of different kinds."

The nun smiled and rubbed her chin with her thumb and the side of her index finger. "Well, you certainly express it well, and with a perspective that no one at this convent could bring to it. Our love is mostly addressed to God and, in a strangely homogenous way, to each other."

"I understand," said Arlene.

Sister Camilla turned to Mary and asked, "Now, Miss Mary—I think I know—but why exactly did you want to bring your friend's work to my attention."

"You do already know," said Mary, "but I need to say it clearly." Her voice was her own again. "We want you to include Arlene's scripts in *The Song of the Abbey*. We don't expect to be paid—we could hardly expect you to fund Arlene's development as a writer—but we want them to be seen. It's a way of starting, if you understand what I mean." Mid-sentence, Mary turned her head briefly to Arlene. *You see, Ar, we did learn something from that awful Mr. Thompson.* Arlene looked back and blinked.

"I do understand, and I think it's a very good idea," replied Sister Camilla. "But this is not a decision I can make by myself. It affects others who have a lot invested in how we are regarded and, particularly, how *The Song* is seen. As you can imagine, for a few of our sisters that is an important expression of their religion."

"We understand," said Mary, as Arlene nodded in consonance.

"May I keep this?" asked Sister Camilla, holding up "Graduation Night."

Mary replied before the question was completed: "Yes, of course!"

"Then, Mary, if you'll just leave your number, I will phone as soon as I have an answer for you." She stood up and began to shift her chair back to the position from which it had come. Mary and Arlene likewise shifted their own chairs in acknowledgement of the nun's kindness.

"Time is a little short today, but the next time you come, I will be sure that you get to see more of our home."

Sister Camilla led them out of the office and signaled silently to one of the sisters who was passing.

"Sister Nelia, would you lead these fine young women back through the maze we live in?"

She spoke no further words and moved gracefully in the direction opposite to which Sister Nelia led them.

On the paved path between the circuit and the gate, Arlene stopped. She looked around for someplace to sit, but there were neither benches nor suitable rocks. Mary looked at her with concern and led her over into some shade just off the path. Arlene was breathing too hard, and her pale features had lost what color they had. She reached up and pulled off her glasses from the bridge of her nose, using her entire right fist and thoroughly smudging the lenses.

"Aren't you feeling okay?" asked Mary. "I thought that went remarkably well."

"It did. It did," Arlene answered between breaths. "I'm not unwell, just overfilled. I don't want to be a nun—I love seeing strangers. You could tell from Sister Camilla that they hardly see anyone but each other. Still..."

"Explain it to me, Arlene. I think you'll feel better if you do."

"Still so much of what is in that convent meets so many places deep inside me. 'Do good and disappear.' They live that. And the obscurity of the abbey, the complexity of its interior, the ancient smell of it mixed with the day that is now. I have to love a place like this, but they didn't have to accept me. I don't mean the writing. I mean that they accepted me and you. They saw who we were and let us in, not just past the door."

"But that was just Sister Camilla."

"No, it was the whole abbey and everyone who lives there. You could feel it."

Mary nodded thoughtfully, taking her point.

"You were right," said Arlene. "I do feel better, even if waiting for their decision is going to seem an interminable torment."

They began walking again, moving out of the shade and back on the paved path that led to the gate, and Mary was glad to see that Arlene's color, such as it was, had returned.

Chapter Fourteen

Arlene spent the next days of her life in light dresses walking the neighborhood and beyond. She had some experience with simply being out of the house with no place to be in order to survive weekends with Charlie. He sometimes went out himself with Bruce, or just to a bar, but during the hours he spent watching television, she, more often than not, would take to the streets. Some patterns evolved. She knew where to find acceptably clean restrooms, inexpensive lunches, places to sit in fine weather, places to huddle when she needed that, too. Strangely, bad weather became her friend insofar as it colored an all-too-familiar environment in interesting new hues. She carried almost nothing with her and used the time to watch people and to think about stories. Some of those became scripts; others were just intricate daydreams that she revisited, refined, extended, and wandered through as if they were alternate but equally real lives.

During those days that followed the visit to the abbey, she called Mary once a day from a pay phone. She made a delicious meal out of choosing the right phone and the right time. They were always glad to hear each other's voices, even when there was no news to report.

Mary, for her part, could continue with her life at home with her family. She felt a special quality of excitement in her usual routine with Hank, David, and Annie. Even washing clothes and the kitchen floor took on a special meaning while she knew she might be interrupted at any moment by the ring of their telephone. Hank knew very well what Mary and her sister-in-law had been up to for the last few months, and even though he had never seen one of Arlene's scripts, he was excited for both of them. As far as he was concerned, anything in Arlene's life that was not Charlie was a good thing, and he enjoyed seeing his wife so filled with anticipation. They were a sound and happy family, but Hank sometimes regretted that he did not have more to give them. He knew that Mary could have had anybody, but she picked him, and he did his best to live up to that. He was never quite sure why she chose him and would never know the simple answer: she chose him because he was exactly the kind of man who would ask that question.

On Tuesday morning, the phone rang. David was out playing, with Annie looking on through the front windows of their living room. Mary tried not to control her rush for the phone.

"Hello, this is Mary Hudson."

Annie now looked over at her mother. A phone call was hardly a new or interesting event in her young life, but Mary's voice and expression were somehow at odds with her plain and familiar words.

"Oh, hello, Sister. I am glad that you called."

Annie raised one eyebrow in vague bewilderment. She knew what a sister was—her friend Doris had two—and she knew that her mother had none, only a brother.

"No, that's no problem. We will be there at ten o'clock on Thursday."

Annie could hear a few more tinny and virtually inaudible words come from the receiver, even though Mary was pressing it very hard to her ear.

"We'll try, Sister Camilla, but we really don't have that many clothes! Thank you for calling."

Mary placed the phone back into its cradle and looked at Annie.

"C'mere, you."

Annie somewhat cautiously approached, only to be swept into a massive hug.

"What is this about?" she demanded.

"Oh, just something to do while I am waiting for Auntie Arlene to call this afternoon." Mary gave one last, squeal-inducing squeeze, before she released her daughter, who went right back to the window, hoping that she hadn't missed anything good.

Arlene and Mary found themselves once again in Sister Camilla's office, but this time the desk was very much in use. The nun sat behind it in her accustomed place, with two chairs drawn up close to the front. The day was hotter, and the women wore correspondingly lighter and simpler clothes. Arlene had on a rose-colored dress with a slightly flared skirt that swallowed her hips. Mary wore a sleeveless light-green dress of a much narrower fit with a small slit at the back to allow her legs to move freely.

Sister Camilla had two copies of two typed pages spread out before her. She rotated them and placed a copy in front of both Mary and Arlene so that they could easily read them.

"The nuns who are mostly responsible for *The Song* read your script and were both delighted by it. In fact, they performed it several times, trading parts. I think that by now all of our sisters have read it, and all who have expressed an opinion think it will be a welcome addition to our modest publication." She paused and smiled at them.

"We are so relieved to hear you say that," said Mary. "I think I am the only one who has read them besides Arlene. We never even got that far with the other places we tried."

"All the better for us, my dear."

Sister Camilla looked down at the papers and frowned.

"This agreement was not drawn up by a lawyer," she explained, "and I am sorry to have even this much formality intrude on your wonderful offering. Unfortunately, our sponsors up the church hierarchy insisted on at least this. The content merely states that you give your consent, as author and agent, to publish free of charge any of Arlene's scripts provided to us. Moreover, the agreement can be terminated by either party with sixty days' written notice. That's essentially all of it. Personally, I don't think it would have much legal standing—and there can be no question of my trust in both of you—but at least it has the virtue of making everyone's intentions clear."

Neither Mary nor Arlene read the document, but each experienced a frisson of excitement when signing over the descriptors "Author" and "Agent." They exchanged copies, signed again, and handed the papers back to Sister Camilla. She in turn signed each copy and handed one back to Mary. Mary took a quick look to see if sisters had last names, but all she saw was "Sister Camilla of the Abbey of Saint Carta."

"The next issue of *The Song* will be out in a week or two, and we'll be including 'Graduation Night.' We try to bring out an issue every month, so the sooner you can let us have your second script, the better. You can send it to the address on the agreement."

"We can take care of that right now," said Mary. Hoping for just this request, yesterday she had been to the same public library at which she had photocopied "Graduation Night" at ten cents per page to make a copy of "Rebellion."

"Here it is. We have lots of others if you don't like this one."

"Let's not even think about that." She glanced at the pages much too quickly to have read more than a few words. "Besides, I have two sisters here who I think will be most eager to read the parts of Marilyn and Danielle."

Over the next week, the Sisters Anna and Monica put together the next issue of *The Song*. They sent it off to be printed and from there it was delivered in batches of twenty-five to ten different churches. The publication was so simple that they did not need to review it before delivery; moreover, the total of two hundred and fifty copies was far more than were ever sold; it was simply the smallest number that the printer would undertake. Typically, half or more were destined for the trash bin. Sister Camilla knew the numbers very well, but after paying for the publication expenses and sharing the small proceeds with each church, there was little enough left for the abbey's general fund. Nonetheless, many of her religious colleagues took so much joy in this virtually insignificant periodical that she thought it best to let them proceed.

This new contribution augmented the pro side of that intuitive ledger, especially since Sister Camilla thought that Arlene and Mary were wonderful young women and the sisters seemed so eager to include Arlene's contributions. She telephoned each of the ten churches that made *The Song* available to its congregants and, without referencing any change of content, asked if they might tell her how things were going over the next few weeks. This was such a small matter that she received immediate assurances from all ten communities that the information would be forthcoming weekly.

Both Mary and Arlene were now at something of a distance from the events. Mary received the first evidence that anything had actually happened about two weeks later. When Arlene made one of her afternoon calls, she asked if they might meet at her house the following morning.

"I am sorry that I cannot meet you halfway this time, but I have both children at home and no one to look after them."

Arlene arrived at about ten. David was already out playing with his friends and Annie, who had been on the porch with one of her dolls, followed her aunt inside, yelling, "Mommy, Auntie Arlene is here!"

Mary came out from the kitchen, carefully drying her hands, then taking off her apron. She was dressed in a sleeveless white blouse, and loose lavender shorts cut about eight inches above her knees.

"Please sit on the sofa. I'll be right back."

Arlene smoothed her aquamarine dress under her, and Annie immediately climbed onto her lap and began attempting to make loose braids in Arlene's hair. Mary returned with a smallish brown envelope and looked at her sister-in-law as if to ask if she should suggest Annie play elsewhere. Arlene answered the question with her eyes and the smallest movement of her head. Annie happily continued her attempts to do to Arlene what her mother so often and so easily had done.

"This, as you will have guessed, "said Mary, "came from Sister Camilla in yesterday's mail. Two copies of the latest issue of *The Song of the Abbey*. I'm not sure why she sent them here, but she mentioned that she had asked that two extra copies be set aside for us. And here they are."

She leaned forward and extended a copy to Arlene, who took hold of it in her left hand since her right arm was needed to support Annie. She looked first at the cover: the same flowers, sea, and sky as the first copy they had seen. She reached around Annie with her right hand to open it. There was no table of contents, so she quietly turned the pages until coming to a right-hand page with the words "Graduation Night by Marla Kraft." Her eyes stopped, and Mary could tell that she was no longer really seeing anything.

"It's amazing to see it, I know, but look at the left-hand page, too."

"Oh," said Arlene, once again able to read. "Oh, that's really lovely."

The facing page was a brief introduction to this new feature that both praised the work and instructed the readers on how it was intended. A few sentences were all that was needed, and they did not differ much from what she and Mary had presented in their interviews.

"It's so different to see it printed like this, not just what comes off my typewriter. But they've still done some things to make it look more like a script. I am not sure what, though. It's beautiful."

"I thought so, too," said Mary. "Congratulations!"

With that, Mary stood up, and Arlene set Annie to the side and followed. They embraced for a few seconds, then Mary released her and stepped back, beaming. I made some coffee and a special little cake for us to celebrate." She looked down and to her left. "You, of course, are included, Annie."

Arlene sat down again and took Annie back onto her lap. The little girl could not understand what her mother and aunt were so pleased about, but she felt warmed and comforted by a sort of contagion. Nonetheless, she frowned up at her auntie, taking two sections of coarse hair back into her small hands.

"Now I'll have to start all over again," she griped.

Early the following week, Sister Camilla got her first reports from the churches that distributed *The Song*. She didn't expect much new information; it was just a baseline. While she entered the messages she received in a notebook, it would not have occurred to her to make a table or a graph. She could easily summarize the numbers to herself.

Almost everyone reports that between ten to fifteen copies were sold, and that only one or two more will be sold within the month.

She had guessed something close to those numbers from the small remunerations that the abbey received on an irregular basis, but now she knew with more certainty that typically only half of the run was actually reaching any readers.

Patience, she sighed.

One week later, Sister Camilla called Mary in the afternoon. Annie answered the phone.

"Hello?"

"Hello, is this the home of Mary Hudson?"

"That's my mom. I'm Annie. Who are you?"

"Sister Camilla. May I speak to your mother, please?"

"But she doesn't *have* any sisters!" The second time with this sister business was too much, and she had to speak up.

"I'm sure that your mother can explain that to you in person much better than I can over the phone, dear. Now may I speak to her?"

Annie held the phone a few inches from her abdomen in order to give her voice more scope:

"Mommy! Someone who says she is your sister is on the phone!"

Twelve miles away, Sister Camilla winced at the volume in her ear, but within ten seconds she heard Mary's voice on the line.

"Good afternoon, Sister. I am sorry about that. Your ears must be ringing. We're doing our best to teach Annie some telephone etiquette, but, as you now know, we aren't there yet."

"No matter, my dear. I am sure she is adorable. And nuns enjoy children especially since they have none of their own."

For an instant, Mary had an untoward thought involving Sister Camilla and Hank and something else that nuns did not have, but it was almost immediately suppressed. She spoke in her most mature voice.

"So, how can I help you?"

"I wanted you and Arlene to know that after two weeks the current issue of *The Song of the Abbey* is nearly sold out at every church that supports us, and this is the first time this has ever happened. Our sisters do a good job with it, and we are proud of it, but the only real difference this time is Arlene's script."

"Wow!" said Mary, minding her volume. "That is very good news, indeed! Arlene will be thrilled."

"Of course, and deservedly so. For both of you. In any case, I wanted to tell you that and that next month we are going to print four hundred copies and see how it goes."

Another "Wow!" was all Mary could manage. Then she added, "It was so kind of you to call and to let us know."

"Not at all, my dear. I should tell you also that I committed you to explaining the wider meaning of sisterhood to your daughter. By the way, before I hang up, may I speak with her again for a second?"

"Of course. Thanks again. Just let us know what to do next."

"I will."

Mary took the phone from her ear and covered the transmitter with her hand. She called to her daughter, who was in the kitchen: "Annie, Sister Camilla would like to talk to you again. Make sure your hands are clean."

Annie appeared at the doorway and looked suspiciously at her mother.

"Why does she want to talk to me?"

"I don't really know, but it would not be nice to keep her waiting much longer."

Annie wiped her hands on her tiny smock and took the phone from her mother. Her look was uncharacteristically diffident.

"Hello again?" This time she was much quieter, almost timid.

"Hello again, Annie. I just wanted you to know when your mother explains sisters to you, that I am as much *your* sister as I am hers. Okay?"

"Okay. Goodbye."

With that Annie hung up the phone rather gently. She looked into her mother's face with an expression of bewilderment that was downright comical. But Mary loved her daughter and did not laugh.

"Now let's go over to the sofa so I can explain to you just what kind of sister Sister Camilla really is."

"Okay," said Annie, meekly following her mother into the living room.

Sister Camilla left her arrangements in place to get progress from each of the churches on the next issue of *The Song*. The results left her blinking at the numbers: all but one hundred or so copies had disappeared on the first Sunday. She talked to one of her correspondents, who mentioned that congregants had been seen thumbing through the publication as if looking for something. "When I took a look myself, 'Rebellion' caught my eye. That sort of thing is new for you, isn't it? And you certainly don't have a Sister Marla, do you?" Sister Camilla confirmed that the scripts were a recent innovation and a less lofty commentary on love than their other contributions.

Along the same lines, two of her other informants had some odd comments. One spoke of visitors coming to the church midweek to get a copy of *The Song*, staying only long enough to pick it up and to deposit a coin or two in the slotted box nearby. Another told her that quite a few readers had purchased more than one copy.

By the second Sunday of its run, *The Song of the Abbey* had sold out at nine of their churches.

The sisters at The Abbey of Saint Carta were delighted. Mary swelled with pride for her sister-in-law when the news reached her and had some left over for herself: she had had a good idea. After an atrocious start, they had succeeded after a fashion, even if Arlene was not being paid for her new-found talent.

Arlene sat on her loveseat in the alcove with her copy of *The Song of the Abbey* opened to Marla Kraft's script about an evening in the life of two young people in love. The sunlight coming through the windowpanes was neither hot nor harsh; the pamphlet's light green pages took on a golden hue. She was not reading the words, but simply accepting the object, processing its presence in her world.

I made this. I needed Mary and Sister Camilla to do it—and I love them for that, and certainly for much more than that!—but it's not wrong to say I made this. And it is something that people want, something from which they can experience being outside of themselves and learning from that. Just as I did when I wrote this.

She looked to the right and down at the cabinet that had concealed her blue typewriter for so many months; her patient friend in hiding from the monster she had married. Her lips tightened, and she turned her head back to the pamphlet.

The gold in that green is now part of me, too, and will be forever. I didn't think it would happen this way. I didn't think it would happen at all. And yet I had hoped this would lead to a kind of freedom, to the resolution of all that still blights me—if that's even the right word. I don't see how that's going to happen yet. But I will sit here and do good work for Mary and Sister Camilla and remain invisible. That should be enough.

With the advent of fall, Sister Camilla's numbers continued to increase, so much so that she suggested to Mary that they begin paying Arlene something for her work. Mary said no for both of them on the spot with no need to consult with her sister-in-law. Arlene continued to write, although she had enough stories to last her for many months. She and Charlie continued in the relationship of cohabitating ghosts. Arlene shopped, cooked, cleaned, washed, and except in one regard did all that a young wife does. They remained unreadable to each other, although both knew that their situation was not stable.

In late October, on the first truly chilly day of the season, Mary received a type-written note in the mail. She opened it with no attention to the return address, and found a single page, dictated by Mr. Brandt, the editor of *Light Breeze*. Mary paused before she began reading.

What in the world?

This was a much tougher call than the offer from Sister Camilla, and she held the letter for some twenty seconds as if this would somehow determine whether or not she would speak to Arlene about it. She decided not yet. She would wait to see what it really meant. Afterall, the letter only stated that Mr. Brandt would like to speak to them and gave a phone number for her to call.

Mary sat on one of her kitchen chairs with a cup of coffee, sipping it absently as she thought through the possibilities and again and again reviewed her decision not to tell Arlene. Finally, inhaling through her nose, she stood up, walked to the phone, and dialed the number given in the letter.

Mary had arrived at the restaurant ten minutes before the appointed time. She looked around to see bright molded walls with a floral pattern, mostly in pink, yellow, and white. The tabletops were glass over a magenta tablecloth, with place settings that included patterned plates, polished silverware, and tan napkins. Everything about the physical environment was cheerful, but there was still an element of something pretentious in the staff and the clientele. Mary wore a dark gray suit, with a skirt that fell below her knees, and a dark green blouse. Her attire was nicely in accord with this latter element of the ambience, if not with the former. She had chosen this outfit precisely for its conservative cut, thinking that the only attention she had gotten in her first meeting with Mr. Brandt was not the kind of attention she wanted again. And this one had not come from any second-hand store. In any case, she was seated, and her legs were hidden by the table of the booth to which she had been led by a sour-faced young man wearing a uniform that suggested formality, overuse, and a wash-and-wear substrate of artificial fabric.

Right on time, Mr. Brandt entered, made inquiries of another employee, who referred the matter to the person who had seated her—the fellow's mood had not improved—and soon this minor figure of an editor sat opposite her.

"You did not make it easy to find you," were his first words; he sounded almost angry.

Mary's face wrinkled slightly. He had asked to meet her, not the other way around, so why this seemingly calculated impoliteness? She decided that civility would cost her nothing; besides, she was apparently getting a fine lunch for her efforts, if nothing else.

"How nice to see you again, Mr. Brandt." Her tone was almost entirely flat. "I am eager to hear just why you took the trouble of finding me."

He began to speak, and Mary realized that he was making no attempt to rein in this loose anger.

"Mrs. Hudson, my life is obviously not glamorous or particularly rewarding on the best of days. These last days have been hellish. Sometimes my home provides sanctuary from my office, sometimes my office from my home. But because of you and your straw-haired young friend, I have had no sanctuary anywhere for the last two weeks."

"What could all of your bad moods possibly have to do with me?"

Mr. Brandt took a short breath and shook his head, although not to communicate anything to Mary. She wasn't sure that the dark rumpled suit he wore wasn't the same as at their first meeting. Perhaps all his suits were dark and rumpled. That would seem to agree well with his personality, she thought.

"Let's order lunch first. The food is good, and *Light Breeze* will pay for it. Do you know what you want?"

Mary nodded yes, and Mr. Brandt raised his left arm to one of the waiters, who promptly came to stand by the table, pad in hand. Mary ordered a small salad and seasoned haddock with rice and asparagus. Mr. Brandt had the ribeye steak with a baked potato and steamed corn—the kind of diner food that one might not expect to find on an elegant menu. Both drank coffee, which arrived within a minute, from virtually translucent porcelain cups with a minute metallic design.

"So, you were going to explain your hard times, Mr. Brandt."

His pale face reddened, which Mary found to be an improvement over his normal unhealthy pallor.

"Yes, Mrs. Hudson, I was." He stopped for a moment, trying to choose his words to reflect his outrage. He looked sharply both to the left and right, and then centered his dark eyes on Mary.

"Three weeks ago, we were putting the October issue to bed. It was all pretty routine with nothing but the usual last-minute cockups. I handled them, and on the way home one night, had the audacity to think that running a small magazine wasn't such a bad way to make a living, even if it meant spending so much time in that suffocating office you visited. When I got home, my wife was going on and on about some little thing that a friend had brought to her attention, a little church publication that had a tiny story in it intended for being read out loud."

"*The Song of the Abbey*." Mary smiled.

Mr. Brandt did not smile; his eyes became smoking black embers of anger.

"Yes, *The Song of the Abbey.*" His voice was sardonic, and he shook his head and expanded his chest like a schoolboy about to throw a punch. "You know what was in there. My wife said that she and her friend had read it four times out loud, trading parts, and how wonderful the whole thing was. It was then I made the mistake of telling her that two women had been in my office to pitch that very idea. I thought it would be interesting for her to hear that." He laughed at his own naiveté. "I thought she might be interested in something to do with how she gets to live in a heated house, have clothes and eat! But instead came an endless harangue: 'You mean, you had a chance at *this*, and you turned it down? You thought this was so worthless that it should be in a church publication that is almost given away? Oh, you're quite the editor, aren't you?'"

At this point Mary's response was a shifting superposition of amusement, gloating, and even a dollop of sympathy. But she kept her face politely and innocently blank, knowing full well that he wasn't finished and having guessed where this was leading. She might at least slow him down.

"I take it that Mrs. Brandt doesn't usually take much interest in your work. So, this was an unusual conversation?"

"Unusual doesn't cover it! Unique! Unique and unpleasant! Whenever I talk about my job, her eyes glaze, and I'm lucky to hear 'That's nice' once a year. I am telling you, she just went on and on about how stupidly incompetent I was not to take your friend's work on the spot."

"My friend, who is also my sister-in-law and might as well be my sister, has a name. It's Arlene. Arlene Zirner."

"Of course. Arlene. I'm sorry to have forgotten."

With that small, but critical shift in his assumption of dominance, Mary's salad arrived. A quiet space followed while she arranged her napkin and silverware and took a modest bite. He waited for her to swallow.

"Well, the on-and-on about my stupidity soon enough changed to the on-and-on of doing something about it. There would be no peace until I at least tried to repair my great blunder. But first I had to find you, and that, Mrs. Hudson, is why we are here."

Mary was taking another forkful of salad, so did not reply for some seconds. She held her fork vertically against the table and looked calmly at Mr. Brandt.

"Just how did you find me?"

She wasn't really curious, and it made no real difference, but now that she understood his purpose, she needed to temporize.

"Well, you left me no contact information, so I traced you back through that convent that publishes that little periodical. A Sister Cinderella finally gave me your address after a proper grilling to make sure I wasn't up to no good." He frowned for a moment, wondering about his own grammar, then continued: "That's how you got the letter and our number."

"It was Sister Camilla, as you well know," said Mary flatly, solidifying her advantage.

The rest of the luncheon was then served. Both were quiet as they arranged their plates. Mr. Brandt cut and speared a few pieces of steak and chewed thoughtfully before continuing.

"So, the long and the short of it is, I am now prepared to pay Miss Zirner twelve dollars and fifty cents for each piece she delivers for a trial period of one year. That's subject to my editorial approval, of course. I can have the papers ready to sign a few days after a verbal agreement. If she says yes, Fanny, my wife, will cease haranguing me. If she says no, at least I can say I made the effort, and sooner or later life at home will once again become bearable."

Mary took some fish and wondered about the wedding of Fanny and Aloysius Brandt. She was then startled by the thought that some element of Arlene's view of life might be rubbing off on her.

"I don't think we need to worry about the quality of Arlene's work," not letting the implications of Mr. Brandt's condition pass. "As for your wife, that might continue to be a problem since I am not sure Miss Zirner will accept your offer. She has an outlet for her work, and I would not be surprised if she didn't remember your dismissiveness at our first interview."

"Then there's no point in offering her more money, is there?"

"Actually, no."

Mary looked down at her plate and resumed eating. Mr. Brandt apparently had nothing more to add and did likewise.

Finally, Mary spoke. "I will put the offer to her, and you can expect to hear from us within a week—let's say ten days at most. I promise to represent your position fairly."

"Well, thank you, Mrs. Hudson. I can ask for no more."

With that they finished their lunches on less formal and correspondingly more cordial terms. When Mary left, she thanked him sincerely for the meal.

I still don't like him, but I wonder how Arlene will react. For all I understand of where she gets her ideas, Fanny and Aloysius may well take center stage in one of her future scripts. The problem is, who'd ever want to play them?

"Well, that's it, Ar. Twelve dollars and fifty cents per script, with Fanny Brandt the wind beneath your wings. How do you feel about it?" Mary smiled with the joy of delivering such good news.

She and Arlene sat on the same bench in the park across from Madison Elementary School on which Arlene had sat with Mrs. Forney when she overheard the exchange that led to her scripts. They held light jackets in their laps since the day had turned warmer than expected. It was just before two o'clock, so the park was empty of children above the age of five. The leaves on the trees were turning but not yet falling and the light seemed to bring a magnification to the paths, plants, play areas and lawn areas of the park. Arlene had often wondered at the special nature of sunlight in early autumn: was there some science to it? If so, she wasn't sure at all if she wanted to know it..

"I don't know quite how I feel," replied Arlene, "except to say it is not how I expected to feel."

"What do you mean? This is great!"

"It is. And, well, if we had gotten this response the first time we went to see Mr. Brandt, I know I would have been overjoyed. But some things have changed... Can I just think out loud with you?"

"Of course, silly. If mothers worried about hearing only organized thoughts, they wouldn't be mothers for at least two reasons."

"Okay. I know that Sister Camilla is at the heart of my unease for at least two different reasons. The first one has to do with... The only word I can think of is property."

"You mean that the work isn't your property anymore?"

"No, that's not it. It *is* mine, and in a way, it will always be mine, no matter where it ends up. But with Sister Camilla and the abbey and the other sisters—even with the congregants who purchased *The Song*, who I will never meet—it was a sharing of something I loved with a place that I loved. And you were part of that, too, Mary. But with Mr. Brandt, the only thing left to love in the arrangement would be you. The reason I never felt I was *selling* my little plays to the abbey has nothing to do with not being paid for them. I wanted them to be part of their world. But Mr. Brandt and *his* world..."

"I see," said Mary softly. "I never thought of it that way, but I do now, and it's perfectly clear. We were very lucky to find a home for your work with the sisters." She smiled again, this time with the depth of her affection for and understanding of this young woman.

"Arlene, was it a mistake then for me to go see Mr. Brandt on my own?"

"Oh, no! I really could not have played any part in that conversation. You were right to go alone."

They sat quietly for a few minutes, each weighing the values that brought them to this hesitation. At last, Mary spoke:

"So, I will tell Mr. Brandt that we are no longer interested and leave him to deal with Fanny."

"No, I don't want to say that yet. Could you give me a few days to work this out? There's that other thing I haven't told you yet."

"Of course, sweetie. It's your decision; I'm just the help."

"Whatever happens, Mary, there is no thank-you big enough for everything you have done since that day I showed up at your house all bruised."

"Whatever happens, no thank-you is needed, Arlene. I've loved every minute of it, except for seeing you hurt."

Early on a wet and foggy morning, two days later, Arlene was alone on the bus to the abbey. She had not phoned ahead, not wanting to waste any of the verbal or emotional energy this visit to Sister Camilla was going to cost her.

The bus was chilly and nearly empty. She pressed herself into the corner of her window seat near the back with a forlorn pretense that she might make herself smaller and warmer in the lined, hooded raincoat she wore. The coat was gray, and underneath she wore a plain, dark blue dress with brown buttons. She would be bringing no Easter to the sisters, this time.

She arrived at the stop, disembarked, and pulled up her hood. She carried nothing but her purse, and ten minutes later stood at the heavy door. She knocked twice and then stood patiently. There was the light shuffle of someone approaching, and then the door opened about six inches. Sister Rose's perfect face appeared. Her well-trained composure lasted less than a second when she recognized their guest.

"Miss Zirner! Come in! You look frozen. No umbrella? Come in, please."

"Thank you, Sister. And please call me Arlene."

"Arlene," she repeated. "Of course. Everyone will be so glad to see you. But how can I help?"

"I haven't made any appointment, but I should like to speak with Sister Camilla. I can wait until she has the time."

"Oh, I don't think that will be a problem. She will be more pleased than any of us to see you. Come, let's see where she is."

And with that, Arlene followed Sister Rose from Nigeria into the dark silent world of The Abbey of Saint Carta.

The two sat outdoors on an ancient wicker love seat. The back and sides were woven from bamboo and extended upward to a canopy with several gaps in the weaving. Still, it was sufficient, with the leaves overhead, to protect them from the rain, with only an occasional drop finding its way to Arlene's hood or Sister Camilla's wimple. Here the exterior of the abbey seemed as dark as its interior, and that quality was as rare as the hues of the refracted light that had once mesmerized Arlene in the Sister's office. Sister Camilla, sitting on the right, again expressed her concern for Arlene's comfort.

"I know it would be warmer inside, but this spot is so lovely at this hour and in this weather. It makes it so easy to speak—or to be silent."

"I wish I could just enjoy the feel of this place with you in silence, Sister Camilla, but I do need to talk with you."

"Well, I welcome the chance to have you here. Perhaps later we can be silent, and after that enjoy a cup of hot tea."

Arlene nodded, and for no reason she could define, abruptly pulled off her glasses. Sister Camilla did not suddenly see a new and unfamiliar face; she saw rather the delicate pale blue of Arlene's eyes and a troubled young woman.

"Whatever it is, dear, we have the resources to handle it." Arlene did not understand how big a thing the "we" in that sentence was intended to convey, but she nonetheless took comfort from the reassurance. She sighed and then began:

"Sister, I have long ago given up on thanking you for your help in getting my scripts into *The Song*, and to do anything that suggests that I am not entirely grateful is unbearable. I am so privileged to be part of your work, and I should ask for nothing more.

"I think Mary saw this as just a beginning, but she, too, respects you and the other sisters and all that you do beyond anything she's known before. I know I am speaking her heart in this."

"Mary is a remarkable woman," interrupted Sister Camilla. "I have scarcely known anyone to whom such honesty, directness, and enthusiasm come so easily. She would have made a fine nun, but that would have deprived her of motherhood, and that was clearly God's plan for her."

"Yes," said Arlene. Her eyes and lips moved in synchrony as if she was discovering something. "And she is such a beautiful woman. Yet there is a plainness about her that makes her even more beautiful, if that makes sense."

"It does," said Sister Camilla, "and I think you put it perfectly. But I think you were getting to something else entirely."

"Yes." Arlene shook her head slowly across a large arc. "And I don't know even how to begin."

"Arlene, please don't look like that—so tragic, as if you are about to disappoint me. Did you ever ask yourself how *Light Breeze* got in touch with your sister-in-law?"

"No, I didn't."

"It was through me. So, I know what this is about, and I applaud your success. We—all of us—are happy for you getting your work before a larger audience, and, yes, you should be paid for it. *The Song of the Abbey* will go on as it did before."

Arlene was all but in tears, shaking her head, but this time more vigorously in specific denial.

"No, Sister, you misunderstand. I did not come here to ask you for that. I want to be part of *your* work until you ask me to stop."

"But what is it then?"

"Because I want your permission to publish my scripts with Mr. Brandt *and* to continue with you. I am asking you first because if you say no, that ends it. I will be content to continue with your convent."

"Arlene, we have no claim to your work; we simply have your permission to print it. Why are you asking? If you have someone willing to pay you and to have your scripts read by more people, why would you hesitate? We, here, certainly won't think less of you."

Arlene put her glasses back on and pulled off the hood of her raincoat. There was enough protection under the trees where they sat for the hood not to matter. A few strands of wet hair nearer her face were clumped together in dampness. She composed herself and looked straight ahead. Sister Camilla, with her head turned to the left, could not see Arlene's eyes. She respected her privacy and looked down at the yellow, saturated leaves that lay on the ground before them.

"Tell me what's happening, Arlene," she said softly, with no hint of a demand.

Arlene thought how different this trip was from the first, with Mary. Then they had been seated inside Sister Camilla's office, ornamented by wonderful splashes of refracted light. Now she sat without Mary in a kind of organic cave, with no dazzling ornaments, just ordinary leaves, dark and wet, and the feel of wet air on her face. Mary could not speak for her now.

Arlene began talking about her life. She talked for a long time.

Arlene got off the return bus that same afternoon eleven blocks from her apartment. The afternoon had turned from wet and cool to hazy and a bit too warm for her raincoat. She did not walk in the direction of her home, but toward a telephone booth that was two blocks north. From there, she phoned Mary.

"Hello?"

"Mary?"

"Oh, Arlene! I am so glad to hear from you. Has something happened? Did you decide?"

"Yes, but first I needed to speak to Sister Camilla on my own. I am afraid you will have to meet with Mr. Brandt alone again. Is that okay?"

"We've come a long way, so, yes, and it will be less trouble than you think. But what am I to tell him?"

"He can print my scripts, but there will be two conditions."

She spoke for a few minutes and was relieved that what she had to say didn't seem of much concern to Mary.

"Okay, Ar, I know exactly what to tell him, and I will as soon as possible."

With that, they hung up. Arlene continued walking in her neighborhood in a place of relative quiescence. She no longer noticed the humidity, and she had made all of the decisions in her power. She realized after passing several pedestrians without the effort to look into their faces to see who was home that she was tired—and hungry. At that point she went directly to her apartment, fixed herself a light sandwich which she ate with a glass of milk. She cleaned and put away the scant dishes. She lay on the sofa and thought that Charlie would not be home for some hours, and after closing her eyes to recall a few images of this morning's darkness and the yellows and greens of the limp, wet leaves, she fell asleep.

The Last Reading

"The Silent Explosion" by Marla Kraft

[Aileen stands in the living room of their apartment, eight feet from the hallway door, next to which are two packed suitcases. She is swaying, and her eyes seem not to be able to focus. Rory stands at arm's length from her. He towers over Aileen, his whole body swollen in anger.]

Rory: What do you mean, you're going now?

Aileen: Is it hot outside today? I hope it is not too hot. I have to carry these bags, you see.

Rory: Carry your bags where?

Aileen: Downstairs and then... Oh, that's a trick. I have to carry them downstairs. They're heavy but I will take them downstairs. That's all.

Rory: For God's sake, Aileen, you can't just take your bags downstairs. And you still haven't told me where you're going or why!

Aileen: Do not worry about me. It is not too hot. I can carry them.

Rory: This is crazy! Answer me in a way that makes sense! Where are you going?

Aileen: Do you know how easy it is to hide if you are a bug. If you are small enough. Nobody would come looking for a bug. I am a bug, Rory, and you will not come looking for me.

Rory: YOU ARE NOT A BUG ALTHOUGH I MIGHT JUST AS WELL CRUSH YOU IF YOU DON'T START MAKING SENSE!

Aileen: No, best to be like water. Not good for crushing but good for evaporating. This is me evaporating. Water evaporates from heat. Anger is a kind of heat. I think I have been evaporated by someone.

[Aileen takes one step toward the door. Rory grabs her by the shoulder and turns her around. Aileen stands passively, still swaying, still unfocused.]

Aileen: Ah, I am water. Or a little bug in water. Anyway, I cannot be crushed or found. So, I will take my bags downstairs. They are big bags for a little bug, I think, but that will not matter.

Rory: Look, Aileen, we have been married for nearly three years. Are you going to tell me we have nothing worth keeping? We got married. We stayed married for this long. There must be something we have between us.

[Aileen moves unsteadily in the direction of a window, stopping about four feet from it and stares out. From behind, and illuminated by the light, her swaying seems especially precarious.]

Aileen: Plants grow together sometimes. They become entangled in ways that make them hard to pull apart without a lot of damage. People do that, too. A wonderful, surprising number of people. Just look everywhere and you will see them paired up, or in larger groups, all tangled together. <u>They</u> have something. Some want nothing. Some are poison to anything that gets too close. Some live to kill others. That's natural if you are a bug, but if you are little enough, nobody cares enough to hurt you.

[She smiles, but not at Rory, and walks back to where she had been standing when he caught her. He is at the limit of his self-control.]

Rory: IN ABOUT FIVE SECONDS I AM GOING TO KNOCK YOU TO THE FLOOR!

[Now more quietly, but in a voice wavering and becoming breathless in frustration.]

Rory: Are you drunk or on something? I am here, and I have every right to expect that you make sense. Where the hell are you?

Aileen: That is a now question. There is no now, and the future question makes no sense. Where does a bug go when it's squished? Where does water go when it evaporates? A milkweed seed just disappears on the wind, and when it is clear and sunny, the brightness makes it disappear sooner.

[She turns and looks at him for the first and last time. She says six words and then disconnects forever.]

Aileen: You were going to hit me. Bugs, water, milkweed seeds. Bye!

[The last word is not addressed to Rory but to the place. She picks up her bags, carries them downstairs, and walks into the not-too-hot day. Rory has no more moves; he watches the door close, hears the now steady but fading footsteps. Aileen is no longer swaying, and her eyes are focusing just fine.

In late spring of the following year, Charlie came home to his apartment early in the evening. There was still some light in the sky, and he came in whistling and carrying a tiny kitten in his arms. He had been almost obsessively feeling the small, brittle bones in the kitten's neck. And its tiny feet. He had picked it up for a dollar at the same pet store from which he had purchased the puppy, the day after he had struck Arlene on the neck. The kitten was not, however, a peace offering. He held it briefly in his left arm alone, while his right hand felt the reassuring hardness of a pair of pruning shears tucked into his jacket pocket. He was ready.

So, you lived with me and ignored me for all this time. Yes, I hit you, but you erased me. Don't worry, I won't hit you again because I know it doesn't hurt you enough. The puppy hurt, didn't it? The thought that the puppy would grow up in the presence of this monster, that hurt so much that you raised that pitiful voice of yours and told me to take it away. I shouldn't have, but that night you had the advantage of surprise. Not tonight, Arlene. Not by a long shot. Tonight, I surprise you, and you won't have a chance to say a word.

Charlie and Arlene had spoken so little for so long, that he didn't think to call out to her. He looked into her alcove, noticing that her elaborate curtains had been removed—probably for cleaning—and then looked into the bedroom, again to find emptiness. He went back to the living room and got comfortable on the sofa to wait for her. She was always out and about these days, but there had been no sign of any special activity. She walked; she spent no money—she had none; and the contact he knew she had with his sister meant nothing.

The kitten crawled into his lap, and he immediately placed it back down on the floor.

None of that, little fellow. That would be pointless. Shall I tell you about the last cat I had anything to do with? His name was Boopers, and to this day, I don't think my sister Mary has forgiven me for pretending to pull off his tail and spoiling her Communion dress. This time it won't be just your tail and it won't be pretending.

He chuckled at that and wondered why this solution hadn't occurred to him sooner. All those months of looking for some way to hurt her, and here it was.

As the night drained the evening, Charlie was getting impatient. He turned on a lamp. There was a magazine he had never seen before on the coffee table, not far from where he was sprawled, and he could see it had been bookmarked. Why would Arlene leave a bookmark in a magazine? It was easy enough to find your place, or you just left it open. Suddenly he was on full alert.

He sat up and then stood up, nearly stepping on the kitten. He went back to the bedroom, looked in the closet and then in their drawers. All empty of her things. He thought of the little cabinet in the alcove where Arlene had a few keepsakes and sewing goods. There was nothing in there but some inexpensive material, which, like a rug long under the weight of some piece of furniture, showed four indentations.

Charlie hurried back to the living room and opened the magazine at the bookmark. He saw a story formatted like a play, something he had not had any contact with since the necessary evil of high school: "Silent Explosion by Martha Kraft." He started to throw the magazine back down on the table when something about the bookmark caught his eye. It was just a rectangular scrap of blue paper, but it clearly bore a script C in a style that was entirely too familiar to him.

He read the script. When he read the words, "Some are poison to anything that gets too close," he understood. His mind froze: it was a paralysis to deflect a panic.

He looked down at the kitten. His plans for it were useless now, so he picked it up and carried it to Arlene's empty alcove. He opened the window, set the creature on the ledge, and then closed it again. Cats were agile; it would somehow find its way to the street. If not, it wasn't his problem.

Charlie stood in the living room about eight feet from the apartment door. His vision was unfocused, and he felt the bones in his face detaching from his skull and from his soul, leaving his unprotected eyes behind. He could only stand there in the harsh lamplight. He had no moves left.

The Last Chapter

Arlene had never been so busy in her life. It began with the contract with *Light Breeze*. She had explained to Mary that she had been to see Sister Camilla, that she wanted two things in her contract with Mr. Brandt: one, an escape clause similar to what she had with the abbey; and, two, the absolute right to continue having her work included in *The Song of the Abbey*. Mr. Brandt didn't care in the least about the first and felt that the small cluster of God botherers who might not purchase his magazine because of this insignificant overlap would cost him essentially nothing. Nonetheless, he did see it as a lever to lower his offer to eleven dollars and fifty cents per piece. Arlene accepted immediately, and her scripts began appearing in a new venue.

Mr. Brandt had only made the arrangement to keep his wife happy, but he had to conclude that for some unfathomable reason, people were buying *Light Breeze* in greater numbers. The rise in sales was similar in profile to what Sister Camilla had seen, but he never shared this information with Mary or Arlene, and they never thought to ask.

Arlene insisted on not keeping the full amount. She knew it was paltry, but she was determined that both Mary and the abbey should be paid three dollars from each check. Sister Camilla understood and accepted the sum gracefully; Mary made more of an objection—she had so enjoyed helping Arlene—but in the end promised to use the money on frivolities for her children. That left Arlene with five dollars and fifty cents each month, which she saved scrupulously.

For the next six months, Arlene spent most of her time writing and avoiding Charlie. She had an occasional visit with Mary, and once spent most of the day traveling to see her mother for about an hour, but as much as she treasured these visits, she wanted to work and to write her scripts faster than *Light Breeze* could publish them. She was working to a plan that she did not expect to bear fruit, but if Mary had known of it—and of the success that Mr. Brandt was having—she would have been far less skeptical than Arlene herself was. In any case, Mary was missing the more active role she had had in the venture in its earlier days.

On a blank winter day in February, Mary was alone at home when the phone rang.

"Yes, this is Mary Hudson.

"Yes, I did more or less represent Arlene Zirner and was asked to sign both contracts for her work. Lately, though, there's been little for me to do.

"Oh, of course, Arlene has no telephone. I am happy that you called, but I am surprised that anyone from Mr. Brandt's organization would have given you my number—or Arlene's real name for that matter. Especially in this connection.

"Sister Camilla? Really! So, I was right about *Light Breeze*.

"Yes, of course Arlene would be interested! In fact, she was the one who insisted on the two-month termination option with Mr. Brandt's publication. It was one of two conditions, and I should tell you right now that she will still insist on the other one: that she be allowed to continue with *The Song of the Abbey*. And it's not just that they were the first to publish her work, but she has a special connection with the place and the sisters there, and they have one with her, too. If you knew Arlene and were ever there, you would understand immediately.

"Well, if that's no problem for you, I'm certain she'll want to meet with you.

"Okay, let me write all that down. Give me a few days to talk with Arlene. She's one of the loveliest people you will ever meet—and she's also my sister-in-law. Anyway, she'll be thrilled.

"No, *thank you*. Bye for now."

Mary walked over to the living room window, and the day was not so blank as it had been. The sun's radiation, so attenuated by the overcast and the season, was now helped in no small measure by her compensatory glow.

They met in the restaurant in which Arlene had first confessed her aspirations to Mary and asked for her help. The sense of dark coolness that she remembered was replaced by a kind of warm coziness owing to the cold weather. They arrived virtually simultaneously and asked for the same booth as last time.

They ordered and Arlene waited patiently. While they had spoken about once every two weeks, they had seen each other very few times since the arrangement with *Light Breeze.* The meeting would have been enjoyable if they had nothing to discuss, but Mary's sense of urgency and choice of venue left Arlene in no doubt that there was some important news to be communicated.

"Well, what's your guess on what this is all about?" said Mary seconds after the waiter had walked away with their orders. Her eyes were wide open and smiling with excitement.

Arlene could only shake her head, shrug, and make some especially bizarre twist of her lips to indicate that she had no guess whatsoever. She had considered that Mr. Brandt might be raising his fees, but that didn't seem right either for him or this occasion.

"Well," said Mary, "you're going to have to end your deal with Mr. Brandt. A national magazine wants to publish your scripts. They want to pay you a ton, and they want to give you an advance."

The numbers were unimaginable to Arlene. For most, the sums would not have changed their lives, but Arlene knew at once that it was enough to make the changes she wanted.

Mary continued to expound on the magnitude of the achievement of getting noticed by such an organization. She wasn't surprised at first that Arlene looked more stunned than ecstatic. But then she realized that there was something else in Arlene's face, and that something was sadness.

"What's going on, honey?"

Two streams of tears began flowing from Arlene's eyes, and she took an unsteady but deep breath. She opened her mouth to speak just as the waiter arrived with their drinks. She tilted her head down and let her loose hair flow past her ears to hide her face.

Mary looked up at the waiter. "Thank you. And could you hold the lunch orders until I tell you we're ready?" He nodded and walked off.

"It's alright to come up now. We've got some space."

Arlene looked up at Mary and began speaking.

"You know I never wanted to be famous or to have a lot of money. I started this because of the simple enjoyment of it. I was engaged in nothing but maintaining a small apartment for a man I could not make happy. It was like the curtains for my alcove: just something that I could do, do well, and do for me.

"But then Charlie hit me over nothing, and that was the first thought I had of getting out, of wanting to disappear from that man's world. That's when I first thought that maybe I could make a little of my own money writing my scripts and when I first talked to you about selling them. Sister Camilla showed me how much it could mean to see them printed and distributed even without any money, but that didn't help with my disappearance. Then came Mr. Brandt—some money but still not enough to get away."

"But if you wanted to get away, why did you insist on giving anything to me and to Sister Camilla?" Mary knew she was interrupting something far more important, but she could not hold her question.

"Because it was right! Because I would have none of the happiness of seeing my stories in *The Song* without you two. That had to be acknowledged. It *had* to."

"Okay, I'm sorry I interrupted, but I still have no idea why you're sad. In fact, it's getting to be more of a mystery."

"Listen, Mary. I hoped that something like this would happen. I didn't expect it, but I hoped for it. And now that it has, I can afford to disappear, and you'll help me do that."

"Of course," affirmed Mary.

"But think about what that means. I want to be so far out of Charlie's life that I never have to think about him and about what I allowed to happen to me—never again. And that means leaving here. Leaving Mutti. Leaving Sister Camilla. Leaving Annie. And most important, leaving you."

Mary started to speak, but Arlene signaled her to be silent just a little more.

"Mary, we *fall* in love with our husbands and wives; we don't fall in love with our parents and siblings. Sometimes we don't love our family, but when we do, we are *born* in love with them. Like I love Mutti. But I fell in love with you, Mary. Not in a way that would ever make Hank jealous or confused, but in a way that slowly acknowledged your goodness and meaning and value to me. That makes leaving so much harder. It means that this unbelievable, unexpected, invaluable success you just shared with me is also the end of our sisterhood."

Mary answered at once. "In the second place, Arlene, there is no place you can go that I cannot visit—and take Annie, too. In the first place, I fell in love with you in the same way that you fell in love with me, so the one thing that you must never question is that I understand. It's funny that I feel like I have always known that there were all different kinds of love, but I thought that falling in love was only meant in connection with romantic love. It's not."

Arlene was visibly relieved by Mary's words, and a few minutes later, Mary signaled the waiter. After their lunches had been set before them, Mary was eager to hear more of Arlene's plans.

"Well, yes, I will tell you as much as I have decided. But before that, we have one more thing to discuss," said Arlene in a serious tone, but somehow serenely.

Mary listened, then argued, but in the end, she could not change Arlene's mind.

Mary sat in the chair in their bedroom, an item much more decorative than functional, waiting for Hank to come home.

"What are you doing hiding in here?" he asked after returning from work and not finding his wife in any of the usual places.

Mary got up and closed the door behind him.

"We've got to talk. I told Arlene today about her new offer. I've got lots to tell you about her reaction, but this has to go first. She is insisting on giving me and Sister Camille about the same percentage as she is now. This is serious money, Hank, and she won't be talked out of it."

Hank's silence and ambiguous look invited her to continue.

"The thing is, sweety, the money from *Light Breeze* was more than I wanted or deserved. This is plain crazy, and it doesn't mean an extra toy for Annie or a new baseball glove for David."

"Then what does it mean?" he asked gently.

"Look, I want you to know that I tried my best to get her to see that this isn't necessary. I never helped her for this reason. She knows that, but she loves me and our family and she is determined that we should share in her success."

"Okay, but what does it mean?"

"It means I want us to save for our own house. It means that we can start saving now, even if I cannot work again until Annie is older."

"Okay. What's your schedule?"

Mary told him.

He took a breath: "Okay."

Later that evening they spoke to the children.

"Look kids, it's important that we have our own house instead of renting this one. We don't have to move far, but for a little while it will mean spending less money, and you both need to understand that.

"I don't care, as long as I can play with my friends," said David.

Annie, who naturally understood less, was more skeptical. She knew a warning when she heard it.

"Once we get this house, can I have a bunny to keep in the backyard? You said I couldn't now because we couldn't make a place for it in the yard."

"Don't you like our cat, honey?" asked Mary.

"I love him, but I want a bunny, too."

"Okay."

And with that single word from Mary, the deal was sealed for all four of them.

On a morning fourteen weeks later, Arlene sat on the floral bedspread that covered an old but entirely serviceable bed in a brightly lit room. The wallpaper was a pattern of blue and white stripes—very close to the pale blue of her eyes—and superimposed on the white stripes were dark blue diamonds about an inch and a half tall at six-inch intervals. One large window dominated the west side of the room, with a flowing chiffon curtain embroidered with small flowers. It was still a bit chilly outside, but the unseen sun was so splendid in its brightness that Arlene had opened the window to allow herself all the better to merge with her new place and situation.

The room had a couple of framed paintings—neither of any value—a chest, a soft chair, and a desk with the kind of sturdy wooden chair one might find in a library. A blue typewriter, none the worse for having travelled over twelve hundred miles, sat squarely and openly on the desk. The desk drawers held paper, envelopes, and a few other office supplies. Finally, there was a small closet, not much bigger than its door, and just deep enough to accommodate a standard hangar.

Mrs. Johns would soon be calling Arlene to lunch. There was one other boarder, but she was working that day, and so it would only be the two of them.

Two weeks earlier, Arlene had arrived by train in a small midwestern town and established herself in the cheapest respectable hotel room she could find. She met

Mrs. Johns in her second week in response to a small ad looking for a boarder in a local newspaper. Arlene showed up that very morning on Mrs. Johns' doorstep. She wore her light blue coat and yellow dress.

"Yes?" said Mrs. Johns on opening the door. She was a woman of medium height and medium build, wearing small oval glasses and a print dress: a light Kelly-green bearing feathered shapes in a consonant tan. Her chin showed some slight puckering of age, but otherwise her skin was almost flawlessly smooth.

"Mrs. Johns? I am Arlene Zirner, and I came about the room." Arlene looked left and right to take in the neat, clean symmetry of the small house.

"Please do come in," said Mrs. Johns with a broad smile that exaggerated the puckering. The smile was just a trifle too pronounced under the circumstances, and a hint of puzzlement was evident in the shape and motion of Arlene's lips. Mrs. Johns noticed that and responded to it.

"You know, Miss Zirner, you are one of the few strangers who ever came to this door and didn't assume I was the hired housekeeper."

"But why would that be? And please call me Arlene."

"Because of this, Arlene." She moved her hands over her face and the exposed parts of her arms and wrists and gestured to her legs below the hem of her dress. It took Arlene some seconds to realize it was about the color of her skin.

"My goodness, that train ride was longer than I thought!"

"I see," said Mrs. Johns. "You are from out of town, and that explains why you'd be looking for a room. Well, let me show you the room and the house, and then we can have some coffee and talk.

The house had a living room, a small dining room off a modest kitchen, and three upstairs bedrooms and a bath. Everything was spotless and nothing looked worn, although none of the furniture seemed new.

"You like right angles, don't you?" said Arlene. That remark carried no risk; her ability to assess people instantly told her that this was a kind and diligent woman.

"I suppose I do. But I'm not mean about it."

The tour ended and Mrs. Johns brought Arlene into the kitchen where she sat down at the table. It was a sturdy metal construction with a ribbed border and a Formica surface bearing a tumble of smooth, overlapping pastel shapes on a grey background.

"So, tell me about yourself. It is a responsibility having a boarder. You would have the west bedroom. Mine is in the middle and the other belongs to Winnie, who has been with me for nearly two years. She's about your age, I would guess. Maybe a year younger."

"Do you have any children of your own?"

"Grown and flown. My husband passed six years ago, so it's just been me and the boarders."

"I'm sorry. I was supposed to be telling you about me." But Mrs. Johns clearly heard that the "sorry" was more about her late husband.

"Yes, do tell me about yourself—although I am becoming more certain by the minute that I like you."

Arlene described her life from its all too hazy beginnings, her parents, high school and her first jobs. She did think it only fair to mention her marriage, but of that she only said that it was a bad choice and had to be ended. Likewise, she mentioned vaguely that she had recently come into a modest income that made it possible to leave what she remembered as her hometown, and that she had chosen someplace small, affordable, and distant. The city she came from was not large on any national scale, but it was larger than she wanted. She added to her own surprise that what she wanted was a kind of retreat without leaving the world.

Mrs. Johns listened thoughtfully and in part reciprocated. Her own early childhood was similarly hazy, but somehow her family had ended up in this town. Her father, an intelligent man with little formal education, had worked tirelessly so that he could buy the house that Mrs. Johns had lived in since she was fourteen. She was an only child, but still after her own marriage and children, the house had become "pleasantly crowded." Her parents died, her children left home and community, and finally she lost her husband. Her boarders had all been young women—"a lot easier to handle than young men"—who had given her the chance to be something of a mother again, although she was careful not to get too close.

Arlene had only one point to raise:

"I need to do some typing almost every day, and I know that will be something you can hear even with my door closed. Is that okay?"

"Yes, indeed, darling, as long as you don't start earlier than seven in the morning and don't go later than nine in the evening."

Mrs. Johns mentioned a number, which included meals, and they agreed that Arlene would move in the day after tomorrow, giving Mrs. Johns enough time to prepare the room for its new guest.

Dear Mary,

I am still happy here. It is now the best part of spring: the days are warm enough to go without a coat, and they are long and still getting longer. It is the perfect time of year. So much has bloomed already. I started to write "bloomed for me," but of course that is nonsense. Still, it feels that way.

I have been working one or two days a week as a substitute teacher at the town's elementary school, for kindergarten through second grade. Mrs. Johns is so nice that I don't need more money, but I wanted to try working with small children. They are lovely! They call me Miss Arlene and will sometimes sit on my lap when they want to talk. The other teachers are nice, too. All but two of them are women, and they span a large range of ages. I had no expectations that they would like me or notice me. Still, as I approached the teachers' lounge on Tuesday to get something to drink, I heard them mention me. I expected to hear something about that strange young woman with the big glasses and twitchy lips, but instead I found that

they rather liked "that nice substitute teacher with the pale blue eyes." I hardly see the two men; one is vice principal and the other teaches shop to the older boys. That suits me well enough. Charlie was enough to last several decades.

The principal, Mrs. Huhnchen, mentioned that in this state you don't need a college degree to be a full-time teacher in the lower grades. She said all I needed was some coursework, and she would be happy to have me as a regular part of her staff. I cannot tell you how exciting that is for me, Mary, but I have not yet made up my mind whether to try. I think I could do it and still write my scripts, but I would hate to disappoint the school, especially the children, if it didn't work out. Right now, the substitute teaching actually helps with the scripts because watching children gives me more ideas for new things. Thinking about how I got started as Marla, maybe that shouldn't surprise me, but it does.

I hope you and Annie will come soon! The train ride was more fun than you would think and might be a real adventure for both of you. I am sorry, but I think it will be years before I am ready to come the other way. Meanwhile, thank you for checking up on Mutti for me. I do write to her, but I do not expect her to write back. I hope she understands why I am so far away.

When I think of seeing you, I only miss you more, but that's given me something else to think about. I so much believe in "Do good and disappear" that I have never considered, even for a second, telling anyone here that I am Marla Kraft. But you know. And Sister Camilla knows. And I <u>want</u> you both to know. Maybe, then, I have never entirely succeeded with "Do good and disappear." Or maybe I have reinterpreted it--for better or for worse--to exclude those I love.

Yours always,
Arlene

ত ত ত ত ত

www.ingramcontent.com/pod-product-compliance
Lightning Source LLC
LaVergne TN
LVHW020702110826
845149LV00012B/2076

* 9 7 9 8 9 9 4 3 4 2 3 0 5 *